A NOVEL ARRANGEMENT

Flos Magicae

ARDEN POWELL

TABLE OF CONTENTS

A
NOVEL
ARRANGEMENT

CHAPTER ONE

A GARDEN PROPOSAL

Elizabeth Turtledove sat in the tropical glasshouse of the Princess of Wales Conservatory in Kew Gardens, warm and glowing with a light sheen of sweat in the enforced humidity. At her side, the petals of the suncatcher flowers shone like stained glass: even their broad, pointed leaves looked gold as the sun glanced through them. They were Elizabeth's favourite flower by simple virtue of their usefulness to her on cloudy days. When it was overcast and the garden was shrouded in shadows, as it often was in England, or during the bleak winter period when the sun rarely showed her face, the suncatchers glowed with a shimmering rainbow of light held over from sunnier times, and allowed Elizabeth to write in her notebook without having to conjure any light herself.

As a matter of safety, the public sections of Kew Gardens didn't house any dangerous magical plants. However, there were a great many friendly varieties to be enjoyed nestled amid their more mundane neighbours, and Elizabeth appreciated every one of them. She found her mind was sharpest when surrounded by nature, however carefully cultivated, but to her chagrin, she had no green thumb herself. So, when she wanted to write, she took herself off to the Royal Botanic Gardens to bask in their greenery: outside in the summer months, or, in the frequent inclement weather, within the vast and many-roomed greenhouses. She was a seamstress by day, and by night, she secretly wrote thrilling romance novels for the hungry public. Her adoring readers devoured her books as quickly as she could finish them, even as the more conservative sect denounced the mysterious 'M. Hayes' for writing such lewd and overly imaginative pulp. She had written all fourteen of her novels in the comfort of Kew Gardens, and was intent on doing the same for her fifteenth, if only she could come up with a plot for the damned thing.

"I worry about repeating myself," she said to Arthur, who sat beside her on the little bench tucked to the side of the walk. "I've written about dukes and princes and highwaymen and pirates and every other romantic hero of which I can conceive—and heiresses, socialites, and governesses—and it gets to a certain point where nothing seems original anymore. How many times can readers buy a book about a secret tryst or a clandestine engagement or a marriage of convenience?"

"Judging by how keen your publishers are to get more from you? Many, I should think. Your readers are the most voracious I've ever seen. If you write it, they'll buy it, surely."

Arthur Leicester wasn't particularly passionate about either botany or the relentless industry of romance publishing, but the fact that he accompanied Elizabeth to the Gardens or lent an ear to her plotting efforts whenever she asked endeared him to her greatly. There were plenty of other things she liked about him besides his steadfast loyalty, but that was what set him so far apart from every other man she'd gone out with, and she didn't take his dedication lightly.

"I'm afraid I might have lost my spark when it comes to romance," she admitted. "Fourteen novels in a row, written and published as quickly as they were, may have burned me out somewhat."

"I hope you're not sick of romance entirely," Arthur said, leaning close to touch her hair.

"I'm still enjoying our romance very much," she assured him. "And those of all our friends. It's just that there are so many relationships I can't touch on whatsoever, no matter how interesting I might find them to write. Like romances between two women, or two men. Or more than two people. And it's just a little frustrating to be fourteen novels deep into this pen name and have this whole part of the human experience closed to me because of marketability reasons."

"I suppose you could take the Marquis de Sade's approach and try the French market," Arthur offered.

Elizabeth hummed, tapping her pen against her notebook as she pretended to give it serious consideration. It would never do, of course; she would never find a mainstream publisher willing to touch those particular subjects. Her work might circulate on the underground market under a different pen, but that wouldn't do her much good. At the end of the day, publishing was a business, and she had never been one to let whimsy get in the way of common sense.

"Stop that," Arthur said, as she pressed the bottom of her pen to her mouth.

"Perhaps the underground market deserves more credit than I give it."

"No, it doesn't."

She flipped open her notebook as if to begin writing a story that very moment. "Maybe homoerotic literature is going to be the next big thing. I could get in on it right from the start."

"It's not; you know it's not."

"I could commission illustrations to go along with it—"

"You'd be done for distribution of obscene materials, Elizabeth!"

"Do you think your Mr. Coxley would do book illustrations?"

Jules Coxley, Arthur's friend and flatmate, was a painter of some renown and ill-repute, and disliked Elizabeth in measures equal to how much they both liked Arthur.

Arthur grabbed for her notebook, laughing as she held it out of reach, coaxing him to lean over her to try for it. "He might, but certainly not for you! Give me that notebook, you little devil—"

She swatted him with it before allowing him to sweep it away from her, both of them grinning helplessly. The sun lit Arthur's hair like a crown, turning the dark auburn bright red and gold, and bringing out the green in his eyes. He was impossibly handsome, and sometimes it took everything she had not to melt into him, no matter where they were or what she was meant to be doing. In her weaker moments she took every excuse to touch him, and he returned the attention without fail. In their early acquaintance he had always been so careful never to instigate such play himself, but in the two years since she had encouraged him to leave such misplaced chivalry behind. Forgetting the notebook, she leaned against his shoulder, and he took her hand in his, clasping it over his knee.

"You'll think of something, Beth. You always do."

"I will," she agreed. "Something involving one man and one woman, as always. Not two men. Nor three, nor a whole squadron of them. And no illustrations, either. I shall restrain myself—even if I do think Mr. Coxley could do a handsome job of illustrating such a book."

"I'll tell him you said so."

"He won't appreciate the compliment, coming from me."

"No, likely not."

Elizabeth sighed and settled against the bench, letting her gaze wander back to the suncatchers. "It's just as well. I don't know how I'd write so many men. Two might be manageable with a little practice, but I can't imagine more than that."

"Are we still discussing your characters, or have we moved on to something else entirely?" Arthur's tone was dry but his eyes gave him away: brimming with fondness, as they always were when he looked at her.

Flipping their clasped hands to put hers on top, she smiled and squeezed his fingers. "Arthur. You indulge me in everything I say, even the nonsense. What am I going to do with you?"

"Marry me?"

Her heart skipped a beat and they both froze for a second. From somewhere out of sight, a songbird twittered, and the leaves shifted and rustled in the breeze made by its wings. Arthur's expression shifted to chagrin.

"Damn it," he muttered. "I had meant to do that over brunch."

Elizabeth found her voice again. "Over brunch?"

"I was going to take you to that little Parisian-style café you like and propose properly. You know: on bended knee, with the ring out and all that." He shut his eyes briefly, tipping his face to the sun. When he looked at her again, he was painted ever so pinkly with embarrassment. "It slipped out a bit early, I'm afraid."

Biting back her laughter, she schooled her face to something more dispassionate. "I see. Would you like to try again?"

"Yes, please, if you don't mind."

She nodded. "Go on, then."

Standing, Arthur straightened his jacket before sliding smoothly to one knee. Elizabeth's heart fluttered into her throat, even though he had already asked. There was something about seeing him kneeling so earnestly at her feet, dashingly handsome in his dove-grey suit, that made her dizzy with excitement. She'd been waiting so long. Unable to hold back her smile, she let it come bursting out, and with it, little sparks of silvery magic that shimmered in the air like dewdrops. She had used to feel self-conscious about showing her magic around Arthur, knowing he didn't have any himself, but he smiled up at her as he always did, the corners of his eyes crinkling. Covering her mouth with her hands, she let her magic sprinkle down over both their shoulders as Arthur withdrew from his pocket a little velvet box in navy blue.

"Elizabeth Turtledove," he said, holding back his own smile by some superhuman feat. Cracking open the box, he offered her the ring inside: a little silver thing with three tiny diamonds set into the band, elegant in its simplicity. "I adore you to bits. Will you marry me?"

"Arthur..." Taking his hands, she drew him close, until he was crowded in right against her knees. The diamonds sparkled in the sun, outshining the flowers and magic surrounding them. "Yes, of course I'll marry you."

His smile broke free, and he reached up to wrap her in his arms as she bent forward to meet him, and their mouths met in the sweetest kiss they'd shared since their first. She ran her hands through his hair, mussing his thick, copper locks and disrupting the pomade, before cradling his face to pepper kisses over his nose and along his jaw, and to each half of his moustache, which was waxed up in perfect curls. When they finally drew apart, he pulled back just enough to look her in the eye, his hands framing her face, fingers curling in her hair.

"Definitely yes?"

"Yes, of course, yes! I've been waiting almost two years for you to ask; you couldn't possibly think I would say no."

"We only met two years ago."

"To the day." She refused to be embarrassed about it.

"Oh," he breathed. "Really? You've been waiting that long?"

She shrugged. "When you know, you know."

"For me, as well. I'm sorry it took me so long. I wanted to ask earlier, I just—"

She pressed one finger to his lips, and he hushed. "I knew you wanted to. I knew you were going to. The waiting wasn't so bad, knowing all that. I could have waited another day. I could have waited ten years, if I had to."

"And what if I never worked up the nerve at all?" Arthur asked, his lips brushing the pad of her finger.

"We're already living in sin. I'm not sure what difference it would have made, really." She paused. "Actually, that's not true. If you hadn't worked up the nerve within the next six months, I was going to buy a ring and ask you, tradition be damned."

"That's entirely reasonable." He held out one hand. "May I?"

"Please." Placing her hand in his, she bit her lip as he plucked the ring from its velvet bed and slid it onto her finger. The silver was a cool kiss against her skin, fitting her perfectly. The diamonds glinted up, catching the sun and making it dance in soft, bright flashes.

"It looks beautiful on you."

"I love it." Standing, she drew him up with her and tucked herself against his side, brushing her hair behind one ear.

He kissed her temple. "Excellent. Now we just have to break the news to your mother."

"Let me worry about my mother," she said firmly. "You deal with Mr. Coxley."

"Jules will be happy for us," Arthur said, though he didn't really sound like he believed it.

Elizabeth didn't believe it at all. In the two years she had known him, Mr. Coxley had never once been happy about Elizabeth's presence in Arthur's life. And it was Mr. Coxley's nefarious presence in Arthur's life that made Elizabeth's mother so recalcitrant to the idea of their engagement.

CHAPTER TWO

ON THE SUBJECT OF ONE JULES COXLEY

"Honestly, of all the ridiculous reasons to warn a girl off marrying a man, the fact that his friend has something of a reputation— Why, I hardly know where to start."

"Saying that Mr. Coxley has 'something of a reputation' is akin to saying that a tiger has 'something of a nasty bite,'" Aaliyah returned, amusement evident in her tone.

It was early April, a week after Arthur had asked the question, and the announcement to her mother had gone just as Elizabeth had expected, which was to say, poorly. Her only allies were her nearest and dearest friends, Aaliyah Kaddour and Jasmine Bailey, who, while supporting Elizabeth's relationship with Arthur, never hesitated to speak honestly on the matter.

In Aaliyah's case, perhaps too honestly. She was the only child of a wealthy silk merchant, in line to inherit the business when her father retired. As a young Algerian woman managing a successful business in the heart of London, she was quite used to fighting in order to get her way, and woe betide anyone who tried to dismiss her on the grounds of her age, her colour, or her sex. Though Elizabeth in no way wanted to trade their places, she had to admit that she admired Aaliyah's approach to solving problems, which was to browbeat them into submission. And the problems generally thanked her for it, afterwards.

Incidentally, that was how Aaliyah had ended up married to Alphonse Hollyhock, a young gentleman of leisure and a man whom Elizabeth had assumed would be a terrible match for her friend (and indeed, for any woman), right up until Aaliyah proved her and the rest of London wrong.

Jasmine and Aaliyah were a study in contrasts. Though both were businesswomen, Jasmine was more interested in art, and her entrepreneurship was a mere vehicle to bring that art into existence. Where Aaliyah was bold, Jasmine was reserved, preferring to speak her mind only in the most private of settings, so as to avoid undue attention. Though her London upbringing had softened her Jamaican accent, it had done nothing to dull the vibrant blackness of her skin, and she caught people's eyes whether she intended to or not. Elizabeth had only made the mistake of confusing her quietness for timidity once, soon after meeting her, and had never been so foolish as to make it again.

They sat around an outdoor table at Elizabeth's favourite café, the trees that lined the street just starting to open their buds and dapple them in early springtime shade. The weather was still cool, bringing with it the risk of night-time frost and prone to dropping sheets of rain at all hours, but spring had undeniably come to stay. The days lengthened one minute at a time, gradually giving way to warmth and fresh blooms. People flocked to the streets and patios perhaps prematurely, but Elizabeth was happy to wear a coat and scarf for lunch if it meant catching some fresh air and a rare spot of sunshine after so many months of dreary grey.

"Mr. Coxley is reportedly an all-around rake, a scoundrel, and a degenerate, and I understand completely why your mother has certain reservations concerning your engagement," Aaliyah continued.

"But his paintings are very good," Jasmine said mildly, sipping her coffee.

"His art is excellent," Aaliyah agreed. "I'm not saying your mother is *right*."

"It's not as if I'm engaged to *him*," Elizabeth protested. "They're only friends! And Arthur is a perfect gentleman in every other way. He comes from a good family, he has a respectable job; he served in the war, for heaven's sake! The only flaw anyone could possibly argue is his lack of magic, and my mother isn't the sort to discriminate based on that. She would adore him, if only she could see past his relations with…"

"They're more than *friends*. They've lived together for years, you know, and I imagine they would have gone on living together indefinitely if you hadn't entered the picture. It's a miracle Arthur's reputation has survived as well as it did. The fact is this: respectable society sees Jules Coxley as a menace, and one misstep will bring Arthur, and by extension you, down with him."

Elizabeth set her coffee down in order to physically wave her friend's words aside. "You'd think he was a dangerous criminal, the way some people speak!"

"He may not be a criminal," said Jasmine, "but he's been nothing but abhorrent to you."

"Yes, but again, I'm marrying Arthur and not Mr. Coxley. That man's personal dislike of me and mine of him has no bearing on anything. His reputation is no more than a load of sensationalist nonsense. I'm to be married in June, and that's the end of it."

"The wedding will be lovely," Jasmine commented, unperturbed by Elizabeth's rising volume.

"Of course," Aaliyah agreed. "I think you and Arthur are a wonderful match, and I'm entirely on your side. I'm just saying: there's a scandal waiting in the wings, and I for one can't wait to see how it plays out."

Elizabeth sighed. "We shall just have to see."

There was a beat of silence, and then Jasmine said, "Why don't you tell us about your next book?" in the most blatant turn of conversation that Elizabeth had ever heard.

Still, she was grateful for it. "I haven't started it yet. I've been so occupied with the wedding dress that I just haven't been able to make the time."

"I can't believe you're making the dress yourself." Jasmine's tone hovered between admiration and judgement.

Not only designing and sewing the dress; Elizabeth was also crafting a series of little charms meant to attract good luck, health, and prosperity, to embroider into the beading. She was only getting married once, after all, and she wanted all the help she could get to ensure both the wedding and her marriage went smoothly.

"She's the best seamstress in London; why shouldn't she make her own dress?"

"Because I have an entire wedding to plan, a business to run, and a novel to write," Elizabeth said with a groan.

Making her own wedding dress had been all her idea, of course, just as the seamstressing had been her idea, and the writing. Her book sales allowed her to keep her dressmaking business afloat, because, though her designs sold decently, their popularity was far from staggering. If she suddenly failed to produce another bestselling novel, her dress shop would suffer from the sudden lack of funds, she was sure.

"I just need a different kind of character for the thing," Elizabeth said. "I've run through all the obvious choices."

"What about someone like Alphonse?" Aaliyah offered.

Elizabeth considered it. Aaliyah's husband was blond, blue-eyed, and wealthy, and therefore a perfect candidate for the love interest in an English romance novel, were it not for one thing.

"I'm not convinced anyone could read about him and come away convinced of his attraction to women," Elizabeth said apologetically.

"Don't be silly," Aaliyah replied. "Most readers wouldn't recognise a queer man if they tripped over him. Tell them he wants a wife and they won't question it. The only ones that would are the ones who are looking for something queer, and they'll certainly never admit such a thing."

"Alphonse would be delighted," Jasmine added. "He's an avid fan of yours."

"Is he really?" Elizabeth took a moment to feel flattered, as she always did when anyone complimented her work. "Wait— Does he know that I'm M. Hayes?"

"Oh, almost certainly not," Aaliyah said. "You could tell him you're doing research on M. Hayes' behalf and he wouldn't question it."

"Jacobi likely knows the truth, though," Jasmine said.

Jacobi was Alphonse's valet and his husband in all eyes but those of the law, and he knew practically everything there was to know. Elizabeth trusted him to keep her secret as he, Aaliyah, Jasmine, and Alphonse trusted her to keep theirs'. It was an unconventional set-up, what the two couples were doing, and not one she was remotely qualified to judge. It made them happy, and therefore she was happy for them.

She hadn't always been. In the beginning when Aaliyah was still scheming how to get around her father's quest to see her suitably married, Elizabeth had been unable to understand how Jasmine could take Aaliyah's husband-hunting with such grace. To watch the love of her life tie herself to someone else for whom she had no affection whatsoever—someone she barely even knew!—seemed an incredibly painful thing to endure. Even with the understanding that Aaliyah and Jasmine had made their own promises to each other and that Alphonse, the husband in question, was in on the whole thing, the situation was unfathomable to Elizabeth. The thought of standing in the pews and watching Arthur at the altar say those words to someone else—

It would be simply unbearable, and Elizabeth thanked every grace she knew that she had the good luck of falling in love with Arthur, and that nothing could stop them from legally wedding and living out the rest of their lives in happy marriage.

Just as soon as Arthur could shake off Coxley's influence.

Jules Coxley had disliked Elizabeth from the moment they met. It had been like introducing an unstoppable force to an immoveable object—Coxley being the unstoppable force, and Elizabeth refusing to budge from her place in Arthur's life. She understood the appeal of Coxley's company, despite his antagonism. He was quick to laugh, though it was often sharp, and his gaze was always bright and interested, if prone to picking out faults. He seemed altogether the sort of man that Elizabeth would in other circumstances want to know better, and all the warnings about his character only made her the more curious.

If only he weren't so dead set on tearing Arthur away from her.

Twenty months earlier, when Arthur had first introduced her to Coxley as his girl, Elizabeth had been taken aback by the man's sarcasm and hostility towards her.

"Does he not think you're good enough for Arthur?" Jasmine had asked bewilderedly when Elizabeth went, distraught, to her friends for advice over tea. "It seems unlikely that a man of Mr. Coxley's reputation should cast judgement on—well, on anyone, really."

"I doubt there's any woman in the world good enough for Arthur, by his standards," Elizabeth replied morosely.

Aaliyah and Jasmine exchanged a glance.

"If it were mere rudeness, I could bear it," she continued. "It's this deliberate cruelty I can't abide. The way he spoke so dismissively, like I was a smear on his shoe! I've never been angrier at a man in my life."

"So, have Arthur cut him off," Aaliyah said bluntly. "If the man won't treat you civilly, have nothing more to do with him. Arthur will take your side in this— unless you think he would be more sympathetic to his boor of a friend than to you," she added, in a tone that suggested Arthur wasn't worth keeping in such a case.

"I'm quite certain he'd take my side." Elizabeth twisted her mouth to one side as she picked at her pastry. "It's just that Arthur has me, and he gets along with all my friends, but from the way he tells it, Mr. Coxley hasn't got anyone else close to him. Not really. And after Arthur came back from the war..." She cleaned her fingers on her napkin, shedding golden pastry flakes. "He doesn't talk about it much, but he relied quite heavily on Mr. Coxley for some time. However poor his treatment of me, I do owe Mr. Coxley for taking care of Arthur then. I don't want to separate them, but I can't stand being treated this way." She looked helplessly at her friends. "I don't know what to do."

Aaliyah reached over to give Elizabeth's hand a reassuring squeeze. "Perhaps Arthur will manage to beat some sense into him," she offered, with some optimism.

"Anyone can see that you and Arthur are a sure thing," Jasmine added. "Eventually Mr. Coxley will come around to the idea."

"Eventually might be a very long time," Elizabeth grumbled, but she allowed herself to be comforted by that hope.

Thus far, *eventually* was two years and counting, and Coxley had shown no sign of warming to her.

"He's afraid of losing me to the banal bliss of married life, I suppose." Arthur had shrugged when she had first raised such concerns to him, but slipped his hands around her waist and drew her close. "I told him not to be so dramatic. He talks like he'll never see me again, when I'm not even leaving the city. He's very much committed to his bachelorhood, I'm afraid, and he doesn't seem to understand—well, any of this."

"What, marriage? Or love?"

"He's very dismissive of marriage as an institution. He always claimed that he would never be caught dead in such a union. But he's an artist, you understand. He's picked up all sorts of radical ideas from the bohemians."

"Has he indeed?"

"He's really not all that bad, though," Arthur had hastened to reassure her. "So much of what's said about him is just gossip and rumours that have spun out of control. He's not *dangerous*."

"Of course he's not, darling. You'd never befriend anyone like that."

But she had never asked Coxley directly whether the rumours had any truth to them. Rumours about his sexual habits, and rumours whispered in even more hushed tones about his magic: that he enchanted his paintings to inspire lust and obsession in their viewers, even that he had caught some portion of his models' souls in the paint and trapped them there. If she asked, she suspected he would say the rumours were all true, and that he was in fact even worse than they claimed— but he would say it with that glint in his eye that meant she couldn't believe a word of it.

CHAPTER THREE

AN UNFORTUNATE FIRST IMPRESSION

Twenty months earlier:

"My friend wants to meet you," Arthur said, looking as if that had taken a great deal of nerve.

"Your friend, singular?" Elizabeth teased.

She had come to visit him at work on his lunch break, bringing him an apple and a sandwich to share. They sat on the steps around the back of the law firm where he worked as a clerk, soaking up the midsummer sun.

"My best friend. Flatmate. But yes, rather. My singular friend."

"Alright," Elizabeth agreed. She had realised in the first month of seeing Arthur that she wanted to keep him, and four months in, meeting his best friend seemed easily arranged, if not belated. Arthur had already met her friends, after all. "When shall we get together?"

Arthur hesitated. "Let me tell you about him first, and maybe you'll change your mind."

"Are you trying to talk me out of meeting him?"

"A little, yes," he admitted.

"Then why bring it up in the first place?"

Arthur dragged one hand down his face. "Because," he said from behind his fingers, "I promised him I would ask you. But you really shouldn't do it. The few girls I've introduced to him before this, he ran them all off. And I know that's my own fault, but I really don't want the same to happen to you."

Elizabeth took a second to process that. "He ran them off," she repeated.

"He goes out of his way to be deliberately rude after asking to be introduced. I think he enjoys breaking up my dates."

"Why on earth do you keep introducing him to your girlfriends, then?" Elizabeth asked, baffled.

"Because I keep hoping that maybe this time will be different." Arthur looked embarrassed and slightly frustrated, tugging on one end of his curled moustache. "Which is silly, I know. But he's not like that normally, you see. He's always perfectly pleasant to my parents and my colleagues and his clients. It's only my girlfriends he takes exception to."

"How many girlfriends are we talking about, exactly?"

"Only three," he said quickly. "And they were all perfectly nice girls, but honestly, they were nothing serious. I mean, we had a good time and all, but I didn't— I never—"

Pleased, she gave his arm a little pat. "Alright. Don't hurt yourself."

Gratefully, Arthur shut his mouth and stopped stammering.

"Why don't you tell me about your friend?" she suggested. "Who is he and why, exactly, should I be trying to impress him?"

"Jules Coxley."

Elizabeth tried to place the name. "The painter?"

"Yes, him. And you don't need to impress him. To be quite honest, I wish he'd try to impress you."

"You've known each other long?"

"We met in school, and we've been living together for a good number of years now. From back before— Well. Since we were old enough to live on our own, really."

From back before Arthur enlisted, she assumed. "Maybe he's trying to protect you," she offered. "Maybe he wants to make sure you find a girl worth your time."

"That's very generous of you, but I somehow doubt it. He's always been very dismissive of the idea of marrying and settling down. Maybe he wants to protect me from that. I don't know."

"Aren't you and he settled down together?"

Arthur laughed. "I suppose, though that's not quite the same thing, is it?"

"Not quite, no." Elizabeth hummed thoughtfully and inched closer to Arthur's side. "Tell me truthfully.

If I meet him, who do you want to come out on top? Him, or me?"

"You," he said immediately.

"You'll take my side if he chooses to behave dreadfully?"

"Absolutely."

"And if I speak up in my own defense, you won't let him turn you against me?"

"I'll have your back whatever you do."

"Well then," she said with a smile, "I don't think we have anything to worry about, do we?"

◆ ◆ ◆

Meeting Jules Coxley went worse than Elizabeth had expected.

They had arranged to rendezvous at the restaurant at seven, and Elizabeth clung to optimism as they waited to be shown their seats. Coxley had been the one to choose the venue; Elizabeth wasn't familiar with it, and Arthur said it wasn't one of Coxley's favourites, as far as he knew. It purported to specialise in seafood, which Elizabeth enjoyed well enough. Unless Coxley intended to poison her with a bad oyster, she intended to make the most of her evening, even if the company turned out to be lacking.

Coxley was already seated and waiting for them, and evidently had been for some time, judging by his half-empty wine glass. Arthur's expression suggested some amount of trepidation, but he greeted his friend as if nothing were amiss.

"Evening, Coxley. Glad you could make it. May I introduce Elizabeth Turtledove? Elizabeth, this is Jules Coxley. Jules—"

"Charmed, charmed," Coxley said dismissively, ignoring Elizabeth's offered hand and not looking at her whatsoever.

Elizabeth dropped her hand, smoothing both palms over her hips. She wore an ivy-green dress with a blue floral print that hit below her knees, with a trendy dropped waist and her strawberry-blonde hair pinned in place with a pearl-decked comb to match the long rope draped over her chest. The dress was one of her own designs, and she'd taken pains to look good without looking like a party girl, or like she was trying too hard to impress Arthur's friend.

Impressing her, or indeed anyone, seemed to be the furthest thing from Coxley's mind.

Elizabeth glanced at Arthur, who rolled his eyes and shook his head minutely at his friend's bad manners before pulling out her chair and then sitting down in between the two of them.

Settling into her own chair, Elizabeth said mildly, "I hope you weren't waiting long."

It was still three minutes to seven; there was no world in which she and Arthur could be considered late, though Coxley seemed to be pretending they were, as if it was their fault he had arrived early.

"Not at all," he replied, lifting his wine glass. "I wanted some time to fortify myself in advance of what I'm sure will prove a tiresome and tedious exchange."

"Jules," Arthur admonished in a hot rush under his breath.

"Come now, old boy, you can't pretend that all such previous encounters have been anything but," Coxley said, taking a drink.

"We've scarcely exchanged two words so far," Elizabeth said. "I have to wonder on what basis you've judged me tedious when you have yet to even look in my direction."

Setting down his glass, Coxley turned the full force of his gaze upon her. She looked back steadily, cataloguing his appearance and demeanour. He had a sharp face with large, dark eyes that looked on her with disdain, his expression giving away no deeper feelings. His hair was thick and dark and given to curls, and in need of a cut and a good combing. He bore a natural tan, at least in the summer, in contrast to both Arthur and Elizabeth's fair and freckled complexions. A shadow of stubble lined his jaw, which, combined with his unbuttoned collar and crooked tie, gave him the appearance of a ruffian. Only his build suggested that he was an artist rather than a thug: he was slight, with delicate hands and fine-boned wrists, and though he was sitting, Elizabeth guessed he was shorter than either herself or Arthur.

She assumed he cultivated such a rough appearance intentionally. He probably enjoyed the attention it afforded: the scorn from polite society that he no doubt liked baiting, as he was baiting her, and the curiosity it garnered from the wilder, younger generation who were drawn to such rebellion.

Elizabeth herself was one such youth, though she wasn't much drawn to rebels outside of fiction. Arthur was proof of that. Furthermore, even if she were intrigued by Coxley's roguish appearance, she had enough self-respect to expect better treatment from a paramour. Coxley, she determined, was little more than an unkempt bully, and once she got through this dinner for Arthur's sake, she would have nothing more to do with him.

As she reached that conclusion, he seemed to have reached some conclusion about her, as well. Before he could voice it—and voice it he would, Elizabeth was sure—their waiter materialised to distribute the menus.

"Let's order now," Elizabeth said quickly, eager to move the evening along. "What do you recommend?"

"The special tonight is clam chowder," the waiter recited dutifully, in the kind of monotone unique to young men who are bored out of their minds. "Cook's got a pot of salmon hash on the stove, and we've got a good stock of fresh jellied eels at the ready."

"I'll have the salmon hash, please," Elizabeth said, "and a bottle of house white."

"The chowder, for me," Arthur supplied.

"Fish and chips, if you please," said Coxley.

The waiter collected their unopened menus and retreated to the kitchen.

Once he was gone, Coxley turned on Elizabeth with a faint sneer. "Salmon hash," he repeated. To Arthur, he said, "Does she always order from the high end of the menu?"

"Excuse me, but poached salmon is hardly a gourmet dish," Elizabeth objected.

"I don't think this place would know a gourmet dish if they tripped over it," Arthur added in a low voice. "Honestly, Jules, if you wanted fish and chips we could have gone to any pub in a five-mile radius. A good, reputable pub where we wouldn't have to worry about food poisoning."

Coxley scoffed. "I've been here before; it's perfectly safe. Anyway: a person's order tells you a lot about them."

"It doesn't tell you anything other than the fact that I thought salmon sounded the nicest out of the three things he listed," Elizabeth said, exasperated. "Besides which, if I did want to order the priciest item on the menu, I would be perfectly capable of paying for it myself. Because that is what you're insinuating, isn't it? That I'm leaving Arthur to foot the bill every time we go out?"

"Of course you can pay your own way," Coxley agreed. "You manage your own business, don't you? A dressmaker, I believe?"

"That's right," she said cautiously.

"Tell me, Miss Turtledove, do you feel the need for such self-employment because you don't trust Arthur to provide for you?"

"Oh, come on, Jules," Arthur complained.

At that moment, the waiter returned with the wine, and Elizabeth plastered on a smile to thank him. The instant his back was turned, she scowled at Coxley.

"Do you not believe women should work outside the home, Mr. Coxley? I shudder to think of your opinion on our right to vote."

"Certainly I think women should be able to vote alongside men," Coxley replied with an expansive roll of his eyes. "By all means, lower your voting age to twenty-one like the rest of us, and yes, of course, work whatever jobs you please. I just wonder, if you're looking for the sort of independence and emancipation that comes with such a job, what do you actually need from Arthur?"

"It's not transactional. Arthur and I are together because we like one another's company. We're not trying to use each other for anything."

Arthur took her hand over the cutlery and gave her a reassuring squeeze and a smile.

"Young love, then," Coxley surmised.

Elizabeth desperately wished for their food to arrive and interrupt the conversation, if it could be called that, or better yet, force a change of subject. When the food didn't appear as a result of her wishing, she used her free hand to pour herself a generous glass of wine.

"You know," said Coxley, watching their display of hand-holding through narrowed eyes, "Arthur told all his previous girlfriends that he loved them, too."

"Jules!" Arthur snapped.

"Is that supposed to shock me?" Elizabeth asked. "I know Arthur's gone out with other girls before. It will take considerably more than that to make me jealous when I'm the one he's walking home tonight."

"Fair enough. I imagine you've slept around with your share of men, after all."

Arthur's hand clenched around her fingers and Elizabeth forced herself to take a drink before replying. The alcohol didn't help diffuse her anger. Putting her glass back down, she said, "Are you really going to cast aspersions on other people's sex lives, after everything I've heard whispered about your own?"

Coxley looked incredibly satisfied, as if he took great pride in such rumours.

"Can you not be civil to a single one of my dates?" Arthur begged Coxley. "You said you wanted to meet her and I *knew* you were going to be miserable, but for god's sake, man, you could have surprised me just this once."

"If you knew I was going to be like this, I rather think that's on you, old chap," Coxley returned. "If you can't find a single girl in all of London who can put up with me for the length of one dinner, then frankly, you're better off without them."

"Unlike those other poor girls," Elizabeth said, "I have no intention of walking away. And if you're going to insist on such needlesome behaviour, I guarantee that out of the three of us, you're the one who's going to be ending this evening alone. Not me, and certainly not Arthur."

"You seem terribly confident in that outcome, Miss Turtledove," Coxley said, leaning back in his chair to look her up and down. He looked like nothing so much as a great, lazy cat, contemplating which delicate vase he wished to bat down from the mantelpiece next.

"She's quite right," Arthur said firmly. "I'm not letting her slip through my fingers like those others you succeeded in pushing away. I wish you could behave yourself just once, Jules. This kind of thing is as exhausting as it is embarrassing."

Coxley didn't look in the least chagrined, but he did adjust his attack. "Very well. I'll concede that Miss Turtledove does have certain irrefutable points in her favour. Pretty, quick-witted, from a decent family and sharp enough to manage a career. Commendable attributes, all around, and certainly more so than any other girl you've introduced me to."

"Thank you," said Arthur.

Elizabeth kept quiet, suspiciously waiting for whatever Coxley had planned.

"Clearly, Arthur would be lucky to have you," Coxley said to her. "But surely you can't think you're a good match."

"Why ever not?" she asked through clenched teeth.

"What on earth can he possibly offer that you can't achieve faster and more successfully on your own? You have your own money, your own career; you're clearly driven. Meanwhile, he's working as a clerk in a law firm. No aspirations of becoming a lawyer himself, mind you, but content to sit behind a desk pushing paper back and forth all day. Don't you want something more from a partner?"

"We're in *love*. I know that must be difficult for you to grasp, as you seem incapable of human feeling—"

"That won't last," Coxley said dismissively. "You've been seeing each other, what, four months? That's nothing. A drop in the ocean."

Elizabeth bit her tongue. Neither she nor Arthur had said *I love you* to each other yet, though she suspected they both felt it was true. She hadn't meant to say it, but it had slipped out, and judging by the way Arthur's hand tightened around hers, it hadn't escaped his notice. They couldn't discuss it then and there, not in front of Coxley, but it was a talk they probably ought to have. Provided they escaped dinner unscathed—an outcome that was looking increasingly precarious—she would raise the subject the moment they were alone. Under the table, she tapped Arthur's ankle with the toe of her shoe in what she hoped was a non-verbal promise of just that.

Aloud, she said to Coxley, "You don't know me."

"I know Arthur," Coxley said. "And he'll never be enough for someone like you."

For a split second, the entire table was still.

Then Elizabeth threw her drink in Coxley's face.

Shoving her chair back from the table, Elizabeth stood, vibrating with adrenaline and barely-contained fury. "You don't deserve his friendship," she hissed at him, "but he is absolutely deserving of mine."

"Badly done, old chap," Arthur said tiredly, standing and taking Elizabeth's arm. "Don't expect me back at the flat tonight. I don't think we have much to say to each other just now."

Retrieving his napkin, Coxley delicately mopped the wine from his face. "I suppose I'll pick up the bill, shall I?"

"Yes, I think you'd better."

Elizabeth turned on her heel and stalked out of the restaurant without even waiting to see if Arthur was keeping up with her. The instant they were outside, she spun around and pressed her forehead to his shoulder, clinging to him tightly for just a second before pulling back to search his face.

"I'm so sorry," they both began at the same time.

"You have nothing to apologise for," Arthur said. "Coxley was a beast. Worse than I've ever seen him. I would have thrown a drink at him myself if you didn't."

"I so wanted to give him a chance, Arthur, I really did, but he rubbed me the wrong way from the very first word and I just couldn't—"

Gathering her close again, Arthur gave her a quick kiss on the forehead. "You were remarkable. I'm amazed your patience lasted as long as it did. I appreciate how you tried to meet him with an open mind. I won't ask it of you again."

"I don't understand how he could take such an instant dislike to me."

"Whatever had him so prickly tonight had nothing to do with you, I promise. I'm going to give him a few days to pull his head out of his arse before speaking to him again. If he offers any apology for his behaviour after that, I'll pass it on to you, though honestly, I wouldn't hold my breath."

"And he's your friend?" Elizabeth asked dubiously, trying to understand what Arthur saw in such a man.

"Not right now he isn't," Arthur said. "But in general, every other time but this? I can't explain it, and I certainly don't expect you to understand after the display he put on for you. But yes, he's my friend, though at times like these I do have to question that."

Elizabeth looped her arm around Arthur's waist and settled in beside him as they walked away from the restaurant.

"Maybe, if we're still seeing each other a year from now, I might give him a second chance and see if I can catch him in a better mood," she said.

"A year from now," Arthur echoed.

"Too far in the future to contemplate?"

"I don't know. I suppose if we're in love, contemplating the future should be well within our wheelhouse, shouldn't it?"

She stopped walking and turned to face him again. "About that."

"Hm?"

"Are we in love?"

"I think we might be."

"Good." She nodded in mock seriousness. "I'm glad we got that sorted tonight, if nothing else."

She couldn't keep her expression straight as he caught her face and kissed her. After a second, she gave up on pretending to be sober about it and flung both arms around his neck, kissing him back and not caring who might see them. In fact, there was a tiny, vindictive part of her that hoped Coxley had left the restaurant and could see them now, happily wrapped up in one another while he was alone and miserable.

But she so disliked being vindictive that she pushed the thought aside until there was nothing in her mind but Arthur, and the feel of his hands against her face, and the taste of his lips, sweet and tart with wine.

"Shall we find somewhere else to go for dinner?" he asked against her lips.

"I could actually go for fish and chips," she admitted.

He laughed against her hair and took her arm once more. "I could as well. I know a decent pub a few blocks from here, if you don't mind the walk."

"Please, lead the way."

They ate haddock fish and chips with salt and vinegar, cosied up in a little booth at the back of the pub.

The next day, they heard that Coxley had got food poisoning from whatever he had eaten at the seafood place.

Elizabeth tried not to feel too spitefully pleased about it, and only marginally succeeded.

CHAPTER FOUR

THE ENGAGEMENT PARTY

Mid-April brought marginally warmer weather and with it, Elizabeth and Arthur's engagement party. Arthur meekly asked to invite Coxley, and Elizabeth hardly intended to be the kind of wife who controlled her husband's life down to the company he kept.

Coxley had never exactly apologised for his behaviour at the seafood restaurant, as Arthur had said he wouldn't, but he had spent the next several months showering Arthur in gifts: taking him out to eat, bringing him lunch at the law firm, bringing home wine and desserts, buying him new clothes and stationery and whatever else he thought might have caught Arthur's eye. Arthur had finally relented and, with Elizabeth's permission, forgiven Coxley before the man could follow through on his threats to buy Arthur a motorcar.

Coxley hadn't taken any such measures to earn Elizabeth's forgiveness, but the next few times they encountered each other, he wasn't nearly as wretched to her. They skirted around one another like two unfamiliar cats, and Elizabeth let herself believe that, having thrown his tantrum and found that it hadn't accomplished anything, the worst of Coxley's behaviour was in the past.

So, she allowed Arthur's invitation to stand. If Coxley was to remain by Arthur's side then Elizabeth would have to get used to him and he to her. The engagement party had enough guests to provide a buffer between the two of them and, she hoped, prevent their mutual dislike from escalating to anything outright uncivil.

The party was hosted at Elizabeth's house, or rather, technically speaking, her mother's. Elizabeth's father had died when she was a girl and left his wife a decent amount of savings, and as such, Elizabeth had grown up comfortably middle class: not wanting for anything, but with a firmly-ingrained idea that she ought to work for a living and earn her own way before marrying. In the past year, her royalties had skyrocketed her far beyond anything her parents had ever dreamed, landing her in the camp of very comfortable indeed. Without her books, her income was modest and unremarkable.

Arthur came from a similar background, though he hadn't lived with his parents since his schooldays. Following his return from the war, he had elected to go straight back to sharing a flat with Coxley rather than return to his parents' house. Perhaps he wanted to avoid their coddling; maybe Coxley was a better flatmate than he seemed. Elizabeth wasn't sure. Arthur understandably disliked talking about his part in the war, and Elizabeth was hesitant to push him for details. In any case, the few times she had met his parents, the company had been somewhat awkward, though they both seemed like perfectly lovely people whom she wouldn't mind whatsoever calling in-laws.

And they seemed to tolerate Coxley's presence in their son's life, which was one less thing for her to worry about as far as the party went. In fact, the only person she worried might cause a fuss at Coxley's attendance was her own mother.

"Just be civil," Elizabeth begged as the party began that evening. She wore a dark blue dress with heavy silver beading, one of the flashier pieces she owned, and she worried at the beads whenever her hands weren't otherwise occupied. "For Arthur's sake; that's all I'm asking. Bare civility."

"I'm not going to be rude to the man," her mother returned, sounding scandalised at the mere suggestion.

She was putting the finishing touches on the table of refreshments, sliding one more plate of cookies into the ensemble. Elizabeth had inherited her penchant for baking, though it generally only made an appearance when Elizabeth was stressed.

"He's a guest in my home. No matter how I might disapprove of his personal conduct, I'm certainly going to be civil to him!"

"I know. I know you are. I'm sorry; it's the nerves talking." Elizabeth managed a weak smile. "This is the first time it's felt like it's really happening—the wedding, I mean. Going out together is one thing, but an engagement party—"

Her mother patted her arm. "Nerves are natural, but we're all friends here, my darling. Or most of us are, at any rate." She nodded pointedly across the room to Coxley, who was engaged in conversation with Arthur's parents, gesturing animatedly as he regaled them with some tale or other. "I'm surprised you invited him at all. You've mentioned nothing but strife between the two of you."

"It's Arthur's engagement, too."

"Are you inviting him to the wedding, as well?"

"I imagine so. Arthur would like him in attendance, and unless Mr. Coxley does something truly wretched, I don't see the harm in it."

Her mother thinned her lips.

Elizabeth sighed. "I know your thoughts on the matter. But can we discuss them later? I want this to be a celebration, not a negotiation." Taking her mother's hand, Elizabeth met her eyes with a faintly pleading expression. "Right now, I just want you to be happy for me."

Her mother softened. "My darling, of course I am. I couldn't be happier."

"Why don't you ask Arthur's parents about Mr. Coxley?" Elizabeth suggested. "They've known him for years. Perhaps they could introduce you to the man lurking behind the rumours and set your mind at ease."

"It's one thing to have your son traipsing around with such a man. It's quite another when it's your daughter." But she allowed Elizabeth to take her arm and steer her over to the trio all the same.

"You never know. You might find that you like him. He is said to be quite charming, after all."

"Charm serves to hide a multitude of sins," her mother intoned. "And I'm not likely to warm to him after all you've told me of his treatment of you. But don't worry: I don't intend to cause any kind of scene or interrupt your party."

Elizabeth tried to find that reassuring, but it wasn't really her mother's potential reaction to meeting Arthur's notorious friend that had her stomach twisted up in knots. Her mother took too much pride in being a good hostess to be anything but polite to the man, no matter her opinion of him. No: Elizabeth's nerves stemmed from Coxley himself, and what he might say or do to ruin her day. Arthur had assured her that no such thing would happen, and if Coxley were to step out of line and show any disdain for Elizabeth, Arthur would remove him from the party himself.

Still, there was nothing she could do for it but hope that Coxley decided to behave with grace.

"Hello, Mr. and Mrs. Leicester. I'm so glad you could come," Elizabeth greeted Arthur's parents.

"Of course we came, my dear," Mrs. Leicester said with a warm smile. "We have to take every opportunity to celebrate our future daughter-in-law, don't we?"

Arthur's mother was brunette and matronly with spectacles that gave her the appearance of a schoolteacher or a librarian, and who exuded the kind of maternal comfort that Elizabeth couldn't imagine turning away from in favour of someone like the abrasive Coxley. Beside her, Arthur's father raised his champagne flute in a toast to the bride-to-be. He had bright ginger hair with a neat beard to match and came off as somewhat sterner than his wife, with echoes of a military history in his stance that weren't present in his son, despite both having served.

"Mr. Coxley was just telling us how the Duke of Edinburgh has commissioned a portrait," Mrs. Leicester explained, holding out one hand to include Coxley in their group.

"Is that so?" Elizabeth said politely. "How exciting. Mr. Coxley, I don't believe you've met my mother yet. Mother, this is Jules Coxley, Arthur's friend."

"Mrs. Turtledove," Coxley said, catching her hand as if he meant to kiss it. "A pleasure to meet you. Might I assume my reputation has preceded me?"

"I've heard your name," Elizabeth's mother agreed neutrally, "and I've seen some of your work in galleries about town. You certainly have a talent, Mr. Coxley."

"Thank you very much. And congratulations on your daughter's upcoming nuptials. I shudder to think what she has said of me behind closed doors."

"Why should I have to close the door before talking about you?" Elizabeth asked innocently.

"She's really only mentioned you in passing," her mother lied. "Why? Certainly you haven't given my daughter any reason to speak badly of you?"

Coxley glanced at Elizabeth, who gave him her best and most insincere smile.

"Of course not," he said. "Force of habit, I'm afraid, to assume people are whispering all manner of salacious things behind my back. To be fair, most of what they say is true. But don't let me keep you from catching up with the Leicesters! Miss Turtledove, perhaps you'd care to introduce me to your friends?"

Elizabeth did not, in fact, care to do any such thing, but Coxley was behaving better than she had expected, so she rewarded him by agreeably walking him over to where her friends were gathered.

"You could tell them about your commission from the Duke," Elizabeth suggested. "That's a fun icebreaker."

"No one our age cares about the aristocracy," Coxley said dismissively. "That's the sort of thing I say to impress someone's parents. It doesn't transfer across generations."

Elizabeth supposed that was true, and seeing as she had nothing invested in whether Coxley felt comfortable around her friends, she didn't say anything more. Her friends were predisposed to dislike the man, as she had been complaining about him from the moment they met. Lending a sympathetic ear to such complaints for two whole years made it unlikely that they would suddenly turn coat and welcome him into their group with open arms.

But Coxley could be charming when he wanted to, albeit in a sarcastic, roguish kind of way. Elizabeth couldn't help the squirm of nerves at the thought that her friends would actually like him and judge her long history of complaints unfair.

She tamped down that thought as she approached, announcing brightly as if nothing had ever been amiss: "Everyone, I'd like you to meet Jules Coxley. Mr. Coxley, these are my friends: Jasmine, Aaliyah and her husband Alphonse, and Alphonse's man Jacobi." She cast her friends a pleading look for them to be pleasant to him.

Jasmine and Aaliyah gave him a cool greeting; Jacobi, unfailingly aloof, merely inclined his head. Alphonse, on the other hand, gave the man a beaming smile, a cheery wave and a, "Hello!" perhaps because he didn't realise it was the same Jules Coxley whom Elizabeth so disliked, or perhaps because he'd taken his cue from Elizabeth's silent plea. She suspected it was the former.

"We've met before," Aaliyah said, "though only briefly. I think it was at your last gallery opening, wasn't it, Mr. Coxley?"

"I believe it was. You took a liking to my painting of the Lady Godiva, if I'm not mistaken. You were especially interested in where I had procured my model for the lady."

Jasmine glanced at Aaliyah. "Were you interested?"

"She had the most striking features," Aaliyah said, straight-faced.

"Her features, yes," Coxley agreed, not nearly so composed as she.

"I mean her hair, of course."

"Oh, yes, her hair. The blackest you've ever seen, tumbling all the way down to her knees in perfect, shining waves. I hardly did it justice."

"And did you find out who this black-haired beauty was?" Jasmine asked Aaliyah.

"I thought it uncouth to share her identity at the gala itself," Coxley said, "but I can tell you now that she was a Gujarati girl come to London for work."

"Jolly good," said Alphonse. "I can hardly imagine having to work for a living, so good on her for earning a wage. Does modelling pay well, do you think?"

"Not generally, but I'm pleased to say her Godiva portrait started quite a trend. Her presence is in high demand, so you're likely to see her crop up frequently over the next few months. In art, at parties, on people's arms, et cetera."

"Is the painting still being displayed anywhere?" Jasmine asked. "I would love to see this Lady Godiva who so impressed Aaliyah."

"Sold to a private collector, I'm afraid," Coxley apologised.

"Not to me," Aaliyah added.

"We'll have to invite her to my mother's garden party at the end of the summer," Alphonse said, nudging Aaliyah in the side. "If she's so popular, the old maternal force will want to meet her, what?"

Aaliyah looked at Jasmine, who raised her brows.

"Mrs. Hollyhock can invite whomever she likes," Jasmine said, "and I'd be very curious to see her, if she made such an impression."

"I've only seen Mr. Coxley's interpretation of her likeness," Aaliyah pointed out.

"All the more reason to see her in person then, no?"

Coxley glanced back and forth between the two of them, his gaze interested and amused in a way that had Elizabeth's hackles up.

"Godiva," said Alphonse. "Was she the one who went riding about naked on horseback through the town square?"

"That's correct, sir," said Jacobi.

"Daring stuff," Alphonse said admiringly. "That must be awfully uncomfortable on the bits, riding a horse like that. I struggle on horseback at the best of times; I wouldn't want to do it in anything less than a sturdy pair of breeches."

"I didn't actually have her on horseback in my studio," said Coxley.

"No? Well, I suppose you'd have a hard time fitting the beast through the door. Not to mention the mess to clean up after, what? Just as well to paint it in after the fact."

Before Alphonse could get too lost in considering the logistics, Coxley asked, "What about you? Would you be interested in modelling for me?"

"Oh no, I couldn't possibly," Alphonse said. "Though I'm told that sitting around and looking pretty are very much the only strengths I have, I'm afraid I would just fall asleep if I didn't have anything else to do, and then what would happen to your painting?"

"You could read a book," Aaliyah suggested, her expression devilish as it always was when she was goading her husband into a bad idea.

"I could," Alphonse hedged. "Jacobi, what do you think, old chap? Should I model for one of Coxley's pieces?"

"If you are so inclined, sir," Jacobi said neutrally.

"Or the both of you," Coxley suggested, looking Jacobi over with great interest.

It had to be said that Alphonse and Jacobi made a striking pair: Jacobi tall, broad-shouldered, and as dark in hair and eye as Alphonse was fair, with Alphonse being the smaller and more slender of the two, favouring light pastels to Jacobi's sensible black and white ensemble.

"Come now, surely you're not going to paint a young gentleman with his valet rather than his wife," Elizabeth interjected with a laugh. Though Alphonse was, to all outside observers, happily married to Aaliyah, there was no reason to start any rumours that he was closer to his manservant than a young gentleman ought to be.

Coxley cut her a sharp look. "Why shouldn't I? Surely you don't think I would go to all the effort of inviting a gentleman to my studio just to mock him on canvas? Any painting I should produce of Mr. Hollyhock and his man would be dictated by his own sense of taste."

"With all due respect, Mr. Coxley, you seem to hold your own reputation in complete disregard. Why should you be trusted with anyone else's?"

Coxley gave her an absolutely humourless smile. "Let's not pretend that you have the slightest concern for my reputation, Miss Turtledove, except for how it impacts Arthur's."

Alphonse looked back and forth between them, radiating nervous discomfort. Jacobi laid a soothing hand on his elbow and Alphonse immediately stopped vibrating.

"Perhaps Miss Turtledove is right, sir," Jacobi said smoothly. "We have no need of a portrait, and surely an artist of Mr. Coxley's calibre would lose patience with an inexperienced sitter."

"Naturally, there is a degree of self-importance one must possess before sitting for a portrait," Coxley said agreeably, "and you seem a man far too sensible to be distracted by such things."

Jacobi politely inclined his head.

"I do like the idea of a portrait, though," Alphonse said wistfully. "I don't mind being insensible or self-important."

"Of course, if it's a concern of reputation, as Miss Turtledove so considerately suggests, there's no need to commit your likeness to canvas at all," Coxley said. "I've had no small number of respectable ladies and gentlemen sit for me, and no one would ever guess their identities. I can paint you as anything you like: a Greek god or a prince or a nymph—anything at all, and no one looking at the final painting need have any idea you were involved."

"You seem awfully keen on getting him into your studio," Elizabeth remarked, not bothering to hide her suspicion.

"Obviously!" Coxley rolled his eyes and waved one hand at Alphonse. "Just look at the man! He looks like he's stepped out of some Wildean fantasy; any painting using him as a model would prove immensely popular with my clientele and I won't pretend otherwise."

Alphonse preened.

"But," Coxley continued, "if you're concerned about your ability to sit still or stay awake for the duration, you could always accompany your man while he sits for me."

Alphonse lit up. "Jacobi! Jacobi, old thing, you simply have to have him paint you as a Greek god. I insist on it."

Coxley's gaze raked the length of Jacobi's figure, gleaming with interest that would have been inappropriate in polite society were he not known to be an artist of some eccentricity. Elizabeth thus put his gleam down to hunger for Jacobi's admittedly top-notch aesthetic rather than some more base physical desire for the man. Nevertheless, she cleared her throat.

"I think not, sir," Jacobi said.

Alphonse deflated.

"A shame," said Coxley. "But, no matter. You know where to find me should either of you change your mind." With a smile, he turned to the ladies. Elizabeth correctly guessed that she was not included in their number. "What about you, my dears?" he asked Aaliyah and Jasmine. "Would either of you care to be immortalised in art?"

Aaliyah immediately declared, "I want to be painted as a Greek goddess."

Coxley blinked at her utter lack of hesitation before giving her a brilliant smile. "Which did you have in mind?"

"Artemis, with her hounds and horses and all. And I have no concerns whatsoever about staying anonymous." She offered him her arm, which, after a quick glance at Alphonse, who merely beamed at his wife's attitude and took a cheery sip of champagne, Coxley accepted. "Shall we discuss the particulars?" Aaliyah asked, swishing him away from the group in her little black dress. "What does your schedule look like? I have a string of meetings next week I can't afford to postpone, but after that…"

Elizabeth would have to thank her later for pulling Coxley away, though she was certain Aaliyah did genuinely want a painting of herself as the goddess of the hunt, and saving Elizabeth from Coxley's company was a mere bonus.

Arthur found his way over to her just as Aaliyah and Coxley departed. "My mother insists that this isn't an engagement party until there's dancing, so, if I may interrupt…?"

"An excellent idea," Elizabeth agreed, pressing against him as the party guests cleared a space in the centre of the room and Elizabeth's mother set up the record player. The music crackled to life and a slow love song filled the room. Elizabeth laughed. "Can't we have something faster for our first dance? This is a party, not the wedding itself!"

"Humour me," her mother called from her place by the record player. "One romantic dance, and then all you young people can choose the music for the rest of the night."

"That does sound fair," Arthur allowed. "Elizabeth?" He extended one hand, inviting her to a slow waltz. "Would you?"

"As if I could say no."

They took their positions as the singer on the record started to croon; too saccharine for Elizabeth's usual tastes, but it hit differently when waltzing with her fiancé, she had to admit. Arthur's charcoal-grey tuxedo with its black satin lapels complemented her silver and blue, and though she wasn't given to flashiness, she enjoyed the thought of every eye in the room being on them.

"Coxley seems to be getting along with everyone," Arthur murmured against her ear. "He hasn't caused any trouble for you?"

"Everything is going incredibly smoothly. To my surprise, I must say. But I still get the sense that he dislikes me, and is merely lying in wait for the opportune moment to strike, like a snake in the grass."

"A little dramatic, surely."

"A little," she agreed, "but I'm not comfortable letting my guard down just yet."

"Perhaps he's finally accepted the inevitable and realises that I'm going to marry you come hell or high water."

"Do you think he's accepted it?" Elizabeth asked sceptically.

"I hope he has. I want him to."

Elizabeth prodded him in the chest with one finger, right in the middle of his bowtie. "That's not a real answer and you know it."

"I think he's making progress," Arthur said. "Coming to the party and making nice with your friends is proof of that. I think he's trying."

Elizabeth hummed and wrapped her arms around Arthur's neck, resting her head against his shoulder, but she still wasn't convinced of Coxley's good intentions.

However, there was too much for her to do to stay distracted by Coxley's behaviour. The wedding was fast approaching, intent on sweeping her off her feet and carrying her away with all its planning and preparations. She had her vows to write and her dress to sew—a decision she regretted as the date neared—and seating to arrange, not to mention the flowers and the dinner and everything else. With Aaliyah at her side as Elizabeth's maid of honour, Elizabeth's mother took over the brunt of the planning with the stoic determination of a general riding into battle, and Elizabeth was only too glad to relinquish the reins to them both.

When she said as much aloud, Arthur replied, "Imagine if we had planned a big wedding. With hundreds of guests and great extended families."

She shut her eyes as if she could block out the very idea. "We could always elope."

"I shudder to think of your mother's reaction."

Because, despite the flurry of activity, their wedding was to be quite small. They had only invited a handful of guests: there were their families, of course, but they didn't go tracking down any distant or far-flung relatives, and they only invited their closest friends. It was to be an intimate affair, tucked away in the countryside rather than in one of London's grand churches. Elizabeth had no desire to feel like royalty on her wedding day. She didn't need a thousand spectators or a designer dress worth her weight in gold. All she needed was Arthur.

"And you have me," he promised, when she said so. "You'd have me even if we were married in a shed, with no one but goats and cows as witnesses. But we're only going to get married once, so let's make it count." Wrapping his arms around her, he pressed his face into her hair as they gently swayed back and forth. "Let your mother fuss over you," he murmured. "If we can placate her this way, perhaps it will keep her from speaking too harshly of me at the reception."

Elizabeth laughed, but tipped her face up to kiss his cheek. "Ever the strategist. Fine, fine. We'll do our best to keep her happy. But she would never be so bold as to criticise you on our wedding day. She really does like you; I don't know how many more times I must assure you of that. She's protective of me, that's all."

"Well, if Jules decides to play nicely, perhaps there's no reason for her to object to me."

The song ended and they pulled apart to bright applause. Elizabeth's mother changed the music to something faster and more people joined them on the floor, throwing themselves into lively dances with different partners. Aaliyah returned to dance the Charleston with Alphonse and then with Jasmine— Jacobi remained on the sidelines, looking serenely stoic as if he had never danced before in his life and never would—before making her way back to Elizabeth at the refreshments table.

"So?" Elizabeth asked. "Have you successfully commissioned a painting?"

"It seems so. I hope you don't see this as me fraternising with the enemy."

"Not a bit. I'm only surprised you warmed to him so quickly. Or at all."

"I'm not trying to steal his best friend away from him, so he has no cause for antagonism towards me," Aaliyah pointed out.

"No, you just normally have so little patience for—well, for men."

"Most men are absolutely boors not fit for human company," Aaliyah agreed. "But I can admit there are a rare few I find tolerable. Alphonse and Jacobi, for example, are perfectly pleasant to be around. I'd stop short of calling Mr. Coxley *pleasant*, but I don't foresee him causing me any trouble." She shrugged. "You learn to get a sense for these things."

"I worry he's still causing trouble for me," Elizabeth returned peevishly.

"Is he really?" Aaliyah looked at her. "*Trouble* would be if he actually disrupted your plans of marriage, and you don't really believe that Arthur would ever choose him over you, do you? Mr. Coxley is a minor inconvenience for you, and a sad one, at that."

"You feel sorry for him?"

"I'm not suggesting you put up with his attitude towards you," Aaliyah assured her. "He needs to pull himself together. I'm just saying that I recognise that in his mind, this entire situation is something of a tragedy."

Before Elizabeth could work out how to respond to that, Coxley himself approached, slinking up to them like a fox to the henhouse.

"May I have this dance?" Coxley asked, one hand extended.

Elizabeth regarded him with no small amount of suspicion. "Are you quite sure you want to?"

"I've already danced with everyone else, and it's your engagement party, after all. But feel free to say no."

Wary of his motives, Elizabeth slowly accepted his hand and walked with him to the dance floor. "I suppose it would be good to talk to you without any friends jumping in on our behalf."

"On your behalf, I think you mean." He gave her a tight smile that didn't come close to meeting his eyes. "I can't think of anyone inclined to defend me against you."

"Why should you need defending from me? I've done nothing but respond to your provocations!"

"My provocations have only ever been in self-defence," he returned. "How would you react if someone swept into your life and tried to turn your closest friend against you?"

"I haven't swept anywhere or turned anyone against anything! You can't possibly accuse me of trying to steal Arthur from you. We invited you here, didn't we? No one is trying to break up your friendship or keep you away from him."

Coxley scoffed. "Invitations to placate me for the time being, certainly, but what about after the wedding? Do you really mean to tell me that Arthur and I will remain as close as we were before you came trampling into our lives? How could we possibly? He'll be off living with you when you don't know nearly enough about him to be able to provide him with the kind of support he needs, and I'll be ignored so you can save your social standing by refusing to have anything to do with me. I know what your mother thinks of me; why should you see me any differently?"

"You are catastrophising," Elizabeth said. "You're spinning scenarios out of nothing but your own fear of the future, when I've given you no good reason to fear any of the things you've just listed. And what do you mean, I don't know Arthur well enough to look after him? I've known him for two years!"

"I've known him for twenty," Coxley countered. "And you are not a suitable partner for him. You're pretty, competent in your business, and perfectly intelligent—all that is obvious, and I can understand what Arthur sees in you. But he is blinded by the rose-tinted glasses of love, whereas I can see you clearly for what you are."

"And what am I?" Elizabeth asked coldly.

"A liar and a hypocrite."

She stared at him. He looked back smugly.

"What?" she finally said.

"I know who you are, Miss Turtledove. And I know that your secret identity is just as debauched and scandalous as the identity I show to the public every day. The only difference between us is that I'm not a coward about it."

"My secret identity," she repeated.

"Indeed. Or should I refer to you as—"

She shoved him hard in the chest and he stepped back with a smirk, deflecting the force of her glare with sheer insolence.

"Don't you dare," she hissed. "Don't you ruin this party for us, you spiteful little menace." Taking a step closer to bridge the gap between them once more, she said in a lower voice, "If you want to discuss our similarities, as you say, then we'll do it somewhere private, at a time and place of my choosing. Do you understand?"

"I think you misunderstand who's in control of this situation, my dear."

"I think you misunderstand everything about me, and about Arthur, for that matter. Now get out before I have Arthur throw you out."

"He wouldn't," Coxley said immediately.

"Do not test him," Elizabeth snapped. "We planned for exactly this scenario, in which you couldn't treat me civilly for a single evening, god knows why not. Arthur is fully prepared to throw you bodily from this house if you won't go quietly of your own accord." She glared at him. She'd never loathed a person more. "Do you doubt me?"

Coxley hesitated for the first time since she'd met him. "He wouldn't," he repeated, though he sounded uncertain.

"He's marrying me," she said flatly. "It's past time you got used to the idea."

An expression of unaccountable hurt flashed across Coxley's features so briefly that Elizabeth couldn't be sure she had seen it at all, and then Coxley turned on his heel and strode away without another word.

From across the room she watched him make his excuses to Arthur and Arthur's parents and her own mother, his smile too strained to be anything but fake. He said his goodbyes quickly—what excuse he offered, Elizabeth didn't know—and departed without a backwards glance. Though she was glad to see him go, his absence gave her no peace. At least when they were in the same room she could keep an eye on him.

"What happened?" Arthur asked quietly when he rejoined her, slipping one hand around her waist so they could speak as privately as was possible in the midst of the party.

"He knows my pen name and I believe he wishes to expose me."

"To what end?" Arthur asked, sounding baffled.

With a sigh and an angry shrug, Elizabeth crossed her arms, leaning her shoulder against her partner's. "Sheer spite, I assume. I'm going to speak to him away from all this and find out what he means to do with that information. Blackmail or extortion or the thrill of dragging my name through the mud, I don't know."

Arthur made a soft, distressed sound. "Blackmail and extortion really aren't his style. I know the two of you are at odds, but I can't believe he would do anything so drastic as that."

"I notice you're not claiming he's above trying to publicly embarrass me."

"I can't deny that he's done worse things to people he considers enemies," Arthur admitted. "But it won't come to that. I'll talk to him and make it clear that if he moves forward with whatever scheme he's plotting against you, I'll have nothing more to do with him."

Elizabeth turned to look him in the eye, and found his expression more serious than she had ever seen.

"I mean it," he said. "If he wants to force my hand to choose between the two of you, then I will."

She placed one hand on his chest. "Are you sure? He's your closest friend, and however much of a cad he is to me, I don't want to be the deciding force that cuts you off from him."

"You're not." He kissed her forehead. "Everything he's doing is of his own volition. If he values my friendship, he'll stop antagonising you. If not…"

"Let me talk to him first," Elizabeth said. "If he already despises me, then let me be the one to deliver your ultimatum. If he doesn't take it seriously, then you can step in, but before that— Maybe he'll listen to reason and back down."

"Maybe," Arthur said, sounding unconvinced.

"I need to talk to him anyway," Elizabeth continued, her anger flaring again. "Because more concerning than whatever threats he's levelling at me is the question of how he found out my pen name in the first place."

CHAPTER FIVE

A CONFRONTATION AND A HESITANT TRUCE

St. James's Park was beautiful in the spring, with fresh raindrops clinging to the newborn flower buds and the tree leaves just starting to unfurl to their full majesty, but Elizabeth appreciated none of that when she went to meet Coxley at the north side of the Blue Bridge.

Coxley, lounging against the side of the bridge, was dressed in his customarily shabby black coat, his collar undone and his hair as unkempt as ever. A few people walked near the bridge's far end, but none near enough to overhear any conversation or threaten their privacy. All the better: the sooner Elizabeth could get this over with, the sooner she could go home and put the whole affair behind her.

"Let's skip straight to the point, if you please," she said briskly the instant she strode up to him, her hands in her coat pockets. "You claim to know my pen name, so I assume you wish to expose me. What is it you want to prevent that? Money? Attention? Or is it the thought of my humiliation that's spurring you on here?"

Coxley pushed himself upright, straightening his coat before slinging his hands casually in its pockets to mirror her pose. "Nothing so base as any of that."

"Arthur said that blackmail wasn't in your wheelhouse, but frankly, I'm not inclined to put anything past you."

"It's actually Arthur who is inspiring my actions in this matter," Coxley said.

Elizabeth fixed him with an unimpressed glare. "Elaborate."

Instead, Coxley gestured to the bridge. "Shall we walk?"

"If we must," she replied through gritted teeth.

Side by side, as if they were amicable companions rather than antagonists, they stepped onto the bridge, walking south.

Coxley said, "It's my concern for his reputation should his fiancée be exposed as the authoress of such scandalous material that's driving me, in fact."

Elizabeth stared at him in silence for several steps before finding her voice. She hardly knew what part of that statement she ought to find most ridiculous. "Scandalous material," she repeated in an undertone. "I'm hardly distributing pornography, Mr. Coxley. I write romance novels for a reputable publishing house. They're not a fraction as scandalous as your paintings— or your conduct, for that matter."

"I think it's only fair if Arthur were allowed to decide the risk for himself. He did with me, after all."

"You think he'd leave me because of my moonlighting as a romance author," she said slowly.

"It's not what you're hiding from him," Coxley said, "but the fact that you're hiding anything at all. And for it to be something so significant, both in its importance to you as well as being a source of considerable income—"

"He knows."

Coxley blinked and, Elizabeth noted with vindictive pleasure, missed a step, stumbling before catching his balance.

"He knows," Coxley repeated.

"Of course he knows. Who do you think proofreads my manuscripts?" She took a moment to enjoy having put him quite literally on the wrong foot before steeling herself for the unpleasantness that was sure to follow.

Their conversation had carried them the full length of the bridge, their fellow pedestrians having crossed ahead of them and left them alone. At no point on the bridge had they lingered to admire the view or any of the park's impressive collection of waterfowl, which in other circumstances might have held Elizabeth's attention quite pleasantly. As it was, she had no patience for charming landscapes or the serene paddlings of little ducks.

"So. You know my name. I ask again: what do you intend to do with this information?"

Coxley scowled, keeping his gaze fixed on the ground directly in front of him. "Nothing. I only rooted out M. Hayes' identity to indulge my own curiosity; it was a pet project. I had no initial suspicion that it might be you and I have no intention of announcing your identity to the public. Truthfully."

"You just thought you could use it to drive me from Arthur. Who else knows?"

"Only the private investigator I hired in the first place."

"Mr. Coxley."

His gaze flickered up to hers, shadowed.

"I had long discounted the rumours I heard of you, as I trusted Arthur's taste in friends. Your deplorable conduct when we first met, I forgave when it didn't happen a second time. For Arthur's sake, I gave you another chance to behave like a decent human being when we invited you to our engagement party. But I can now safely say that you are every bit the wretch people say you are. I should have believed you the first time you showed me your personality. You should try reading my books sometime," she said icily. "Perhaps you could use them to learn a thing or two about functional relationships."

As they stepped off the bridge together, it was Coxley's downturned gaze that allowed him to be taken by surprise. One of the aforementioned waterfowl, a swan of magnificent size, perhaps insulted at the lack of appreciation Elizabeth and Coxley had offered, charged up the bank, wings spread, to buffet Coxley about the legs, all while hissing ferociously.

With a curse that came out more like a startled yelp, Coxley lost his footing and tumbled straight into the water from whence the bird had come.

Elizabeth froze, staring at the empty space where he had been a second previously, before the wild thrashing from the water prompted her to action. As Coxley fought his way up the bank, soaked and heaving for breath, Elizabeth collected herself and reached to meet him halfway, instinctively offering to help him out of the water. Still cursing, he batted her hand away—to be fair, perhaps accidentally, as he was flailing to keep his balance against the slippery slope of mud—which proved to be her last straw. The instant he hauled himself ashore, bent double as he coughed out a mouthful of water, she lit into him with two year's-worth of frustration.

"I do not have the time, the patience, or the inclination to deal with you!" Elizabeth exclaimed. "I'm getting married in June, and there is nothing you can do about it. I say this not as a challenge, but as a fact. You cannot stop Arthur and I from marrying. If you try, Arthur will cut you off for good."

"Miss Turtledove—" he began wetly.

She held up one hand to forestall his argument. "You still don't understand. There is no challenge here. You think you can stop him from choosing me, but it's already over. He chose. All you're doing is forcing him to reaffirm his choice every time you come against me like this. You're ensuring that he'll gain a wife but lose a friend, and for heaven's sake—to what end?"

She stared at him, demanding an answer. He stared back, dripping from head to toe and looking as taken aback by her assault as he had been by the swan's. The combination of his expression, his being soaked, and the fact that he had very clearly lost the fight between them made him seem for the first time not a challenge for her to best, but a pathetic little man more worthy of her pity than her loathing.

"What on earth is the point of all this antagonism when you could simply be happy for him?" she asked desperately.

"I would be happy for him," Coxley replied tightly, his hands curling into fists by his sides, "if it didn't come at such high cost to myself."

"What cost? You could be losing a flatmate, nothing more. He would have had you as his best man if he could trust you not to go for my throat during the ceremony; instead you seem insistent on forcing him to denounce you entirely. What is it about me that's so abhorrent that you would rather ruin your friendship with him than accept me as his wife?"

"I don't expect you to believe me, but it's really not personal at all."

"You're right. I can't believe that."

He gave a stiff shrug. "There is nothing abhorrent about you, Miss Turtledove, save your interest in him."

"Do you hate all women?"

"Not remotely. Only the ones set on marrying him."

"You'd consign him to perpetual bachelorhood for the rest of his life? With you?"

Coxley didn't answer.

"You're scared of losing your friend. I sympathise: I know you care for Arthur very much. But has it occurred to you that you stand a much better chance of keeping him close by supporting his marriage, as opposed to sabotaging it?" She leaned in. "He loves me, and I intend to keep him. Don't drive him away. I can't imagine you have many friends to spare."

When Coxley didn't immediately reply, Elizabeth forced herself to turn and regard the water. A flock of ducks milled around dipping for food, little flashes of white catching the sun every time they went tail-up. Nearer the bank, Coxley's swan patrolled up and down with a mean look in its eye.

"Very well," Coxley finally said. "I know when I've been beaten."

"Mr. Coxley, this truly doesn't have to be a competition."

"Does it not? It's quite alright, my dear. You've won him, fair and square. The least I can do is retire with some modicum of grace."

"I don't believe you've ever done anything with grace in your life," she said bluntly, and then paused to consider the situation.

Either Coxley was genuinely conceding defeat, or he was the best actor in England, and he struck her as being far too rash to play a long game. Looking at him now, he didn't seem like a wild animal, cornered and about to lash out. He just looked embarrassed, and under that, tired. And wet, obviously, and starting to shiver. Perhaps it was fanciful to see loneliness in him, too, but she suspected it was true. Aaliyah's words came back to her: that Coxley was a sad man, convinced he was trapped in some tragedy.

"Let me suggest an arrangement," she said, weighing her words with care. "You don't speak to Arthur of the wedding or the marriage again unless he asks you directly, and in return, after the honeymoon, I'll encourage him to keep in contact with you. If we survive this afternoon together without any public violence, perhaps the three of us can go to dinner. Regularly, even."

"A truce," he said slowly.

"We're not at war," she countered.

"This is rather my running up of the white flag."

"Very well. If this is your surrender, then I shall endeavour to be merciful." She eyed him. "As long as you don't shoot me as soon as my back is turned. Do we understand each other?"

"We do."

"Excellent."

Exhaling, she let go of her animosity. She would give him this last chance. If he could behave civilly for the rest of the day, she would report back to Arthur that perhaps things were mended. If he picked another fight—if he offered a single unkind word—then it would be over. Drawing a quick symbol in the air, she uttered a drying spell and cast it over him. Coxley held very still, wide-eyed as her magic evaporated the water from his hair and clothes in the time it took to snap one's fingers, leaving him as dry, if somewhat more dishevelled, as he had been when he first set foot upon the bridge. Though her strength lay with charms, she had a handful of spells at her disposal, mostly ones that came in useful at the sewing machine or around the house. Drying was hardly glamourous, but it had been the second spell she had mastered, after the classic spell of illumination, and it made the laundry and washing up so much more efficient.

"Let's not talk about the wedding anymore," she said, with forced lightness. "Tell me about your work, Mr. Coxley. I don't know anything about the particulars of painting."

Coxley accepted the change of conversation without protest. He seemed as unsure of her as she was of him, both of them testing the waters. Their conversation was stilted at first, both speaking awkwardly of the weather and superficially of their work, before the frost finally thawed. Coxley was on his best behaviour, courteous and perfectly respectable, and when he realised that she wasn't going to hold her victory over him, he gradually relaxed, and their talk grew livelier. Dancing around more sensitive topics, skirting the edges of politics and carefully avoiding any mention of weddings or romance, the rest of their walk passed in a blur. As they came upon the edge of the park where it met the main thoroughfare to rejoin larger society, Elizabeth was surprised to admit that she had ended up enjoying herself, and she told him as much.

He cast his gaze down, his dark lashes painting his cheeks. "You're likewise a fine conversationalist, Miss Turtledove. It's a shame I was too pig-headed to recognise it sooner."

"As long as you avoid any such pig-headedness in the future, I could be persuaded to let it slide."

Frowning, he met her eye. "I've been nothing but horrible to you. Why should you forgive me so easily?"

"Because I believe you're better than that, when you're not feeling threatened."

"Threatened—"

"And because you make Arthur happy," she added, in a gentler tone.

He shut his mouth.

"I was telling the truth when I said he wanted you as his best man, you know."

"Yes, I imagine he did," Coxley said quietly.

"He hasn't asked anyone else, yet."

Coxley glanced back at her. "No?"

"Should he ask you?"

It was a challenge, and they both knew it.

"Let me make things up to you," Coxley said immediately. "To the both of you."

Nodding, she offered him her hand. When he accepted it, his touch was firm but cautious.

"Then I'll see you at the wedding, Mr. Coxley."

CHAPTER SIX

IN WHICH VOWS AND DANCE PARTNERS ARE EXCHANGED

The rest of the spring spun by in a whirl, turning to summer without pausing to catch its breath. The days warmed and lengthened, flowers bloomed, and trees burst green and full of birdsong. Elizabeth scarcely noticed, so busy was she with the wedding plans and all that accompanied them. Her dress was one thing, but she couldn't prioritise it over her clients' work, and then there was the matter of finding a house to buy. Her book, unrelated to her wedding, she set aside for the time being, with a promise to herself and her publisher both that she would see it done by the fall and no later—but certainly no sooner, either. House-hunting she found rather tedious, but Arthur took to it with the same meticulous attention to detail he took to his clerical work, so she trusted he would find something suitable without needing her input.

The day of the wedding dawned bright, the June air hanging heavy even before the sun slipped her fingers over the horizon. They had fled London for the ceremony, Elizabeth staying overnight in her mother's country house and Arthur arranging to travel out in the morning. They were to be married in a small church amid the rolling yellow hills of the countryside, the sky vast and blue overhead, promising a day of thick, billowy heat.

"Are you nervous?" Aaliyah asked as she and Jasmine buttoned Elizabeth into her dress.

They were in a tiny room on the church's second floor, tucked away from the guests and stirring excitement of the ground level. Elizabeth stood in front of an old full-length silvered mirror propped against the wall.

She smoothed her hands down her dress's body as she exhaled in a rush. "A little," she confessed. "But it's a good kind of nervousness. My only worry is whether Mr. Coxley will make some last-minute attempt to stop Arthur from going through with it. I don't think it's likely at this point, but if I've read him wrong and he is capable of such a drawn-out trick, today is his last chance to throw a wrench in our plans."

Coxley had thus far kept his word and not interfered with her relationship any further. She only saw him when the wedding plans threw them in each other's paths, during which times they were unfailingly polite to one another, she in a whirlwind of to-do lists and he skittish and seemingly unsure of himself. Arthur promised that Coxley had shared no more negativity surrounding their match, seemingly dedicated to his role as best man, and equally dedicated to staying by Arthur's side as much and for as long as possible.

"He'll be fine," Aaliyah said firmly, finishing with the line of pearl buttons that ran up Elizabeth's back.

"Not even Jules Coxley would be so shameless as to interrupt your wedding," Jasmine added, fixing a tiara of flowers to Elizabeth's veil.

Elizabeth studied her reflection. Her strawberry-blonde hair framed her face in carefully-sculpted finger waves, swooping over her ears to gather in a chignon at the back. Over her hair sat an ivory cloche cap to which was fixed her veil, which Jasmine had pinned in place with magic-crafted flowers that circled her head like a crown. Like Elizabeth's suncatchers, they seemed made of stained glass, glowing green and gold and pearl in the sun, a bright tiara made of her friend's magic.

The veil was a shimmering length of the thinnest silk to match the satin ivory of her shift dress. Elizabeth had hand-sewn every white and gold stitch of that dress, painstakingly embroidering the body and the hem with tiny beads and good-luck charms of her own crafting, which glimmered with a faint aura of magic even weeks after completion. A line of pearls ran up the back and the skirts hung straight down in elegant sheets, sweeping over the floors as lightly as clouds. It felt like wearing air.

"You look like a queen," Aaliyah told her, smoothing down her veil.

Elizabeth's breath caught in her chest. She looked like she had stepped from the pages of a fairy tale, bedecked in flowers. And her prince was waiting for her at the altar. "I feel like one."

A short knock at the door announced Coxley's arrival. He was dressed presentably for the first time since Elizabeth had met him, in a navy-blue suit with a pale pink bowtie and pocket square, and, glancing down, Elizabeth saw matching pink socks peeking out above the tops of his brown Oxfords. His hair was still unruly, but Elizabeth was beginning to suspect that had less to do with effort and more to do with some inherent wildness that simply couldn't be tamed with pomade and a comb.

"Everything's ready for you," he said from the doorway.

"Are you supposed to be here?" Elizabeth asked.

"It's only the groom who can't see you beforehand."

"Yes, but aren't you supposed to be staying with the groom?"

"Technically." Coxley shrugged. "But Arthur is nearly vibrating out of his skin with nerves, and he seemed reassured by the idea that I might come to check on you. So, here I am."

"Everyone's waiting for me?"

"There's no rush. They can wait a while longer before they get restless if you need more time."

"No, no. I don't want to stall; it will only give my own nerves an excuse to start up." She adjusted her veil, took a deep breath, and held out one hand to Jasmine, who presented her with her bridal bouquet.

"Are you ready?" Jasmine asked.

She had never been more ready for anything in her life. The butterflies swirling in her stomach urged her to run downstairs to the altar, but she wanted to draw the moment out eternally, too.

"I'm ready." Turning to Coxley, she requested, "Walk me downstairs?"

He balked. "I'm not sure that's appropriate."

"Not down the aisle," she chided. "I'll give you plenty of time to get back to Arthur's side before I make my appearance."

"Ah. You just want to keep your eye on me until the ceremony starts."

"Yes," she agreed without hesitation. "If you don't mind."

"It's a bit late for me to try to disrupt your plans at this point. Unless you expect me to stand up and publicly object at the last minute?"

She eyed him.

"I haven't earned your trust yet?" His mouth was a crooked slant like he expected the worst from her.

"You're here, aren't you?" she returned. "You've been earning it. I hope you'll earn the rest of it today."

He blinked. "Right. Well. I won't object. Whatever my word is worth, you have it." He offered her his elbow. "Now: shall we?"

They descended the stairs arm in arm with Aaliyah and Jasmine flanking them on either side. Elizabeth held her bouquet in both hands: a bundle of wildflowers picked from the garden outside, cut fresh that morning and tied with a white ribbon, interspersed with those suncatcher flowers Jasmine had sculpted from raw magic, matching the ones in the crown of her veil. They glowed gold and green, washing her hands in summer colours.

When they reached the bottom of the stairs, Aaliyah, Jasmine, and Coxley left her, slipping past the congregation of guests in the pews to take their places by the altar. Alone, with the aisle stretching straight before her and seemingly infinite in its length, Elizabeth shut her eyes for a second, breathed in the flowers' sweet perfume, and nodded. When she opened her eyes, on the other side of the church Aaliyah gave the signal to the organ-player, and the familiar tune of the wedding march filled the church hall. Mr. Leicester came to Elizabeth's side, waiting for her to take his arm and begin their walk. He was dressed in his military best, grand and imposing, but as she looped her arm through his, he gave her a smile so fatherly that she couldn't find him intimidating whatsoever. In the front row of pews, Elizabeth's mother was turned around in her seat to beam at her, eyes already shining with unshed tears.

And at the altar, Arthur waited, resplendent in his dove-grey suit, a wildflower tucked through his buttonhole to match the ones she wore and carried. To his left, standing some paces behind him, was Coxley, his face a mask of neutrality, but he and her friends, family, and all the guests faded into obscurity as soon as Elizabeth took her first step down the aisle. She only had eyes for Arthur, whose gaze tracked her every move, his hands clasped before him to keep them from trembling. He looked beautiful, barely contained by the ceremony, like he wanted to run down to meet her and sweep her off her feet then and there, vows be damned.

But he held his ground.

His best man wore navy and her bridesmaids wore blush-pink, with wildflowers pinned in their hair. The petals of Elizabeth's bouquet brushed her fingers as she walked, leaving tiny smudges of pollen in their wake, painting her gold. The butterflies in her stomach swirled all the way up to her throat, threatening to spill out in giddy laughter.

Finally, Mr. Leicester left her side to join his wife in the front row, leaving Elizabeth to walk the final steps on her own. As she reached the altar, she was smiling so widely under her veil that she felt her face could split. Arthur could see it through the silk, she was certain, and his smile grew in response, his fingers twitching as he held himself back from reaching for her. When they faced each other, the rest of the world fell away. The priest's words were a mere murmur in the back of her mind; the thrumming anticipation from the audience was nothing compared to the racing of her heart.

She stared at Arthur, the sun slanting through the stained-glass windows to light up his auburn hair like burnished copper and paint his skin with a warm glow. He was the most beautiful man she had ever seen. He touched her veil as if tempted to remove it ahead of schedule, though he was careful not to upset the myriad pins keeping her hat in place or the crown of flowers nestled atop. When he finally met her eyes through the silk, his expression was impossibly fond and she fell in love with him all over again. Grasping his hands, she tried to communicate that, as if he couldn't read it plainly on her face. Happy tears welled in her eyes and she blinked them back, mortified at the prospect of crying in front of so many people, even if it came from joy.

"I, Elizabeth Turtledove," she said, fighting to keep the tremor from her voice, "take this man, Arthur Leicester, to be my lawfully wedded husband. I promise to honour and protect him, to cherish him, to care for him when he is sick and lift him up when he is well, and to love him with all my heart, as fully as I am capable, till death do us part." Her voice broke at the end and she swallowed hard, but Arthur just beamed back at her, his own eyes equally bright with tears.

"I, Arthur Leicester," he said softly, gazing deep into her eyes, his fingers clasped around hers, "do take Elizabeth Turtledove to be my lawfully wedded wife, whom I will honour and protect in sickness and in health, whom I will defend and love whole-heartedly and whose side I will never leave, till death do us part."

"Do you have the rings?" the priest intoned.

Coxley stepped forward from his place behind Arthur, a shadow to Arthur's golden glow. His gaze flickered to Elizabeth's and she met it just long enough to take in his expression: a half-smile and something wistful in his eyes. Elizabeth blinked and it was gone. With a shallow bow, Coxley presented the rings—pale gold bands, plain and simple—on a black handkerchief. Arthur took Elizabeth's and slipped it onto her finger, and she took his and did the same. The metal was warm against her skin and immediately felt like it had always been a part of her, just waiting to be returned to its rightful home.

"Now, Arthur Leicester, you may kiss the bride."

Arthur lifted her veil with deceptively steady hands, but when it was settled around her shoulders, he stilled, as if lost in her and incapable of continuing. Without waiting for him to make the next move, she threw her arms around his neck, crushing her bouquet against his shoulders. They met open-mouthed and laughing, their teeth bumping and their noses getting in the way, but she didn't care. Above them, a shower of silver and gold sparks rained down, a variation of one of Aaliyah's illumination spells she had crafted specifically for the occasion, and the magic glittered where it clung to their skin and clothes. Elizabeth let her own magic spark out like little fireworks to join it—nothing so wild as to be embarrassing, but wild enough to be improper in a church, perhaps. Arthur turned his face up to bask in the light and she followed him, her cheeks wet with tears. She pressed her face to Arthur's, her fingers tangling in his collar and smoothing over his hair. His rested at her waist, pulling her close and holding her so tightly that maybe they would never let go. It was all terribly indecent, and she had never been happier.

Elated, she kissed him again and bit his lip before parting, and when they finally turned, hand in hand, to face the crowd—all on their feet, applauding and cheering themselves hoarse—they were both flushed and bright-eyed, and smiling so widely it hurt. She felt drunk already—from their kiss, from their vows, from the explosive applause and the knowledge that when they went to their new house that night, they would do so as husband and wife.

"I love you, Arthur Leicester," she whispered fiercely.

"I love you, too."

As they waded into the crowd to accept their congratulations, Coxley circled around from his place at Arthur's side to intercept them.

"Let me be the first to offer my best wishes. I hope you'll both be very happy together."

"I'm just glad you didn't lose the rings," Arthur replied, still grinning, before he enveloped his best man in a crushing embrace. Coxley stumbled into it, wide-eyed as Arthur grabbed his face and planted a smacking kiss on his lips. "Thank you," Arthur said, holding him by the shoulders so he couldn't escape. "I really thought for a second there you might go and cock it up, but you didn't, so— Thank you, Jules."

"I wouldn't have," Coxley protested, recovering and clasping Arthur's hands with his own. "Not today. You couldn't think—"

"Of course you wouldn't have," Elizabeth interjected, brushing her husband aside to lean in and press her own kiss to Coxley's cheek. "You were a brilliant best man, Mr. Coxley, and we're ever so glad you're a part of this."

The crowd jostled, their immediate families growing impatient and surging up to meet them. Coxley stepped back, faintly pink from the attention.

"We'll see you after!" Arthur called to him, before he and Elizabeth were swept up in congratulatory affection by friends and family alike.

The afternoon passed in high spirits and champagne, swirling by like a rush of paper confetti. At some point she removed her cloche hat and veil to sit her tiara of flowers directly on her head, less a bride and more a fairy tale princess. Later, Elizabeth would only be able to remember individual moments: her mother holding Elizabeth's flushed face in her hands, Arthur's mother crying as she wrapped Elizabeth in a warm hug, his father misty-eyed as he proclaimed Elizabeth his daughter, and the best he could have wished for his son. The feeling of Arthur's ring around his finger when she held his hand. The heat of Coxley's stare from across the room as he watched them together.

It wasn't until evening that time slowed down enough for her to catch her breath. They were halfway through dinner, the food doing wonders to ground her against the giddy effects of the alcohol, and the speeches from their friends and families were well underway. Aaliyah had just concluded hers to laughter and applause when Coxley rose, tapping his spoon to his glass to cut through the ruckus.

"Last chance for things to go south," Elizabeth murmured to Arthur.

"You think they will?"

Coxley coughed lightly. "I promised Arthur I'd keep this short; he was worried about me saying something inappropriate, I think. Any other time, I'd prove him right, but not today. Today calls for sentiment." He paused. "I'm not particularly given to sentimentality," he confided to the crowd, which responded with amusement. "So: short and to the point." Coxley raised his glass, and everyone raised theirs' in turn. "Arthur is my oldest friend. He's known me the longest out of anyone in the world, and I've known him the longest out of anyone in this room. Save his parents, naturally." He nodded to the Leicesters. "And for all that I've tried to be a terrible influence on him, it's clear to see that I have completely failed on every count. Arthur deserves a wife determined to bring out his best in equal measure to my attempting to bring out his worst, and I believe he's found that in Elizabeth." Coxley found Elizabeth's gaze and held it. "In fact, I know he has." Breaking eye contact, he cleared his throat. "So! To Arthur and Elizabeth Leicester. May they be a force of good in each other's lives."

"To Arthur and Elizabeth!" the crowd echoed joyously.

"Thank you," she mouthed to him, and he inclined his head in acknowledgment before they both took another drink.

Dinner turned to cake, where she got her fingers sticky cutting into it for the first time and barely resisted Arthur's indecent offer to lick them clean, and cake turned to dancing. Her first dance was with Arthur, and they took the length of their gentle foxtrot to let the rest of the party fall away, enveloping themselves in a quiet moment where they were the only people in the world. Shutting her eyes, Elizabeth pressed her cheek to Arthur's shoulder and thought only of the feeling of his suit against her skin, the warmth of his hands and the easy rhythm of their movements, flowing forward and back over the dance floor.

The end of the song and the burst of applause accompanying it brought them crashing back to earth. Elizabeth blinked, momentarily startled.

"There will be plenty of time for peace and quiet when we go home tonight," Arthur said. "I don't think we can get away with waltzing by ourselves for the rest of the party."

"Perhaps not, but it would be nice, wouldn't it?"

Laughing, Arthur gave her a little push towards their waiting families. "You have too many other people waiting in line for their chance to dance with you. You can't disappoint them."

Elizabeth waltzed with her mother, who was inspired to a fresh burst of weeping, and performed a very tame samba with Arthur's father—she was delighted to learn that he was familiar with the dance— at which point the floor began to fill with other couples. When the samba ended, Aaliyah called for the band to strike up a jazzier tune, and she and Alphonse flailed their way across the room in a lively Charleston, urging Elizabeth and Arthur to join them until, laughing, the bride and groom gave in.

The pace picked up as Aaliyah took control of the band, and the dances grew faster and more energetic with every song until finally, even as tipsy and elated as she was, Elizabeth was forced to admit that she was in need of a break before she sweated clean through her wedding dress.

"You two should dance!" she told Arthur and Coxley next time the music shifted and people were looking for new partners.

"Should we?" Arthur asked, bemused.

"I really don't think we need to," said Coxley.

"I need a second to catch my breath," Elizabeth said, "and at least one of the married couple has to stay on the dance floor. Who better to entertain him while I'm gone than you?"

"She's right," Arthur said, catching Coxley by the elbow when the man tried to escape. "Who better to dance with me than my best man?"

"You'd think I was the only person left in the room," Coxley grumbled, but he didn't pull away.

"Come on," Arthur pleaded. "It's my wedding."

"I know."

"Oh, go on." Elizabeth pushed them lightly towards the dance floor. "Humour me, the both of you."

Laughing, Arthur did as she asked, and pulled the barely-resisting Coxley into position as the music struck up a bright waltz. Pleased at having got her way, Elizabeth traipsed through the crowd of dancers and minglers to find her friends. Aaliyah and Alphonse had commandeered the cake table to eat spoonfuls of frosting like children sneaking into the kitchen after hours, while Jasmine stood by sipping her drink as she pretended not to know them.

"Here she is!" Aaliyah crowed as Elizabeth joined them. "The woman of the hour."

"I have to say," Alphonse said around his icing spoon, "this is a spiffing party, Elizabeth. My mother could take a page out of your book."

"I'm quite looking forward to your mother's big garden party, as a matter of fact," Elizabeth replied. "You probably only like this one because she's not here to fuss at you."

"Glare at me like a great mean-spirited hawk, more like. But no, her parties always have a great deal more talking and not enough dancing, in my opinion, so yours wins out regardless." He raised his spoon to her in a sugary toast. "On that note, I'm off to rope someone into another foxtrot. Cheers!"

As Alphonse jogged off, Aaliyah tucked herself to Elizabeth's side. "How are you doing? Feeling overwhelmed yet?"

"Still basking in it," Elizabeth admitted.

"As you should. Where's Arthur got to?"

"I handed him off to Coxley so I could refill my drink."

"Shouldn't you have someone to do that for you at your wedding? Here, give me your glass, let me do it. If there's ever a day when you should be catered to—"

"I wanted to do it myself," Elizabeth said, though she made no objection to Aaliyah pouring her another drink. "Take a moment to clear my head, you know? I feel drunker than I am, and I want to savour this. All of it."

Aaliyah paused, gave Elizabeth a good once-over, then set aside her newly-poured drink to fetch her a fresh glass, filling it with water. Elizabeth accepted it without complaint. It tasted sharp against the dry champagne and sugared frosting still clinging to her palate.

"Thank you," she said. "I can't imagine much worse than spending the first day of my honeymoon hung over."

"As your maid of honour, it's my job to keep that from happening. Hopefully Mr. Coxley is doing the same for Arthur."

"They make a handsome pair," Jasmine observed, nodding to the groom and his best man on the dance floor.

"I have faith in them both," Elizabeth said, sipping her water. "I sent them off together so I could take a moment to stand still. Everything's been passing by in such a rush—a wonderful rush, but I feel I need to catch my breath so I know it hasn't all just been an especially vivid dream."

"How romantic-sounding," teased Aaliyah.

"I'm somewhat worried I'm going to end up spending my honeymoon trying to catch up on lost sleep."

"I'm sure Arthur would be thrilled by that outcome."

"Well. Sleep and perhaps one or two other activities."

Aaliyah raised her glass. "To marriage! May yours spare your sex life."

"I don't think it's in danger of fizzling out anytime soon."

"You have to be careful. They say familiarity breeds contempt, and so many couples fall prey to it." Aaliyah took a swig of her drink before giving Elizabeth a mischievous smile. "I, for one, have certainly never had sex with my husband."

Elizabeth swatted her. "Arthur and I are going to be terribly happy together for the rest of our lives, in bed and out of it, thank you very much."

"I know you are. And I absolutely believe Arthur feels the same."

"I wouldn't have married him if he didn't," Elizabeth replied, intending to match Aaliyah's flippant tone, but her voice came out far softer.

Drinking her water, Elizabeth watched the two men dance, studying the way their bodies fit together, the sharp angles of their suits softening to something graceful when they moved, hand in hand with their steps synchronised like they had done it before. Maybe they had, Elizabeth considered. Maybe they had taught each other to dance in the absence of any female partners before she had entered Arthur's life. The thought stirred in her something fond for Coxley, something she hadn't previously felt, not even when she had kissed his cheek following the ceremony.

"I'm glad you and Coxley are getting along," Aaliyah said. "It would have been terribly awkward if you had continued going for each other's throats when I was getting along so well with each of you separately."

"Yes, that's the only reason it would have been awkward," Elizabeth replied, smiling as she rolled her eyes. "I take it your portrait is coming along to your liking, then?"

"Oh, it was finished last month. I have it hanging in my study. I would have put it in the bedroom, but Jasmine said that was a bit much, and as she is the designated artist of the house, I can only defer to her judgement."

"She has enough ego without hanging up a painting of herself as a literal goddess to look at while she's in bed with me," Jasmine said. "It went in her office."

"You'll have to come and see it once you're settled. I would have had you over to show it off sooner, but you've been so busy, and I wanted to be sure you and Coxley were in each other's good books beforehand."

"And you're happy with it?"

"It's exquisite," Aaliyah said. "He really is marvellously skilled with a brush, and you know I don't toss compliments around casually."

"I do know. What was it like modelling for him?"

"Better than you might think. You've only caught glimpses of his charm up until now, and of course he's been tiptoeing around you what with the threat of Arthur cutting him off. But he's surprisingly good company when he's at ease, and I enjoyed myself immensely. In fact, I would happily model for him again, if only time and patience were on my side. Unfortunately, I can't justify spending so many hours lounging around when I've already got one painting out of it, so." She shrugged.

"I have to say, I'm rather curious about it," Elizabeth admitted. "Did you really spend hours at a time with him in his studio?"

"It turns out that most of the time put into a painting is waiting for the oils to dry. But as for him actively painting me, yes, I did spend a fair few days sitting around in his studio mostly naked while he stood mixing colours and documenting the light. If he weren't such a decent conversationalist I'd have got fed up and walked out without waiting for it to be finished. If that's not a testament to his character, I don't know what is."

"Fair enough." Elizabeth paused. "Mostly naked?"

Aaliyah grinned.

Arthur and Coxley's song ended and the two men came over to the cake table, Arthur grinning and Coxley looking more reserved, but still bright-eyed.

"My turn to top up my drink," Arthur announced, swooping in to kiss Elizabeth before pouring himself another glass of champagne.

"Then it's my turn to return to the dance floor," Elizabeth said. "Mr. Coxley, will you dance with me?"

"Arthur—"

"Please do," Arthur said from behind his drink. "I could use a minute, and I think my mother wants a word anyway."

"There you are, then." Elizabeth held out her hand to Coxley, one brow arched imperiously. "Don't tell me you need a minute to catch your bearings as well."

Coxley smiled and accepted her hand. "If Arthur has exercised his right of first refusal, then no, not in the least."

As they threw themselves into a whirlwind of a dance, Coxley asked, "So? Has the day been everything you'd hoped for?"

"Yes," she said honestly. "And you? Has it been as bad as you feared?"

"Not entirely," he admitted. "Though I should probably head out sooner than later, before I get too drunk."

"Do you tend to make poor decisions under the influence?"

"No worse than usual, but I have the feeling I might tend to the morose rather than the exuberant this time, and I don't want to inflict that on either of you today, of all days."

"What reason do you have to be morose?" she asked, concerned.

"No reason. I'm just given to moods sometimes, that's all."

"Well. As long as you're sure it has nothing to do with the day."

"Perfectly sure," he said with a smile, and perhaps if she had been less tipsy, she might have questioned his truthfulness. But, as she had been drinking all afternoon, she didn't.

The evening dashed ever onwards, champagne and music flowing liberally, until Elizabeth's day finally caught up with her, and she wanted nothing more than to retire somewhere quiet with Arthur and no one else, and stay there until she had recovered.

"Things are slowing down," she said in an undertone in Arthur's ear. "Let them finish up the rest of the way without us."

"You're ready to go?"

"I'm very ready. I'd like to go somewhere quiet with my husband now, if you don't mind. Where we can be alone."

His eyes were warm and dark as he replied, "I should be delighted to facilitate that."

And so, at a quarter past one in the morning, Elizabeth and Arthur escaped their own wedding reception to be alone together for the first time as a married couple.

CHAPTER SEVEN

A CONVERSATION IN THE DARK

"Husband." Elizabeth's lips grazed Arthur's cheek as she pressed her face to his, arms wrapped tight behind his neck as he carried her over the threshold of their new home.

"Wife," he returned.

"We have a house."

"We do. And we have it all to ourselves."

Elizabeth kicked the door shut behind them. "I want to have you in every single room of this place."

His brows lifted. "Not all tonight, I hope, because I'd hate to disappoint you."

"We can work at it gradually," Elizabeth agreed magnanimously. "You can start by taking me to the bedroom."

"As you wish."

He carried her up the stairs like it was his honour to ferry her wherever she wished to go. When they reached the bedroom, he gently set her down halfway to the bed, nudging the door shut to cocoon them in quiet intimacy.

Elizabeth smoothed her hands over her dress, feeling unaccountably shy now that they were properly alone for the first time all day.

"Isn't it silly how we've done this a hundred times before, but being able to call you my husband makes it feel like something new?"

"I don't think it's silly at all," he said softly, bringing his hands to her hair to undo the elegant twist of her chignon before beginning the process of removing all the little pins and flowers. "It *is* new, being married."

"It hasn't really changed anything, though. It hasn't changed us."

He lifted the tiara from her hair and set it on the vanity table. Kissing her forehead, he said, "You can't logic your way through the tempest of love, Beth. You just have to let yourself feel what you're feeling."

With a smile, she returned his kiss. "My beautiful romantic."

"My perfect pragmatist."

"Please take off my dress so we can feel some of our feelings together?"

"I would love to."

In a mirror image from that morning, Arthur unbuttoned her line of pearls, starting between her shoulder blades and finishing in the small of her back. She let the fabric fall away, beads, embroidery, and good-luck charms tumbling to the floor in a glittering pool as she turned to face him in her chemise and stockings. He drank in the sight of her, hands clasping her shoulders as she worked loose his bowtie, sliding the fabric from his collar to drape carelessly across the vanity. She unbuttoned his shirt as his hands drifted to her waist, impossibly hot through the silk.

When he was topless she stepped back, slipping the straps of her chemise over her shoulders to let it fall off her in a whisper of silk. A breath away, Arthur unfastened his trousers and likewise stepped out of them, kicking off his shoes as he draped his clothes over the back of the vanity chair, never taking his eyes from her. With one hand on the vanity for balance, she wordlessly offered him one leg, and he caught her thigh around the blue ribbon of her garter. His fingers were light and clever as he rolled her stockings down one at a time until he could pull them over her pointed toes, draping the white gossamer silk over his clothes on the chair. She held her breath, her bottom lip caught between her teeth. He was beautiful in his focus, his gaze dark and steady as he finished undressing her.

Naked, they stepped into each other's embrace as they had done so many times before, their hands in each other's hair, pressing skin to skin and mouth to mouth as they fell into bed. There was nothing new in any of their actions, but it was the first time they had made love as husband and wife, and though the act was familiar, the novelty of marriage made each kiss a little sweeter, each stroke a little more passionate, each gasp and uttered prayer a little more heartfelt.

When they were finished, they lay side by side on their backs as they tried to catch their breath, sticky and gleaming with sweat. Arthur, ever diligent in his duty, had ensured that she had come first, and then again with him for good measure.

"Was that the best it's ever been?" she asked, groping blindly to pull his hand to her breast where her heart galloped behind her ribs.

"You asked that last time," he said hazily, "but yes, I think so."

"Good. Let's keep getting better."

They drifted off together somewhere in that dreamy place between sleep and waking where everything felt good and heavy. When they next came to they went again, and if they didn't beat their previous record, they certainly didn't fall short, either. When they had both finished, Elizabeth draped herself over Arthur's chest, careless of the fact that they might get stuck together.

"It was a good wedding," she declared sleepily.

"It was certainly the best I've ever had."

"Everything went perfectly. Even the weather cooperated."

"Your good-luck charms paid off," he agreed, lazily kissing her hair without any real intent.

"Coxley behaved, too."

"He rose to the occasion admirably."

She nuzzled under his jaw, cracking a yawn before settling in to fall asleep again. "I'm glad you get to keep your friend," she informed him, and dozed off before she heard his answer.

In her dreams, Arthur and Coxley whirled across a glittering ballroom, arms around each other and steps perfectly in synch as a million crystals glinted off them, like two butterflies dancing under the summer sun. She wasn't present in the scene with them, but rather watched as if they were dancing over the pages of a picture book she held in her lap. Though she longed to join them, beautiful as they were, she was equally content to admire them from afar. Their embrace was light yet sturdy, their posture perfect like they were made to dance in each other's arms.

She woke feeling content, but also like there was something waiting for her just out of reach. It didn't give her the sense that she was missing something, but rather like there was a puzzle waiting to be solved whose completion would somehow make her life more fulfilled.

She couldn't imagine what she might be lacking, now that she and Arthur were wedded. It was likely no more than some lingering emotion caused by the dream itself, with no bearing on the waking world.

Yet she couldn't shake the image of Arthur and Coxley's dance from her mind's eye.

Beside her, Arthur slept on, seemingly oblivious as to his activities in her dreams. Laying on her stomach, Elizabeth pillowed her head in the crook of her arm to watch him. He lay on his back, his face turned towards her like a flower to the sun, one hand draped carelessly over his ribs with the other by his side. He looked perfectly at peace, and in that moment, in the small hours of darkest morning, she would have been content to look at him forever. His hair was mussed, the neat style that he wore during the day utterly wrecked, auburn strands splayed against the pillow like a halo. His skin was still flushed from their earlier exercise, and his breaths were deep and steady.

She had learned early on that he had nightmares, sometimes. Not often enough to say he was prone to them, but enough that Elizabeth had witnessed them on more than one occasion. When they came, his breath hitched and a tiny groove of worry dug into his forehead right between his eyebrows. Then his fingers would twitch, his muscles tense, and his breathing come quick and shallow. Yet, he never lashed out and he never made a sound.

Elizabeth couldn't decide whether his silence was better or worse than if he talked in his sleep. The nightmares were about the war; she knew that much. But when he woke, whether on his own or if she called to him, he never elaborated. He would only fold himself into her arms, his face pressed to her shoulder or her breasts, and let her hold him until the tremors passed. She would talk to him, telling him inconsequential things about her clients or her writing, or she would read to him by lamplight until they both drifted back to sleep.

No terrors plagued him on their wedding night.

They would return at some point, and her heart would break for him, but she took comfort in the fact that she would be there to chase them off when they came.

Moving slowly, she pressed her thumb between his eyebrows where his worry liked to etch itself. She smoothed the groove away as much as she could whenever it appeared, which never failed to make him smile. Though there was nothing to smooth in that moment, she repeated the motion anyway, like she could leave her mark there for him to use in the future when he needed it. He stirred under her touch and she smiled, tracing a line down his nose to his lips, which still held her kisses, into the dip between his bottom lip and his chin. When he opened his eyes, his gaze soft and sleepy in the dark, she moved her hand to his jaw so she could kiss him.

"I want to see you," he murmured, when they had parted far enough to look at each other again.

He didn't often ask for her magic, but when he did, she never refused him. She didn't make a point of hiding it the rest of the time, but she certainly didn't flaunt it around him, either. In certain circles, a lack of magic was a shameful thing. It wasn't unusual to be short of talent when it came to specific spells, or to suffer insufficient strength and only be capable of the simplest conjurings. Of course, servants and the lower classes weren't expected to have much magical talent at all, never mind any higher knowledge of spells, potions, or incantations. But for a middle-class man from a good family to have no magic whatsoever was generally agreed to be an embarrassment.

When Arthur had first admitted to his lack of magic early on in their dating, he had clearly been braced for rejection. His shame and discomfort had been a physical thing, like a shadow looming over them. Elizabeth had been taken aback, to be sure, not because she required magic in a partner, but because her own magic flowed so comfortably that she couldn't imagine a life without it. She wasn't especially strong, but she was competent, and good with charms. To have no magic at all was an alienating thought.

"Does my having magic bother you?" she asked him, concerned. They had been walking arm in arm through the park admiring the daffodils as the sun started to emerge after a morning of showers.

"No!" he said quickly. "No, not at all."

"Because I know some men might find it emasculating to be with a girl who can do something they can't."

"That's definitely not the case," he assured her, ducking his head to hide his smile and the way his ears were going red. "I quite enjoy your competence, as a matter of fact." Sobering, he continued, "I just wanted you to know that I have certain shortcomings that can't be improved upon. And if that bothers you—"

"It doesn't," she said, just as quickly. Taking his hands, she coaxed to him to meet her eye again. "Mine's nothing so special anyway. It's not like I show it off on a regular basis."

"I wouldn't mind if you did. I don't want you to hold back on my account. Anyway," —his smile slipped a little— "I rather like the look of magic. I would never want anyone to smother or lose theirs just to make me feel better. What an awful world that would be."

"Would you like to see it?" she asked tentatively.

He hesitated, seemingly torn.

Elevating one hand, she spoke the word for illumination, and a tiny ball of soft white light came out of her fingertip to hover in the air between them like a soap bubble. With a nudge, she sent it towards him, and he broke into a smile like he was seeing an old friend for the first time in years. He offered it his hand, unsure if he was allowed to touch. With an encouraging gesture, Elizabeth sent the light closer until it bumped into his fingertip and burst like a water balloon, sending little drops of light scattering over his knuckles. A delighted laugh escaped him and he stepped through the lingering sparks to grasp her hands.

That had been their first kiss.

He had asked to see her magic every once in a while since then, encouraging her to let it out when she was happiest, or use it to make certain menial tasks easier. There were times when it seemed that he simply wanted to bask in its presence, and she always indulged him. However, he only asked when they were both in good spirits; never after a nightmare. She sensed that, despite his enjoyment of her magic, it was still a sensitive subject, so she didn't press him to talk about it, and she didn't offer to show it off after that first time.

Which was all to say that, when he said, "I want to see you," as they lay in bed together on their wedding night, she didn't hesitate to let the light come bubbling out of her. A dozen orbs of white and gold hung in the air above their bed like paper lanterns, bathing them in the gentle glow of so many illumination spells. Arthur looked otherworldly in their light, like they were laying together in a summer meadow during the warmest, goldest hour of the evening.

"No," he said softly, touching her face. "Let me see the real you."

She knew exactly what he meant, though he'd never asked it of her before. Shutting her eyes, she let her magic pour out without any spell to shape it. As it pooled around them, silver and blue, they seemed underwater. It ebbed and flowed, drifting against their hair and rippling over the bedsheets in gentle currents.

"You're so beautiful," he whispered, his gaze reverent. "I love you terribly, Beth."

She kissed him soundly, letting her magic rush out full-force, revelling in the sensation of such strength and freedom, like a waterfall crashing over them both. It only lasted a second before she withdrew from him and pulled her magic back inside, biting her lip as she searched his face for his reaction. It was the first time she had let go so freely in his presence.

His eyes stayed shut a moment longer, just as they had been during the kiss. When he opened them, they were soft and full of the most awful yearning.

She blinked, unsure of herself now that the room was blue and fuzzy again. She must have misread his expression in the dark.

"What are you thinking?" she asked.

But he shook his head. "Tell me what *you're* thinking," he said instead.

"Hardly anything at all. That I'm happy. That I love you." Settling down again, she rested her chin against his shoulder, tracing constellations in the freckles that mapped his chest. "I dreamt about you. It was like walking through our wedding all over again. It was lovely; there was dancing..." The memory or the dream image of Arthur and Coxley waltzing in each other's arms rose to the forefront of her mind. "About my next book," she began, the words coming without conscious thought. "What if I wrote about two men?"

Arthur stilled in his process of combing his fingers through her hair. "Do you want to?"

She hadn't given it a thought, despite her teasing him about it, months ago in Kew Gardens. But there was something to that dance that she wanted to immortalise. She wasn't sure she could explain the way it made her feel, the sight of them together, or why it seemed important to hold onto.

"You'd be brought up on indecency charges, darling," he said after a moment, his tone gentle.

With one hand resting lightly on his chest, she searched his face. "Would you read it, though, if I did write one? Or is the thought of reading a romance about two men indecent to you, as well?"

"I'd read it if you asked me to, but I'd discourage you from publishing it. In as much as I can discourage you from anything." He cupped her cheek in one broad palm. "Not because I agree with the indecency laws, but because I wouldn't see you dragged through such a mess as that."

Leaning into his touch, she nodded. "I'd not put you through it, either."

It was no sacrifice on her part. Writing a book she couldn't sell hardly felt motivating, in her current state.

And there was another part of her that was secretly pleased at the thought of keeping their dance all to herself; something private and untouchable.

Nestling closer, she asked, "Have you ever met a man with such inclinations? Besides Alphonse and Jacobi, I mean. Out in the wider world, beyond our insular friend group."

Is Coxley such a man? was what she really wanted to ask. With the rumours surrounding the young men he hired to model for him, the sexual nature of so many of his paintings— But she couldn't ask that. It felt inappropriate, even in a setting as private as their bed.

In any case: Arthur's reply had nothing to do with Coxley. "There were times in the army when the men turned to one another for company, but I can't say whether that's the same. Necessity breeds adaptability, you know?"

Her heart skipped a beat at the prospect of discovering something new about her husband. "Did you ever—?"

"What, in the army?"

She prodded him. "At all."

"I've certainly never had a romance with one. There were a few times—after we'd had a few drinks, you know—but never properly. That is to say." He cleared his throat, his face gone pink.

Delighted, Elizabeth propped herself up on both elbows to gaze down at him. "But you have done *something*."

"I hadn't realised it would be of interest to you," he confessed, covering his face with one hand. "I hadn't expected to speak of it at all, in fact. Not to you, and certainly not to anyone else."

A pang of sympathy unfurled in her chest. That Arthur loved her—that he loved making love to her—she had no doubt, but she ached for all the men who preferred the company of their own sex and were compelled to either give it up or else live their lives in perpetual bachelorhood, which of course only attracted further rumours. To be a woman was confining enough with so many limitations on one's behaviour and the proper expression of one's passions, even in the twentieth century's broadening horizons. To be such a man—

"I love you very much," she told Arthur, laying her head on his chest so she could hear the steady thumping of his heart. "I want to give you everything you could ever want."

Wrapping his arms around her, he nosed at her hair and thumbed over the soft skin of her shoulders. "You already have. What more could I possibly need?"

"I don't know, but if you ask, I'll move the heavens to see you have it."

He stilled. "I don't want—*that*. If I've said something to mislead you…"

"No, not at all." Sitting up, she brushed his hair from his forehead with a reassuring smile. "I was only thinking of the sacrifices some people give up in their marriages. Other people. And if there was anything you ever set aside for my sake, I want you to reclaim it. Heaven knows you've supported me: my job, and my writing. I want you to be as happy in this as I am."

"Of course I'm happy. I can't imagine being happier. All I've left behind is my bachelorhood and the army, and I'm more than glad to see the back of those." Catching her hand, he kissed her fingers, over her rings. "I couldn't ask for a better wife."

"You don't miss living with Coxley?" she asked carefully.

He hesitated for an instant, and in that hesitation, she had her answer.

"I'll still see him plenty," Arthur said, after too long a pause. "I couldn't have gone on living with him forever. Eventually, a man does have to grow up."

She smoothed her hands over his chest before nestling down against him once more. "Yes, I suppose so," she conceded, even as she set herself to the task of bringing Coxley further into their lives so as to make Arthur more content.

CHAPTER EIGHT

IN WHICH A PAINTING IS GIFTED AND A LETTER IS DELIVERED

They took a week off for their honeymoon and used it to settle into their new house. It was perhaps less romantic than Elizabeth might have imagined as a girl, and certainly less romantic than her own stories dictated, but she rather enjoyed it. Her authorial career aside, an excess of romance had never suited her. She and Arthur found themselves mired in domesticity quite quickly. They had to familiarise themselves with their new house, which, now that she was actually living in it, was considerably larger than she had thought based on her initial tour of the place. They also had to familiarise themselves with the patterns of their new housekeeper, Mrs. Patel, whom they had hired on Coxley's recommendation: an Indian immigrant just past middle-age who regarded them with a maternal air, simultaneously strict and indulgent.

"She's going to be running this house within a month, you do realise that, don't you, dear?" Arthur asked on the third night as they lay tangled together under the bedcovers.

"Oh, I'm counting on it," Elizabeth replied. "But let's not talk about the housekeeper in bed, hm?"

And then talk moved on to better things: soft gasps and muffled laughs, and fewer actual words. That part of their honeymoon, at least, was going the traditional route, and Elizabeth was enjoying it immensely. She and Arthur had of course slept together before marriage, and slept with other partners before ever meeting, but Elizabeth could confidently say that their honeymoon sex was the best she'd ever had. While she knew there was no quantifiable difference between the Arthur before their wedding and the version of him that came in its wake, she nonetheless thrilled at the fact that they could now go to bed as husband and wife. It was her husband who pushed her down against the pillows, her husband who pressed himself to the line of her back and curled against her, who kissed his way along the delicate skin of her innermost thighs, who tasted the salt of her and knew all her most intimate places. And from the way he looked at her, he felt the same about calling her his wife.

Still, they couldn't stay cocooned in bed forever, and the bright summer of the outside world beckoned. With some reluctance, they rejoined it on the morning of the fifth day.

"Jules is demanding a dinner invitation," Arthur informed her over breakfast, waving the letter that had been waiting for them by the front door.

They had avoided connecting their phone line for the first few days, wanting to keep the world at bay until they had worn themselves out in bed. Apparently, Coxley had got fed up trying to ring them and resorted to more traditional methods of contact.

"He's quite insistent; I don't know how long I can put him off."

"Why on earth would you do that? Invite him!"

"What, really?"

"Why not? I think he knows perfectly well where he stands. He and I have come to an understanding, and I intend to hold up my end of the bargain. So, by all means, invite him around. If he behaves out of line, I shall set Mrs. Patel on him." Elizabeth wasn't in the least concerned, but Arthur was, so she fixed him with an appraising look. "You talk as if it's a wild dog asking to be let in the house, rather than your closest friend. The wedding went well with him as your best man, didn't it? He gave a perfectly good speech and everything. What do you expect him to do if we have him around? Start chewing the wallpaper?"

Arthur smiled, though it looked pained. "No, of course you're right. It's just habit, you know. Precaution. What with the way people talk."

"We're married now, with our own house, and no interfering relatives to watch over our shoulders—or at least, not from so close a distance. We can entertain whomever we like, no matter how disreputable. Heaven knows we have the room for it." She rose and crossed around the table to press a kiss to his cheek. "Not that Coxley is half the monster he's made out to be."

Arthur returned her kiss and stretched his legs. "No, he's really not. Not in the least."

Jules Coxley turned up on their doorstep that very evening, wearing his usual black coat and a smile that looked slightly too bright to be anything but nervous. Under his arm he carried a flat package wrapped in brown paper, which he thrust into Elizabeth's hands the moment she opened the door.

"Mrs. Turtledove! Mrs. Leicester, rather," he corrected himself immediately. "Apologies."

"That's quite alright," Elizabeth said. "I'm still adapting to answering to Mrs. Leicester, to be honest."

"Oh, good. I'm afraid 'Mrs. Leicester' is still Arthur's mother to me."

"In that case, I won't tell anyone you're still calling me Turtledove as long as you don't mention it, either."

"It's a deal," he agreed. "It's lovely to see you again. You look entirely fetching; I take it married life is to your liking, besides the confusion of a new name."

"Thank you, Mr. Coxley. And thank you for?" She hefted the parcel and he beamed, shedding his coat and hat and foisting them into Arthur's waiting arms.

"Your wedding present, naturally."

"Jules, I told you not to bother about a gift," Arthur admonished, depositing the hat and coat in the closet as Elizabeth turned the parcel over in her hands. It was about the length of her forearm, roughly square, and

116

quite flat: almost certainly a painting, if the man's nerves were anything to go by.

"Thank you very much," she said, offering Coxley a warm smile. "Come in, please. We'll have to give you the tour, of course. You haven't seen the house yet, have you?"

"Not yet," Coxley said cheerfully, folding his hands behind his back as he followed them through the foyer. "It looks like you've settled in already though, haven't you? A charming place."

"Large enough that I've walked into the wrong room once or twice," Elizabeth said. "There's enough space for each of us to have our own office with plenty of room left over. I hardly know what to do with the place."

"Mrs. Patel will help with that, I think," said Arthur.

On cue, the housekeeper poked her head out from the kitchen to give Coxley a polite nod. She wore rectangular glasses, a neat bun, and a simple burgundy shift dress in spotless condition, despite having spent the last hour in the kitchen.

"Mrs. Patel! How are you liking work in the Leicester household?"

"It's early days, Mr. Coxley," she said neutrally. "Time will tell, will it not?"

"And how is she treating you?" Coxley asked Arthur and Elizabeth. "Have you given her the run of the place? That's the way housekeepers ought to manage things, I always thought. Housekeepers and valets both. Not that I've ever had the opportunity to employ either."

"We're very happy for her to take as much control of the house as she feels comfortable doing," Elizabeth said pleasantly.

"And the food is excellent," Arthur added. "She's a top-notch cook, and we can't thank you enough for sending her our way."

Mrs. Patel looked modestly pleased.

"And how is your daughter?" Coxley asked her. "Well, I hope. You'll have to say hello to her for me."

"I imagine you'll see Deepa next before I do, Mr. Coxley," Mrs. Patel replied, sounding dryly amused. "She is a very busy girl these days, thanks to you."

"Deepa was one of my models," Coxley explained to Arthur and Elizabeth in an aside. "It was through her that I learned Mrs. Patel was looking for a position. And now, here we are."

"Dinner is ready," Mrs. Patel said. "Would you like me to keep it warm for you, or are you eating presently?"

"We're going straight to the dining room," Arthur assured her.

With a satisfied nod, Mrs. Patel retreated to the kitchen to plate their meal.

"The only question is whether we should open our wedding present before dinner or after," Elizabeth said.

"We'll open it now," Arthur said, eyeing the package with a degree of fond mistrust. "He'll want us to fawn over it for as long as possible, if it's one of his."

"Of course it's one of mine! But you aren't required to like it. In fact, if you don't, I can have a buyer lined up within the week, so don't be shy."

"I've yet to see any of your paintings in person, Mr. Coxley," Elizabeth remarked, leading both men into the dining room, where a tall white candle flickered in the table's centre. "I've seen your work in the papers and on postcards, but Arthur tells me that can't compare to the real thing."

"He's very generous."

"I am not," Arthur retorted. "You're a brilliant artist and you know it."

"But not brilliant enough to show me off to your wife?"

Elizabeth rolled her eyes before turning with the parcel in both hands. "Well, I shall see it now, and I'm sure it will be very lovely indeed."

She wasn't sure at all, in fact. Oh, she was sure it would be very well painted, a testament to his artistic skill, but 'lovely' was a descriptor that seemed ill-suited to the man.

"I hope it's not one of your naked ladies," Arthur commented mildly, coming up to face Elizabeth and tug loose the ribbon holding the brown paper in place.

"Would you rather it one of my naked men?" Coxley asked innocently.

"I would rather there be no nudity whatsoever, if you must know."

Elizabeth did not particularly want to hang any matter of naked person on her walls, but her curiosity was piqued, and she slipped the paper away to reveal the canvas, propping it up atop the dinner table to examine it in detail. The first thing she noticed was the colour: an overwhelming rush of pink from one edge of the canvas to the other, broken here and there by rich purples and greens and streaks of paler pink, almost white. The second thing she noticed was that while it was not a naked person, it still served to make her blush hotly from her cheeks all the way down her chest, so suddenly that she felt lightheaded.

Arthur put his hand on the small of her back and made a considering sound.

"Do you like it?" Coxley asked.

Elizabeth took a deep breath and turned. "Your talent wasn't exaggerated in the least," she said, fighting to rein her blush back under control. Coxley had to have noticed it, and if his creeping smile was any indication, he knew exactly what she was thinking. "This is exquisite."

"Is it," Arthur said flatly, in that way he had of trying not to let his amusement show.

"Oh, it's nothing," Coxley deferred. "A slapdash of brushstrokes, I assure you."

The painting was of a flower, but from so close an angle that it was almost lost to abstraction. The petals splayed wide around the edges of the canvas, but the centre was devoted to the flower's innermost folds, where the labellum narrowed and curled inwards, and the delicate fabric of the petals grew thicker, the pink darkening to something rich and lush where it rippled and grew firm before disappearing down the column into the dark.

"An orchid, dear boy," Coxley said. "Surely you have no objections to a flower! I thought it made a perfectly innocuous wedding gift."

"Oh, indeed," Elizabeth said, nudging Arthur with one elbow. "We do enjoy flowers, don't we, darling?"

Arthur heaved a long-suffering sigh. "And I expect you'd have us hang it up, as well."

"It would look splendid in your sitting room."

"Where we bring guests for tea. Where we would bring our families, Jules. Our—our mothers."

Coxley's eyes were positively glittering. "Why should your mothers have any objections to orchids? They must have seen them before."

Arthur pinched the bridge of his nose and Elizabeth laid her hand on his arm. "I'm sure we'll find the perfect place for it, Mr. Coxley. It's a beautiful gift."

"It is," Arthur agreed, eyes still closed. "I'm sure we'll find somewhere decent to hang it. In the meantime: Mrs. Patel is waiting to bring us dinner, so we ought to oblige her before it gets cold."

"Excellent," Coxley agreed.

Elizabeth could not be shaken by the sight of a flower, no matter how provocative. Coxley watched her closely through dinner as if cataloguing her every habit and reaction for further study, and though his gaze prickled over her skin, she allowed it. She smiled charmingly and laughed in all the right places when he spoke, playing the part of the perfect hostess, and though Arthur kept looking back and forth between them with a cautious air, he didn't intervene.

Elizabeth allowed Coxley to test her as they ate. She would permit him to poke and prod to his heart's content, at least for now, because there was absolutely nothing he could find that would break the bond she shared with Arthur.

Though, she noted that this testing had little in common with his earlier barbs when he had been hunting for weakness between them. This seemed to be more a testing of the waters, as if he were circling the outermost edges of her character, trying to work out how best to approach and carve himself a place in her life. That was fine. And if, until he found that space for himself, he wanted to foist more inappropriately-painted flowers on her—well, she would smile and accept them. And then she would hang them up in the sitting room, because they were really quite beautifully done.

"I think it would look excellent right there," Coxley said, nodding to the expanse of wall behind Arthur's head. "It's a lovely house you have, but it could use an artist's eye to decorate. I am of course willing to volunteer for such a task; I could even donate another painting or two to fill the space. I'm sure I have some laying around the studio that are as yet unspoken for. There's nothing worse than an empty wall, you know."

"That explains why our flat always looked like a bomb had hit it," Arthur said.

"Might I see your studio?" Elizabeth asked. "Having made your acquaintance to this extent I find it safe to assume that it's not actually the den of iniquity rumour would have me believe, and I should very much like to see further examples of your work. Especially if this orchid is, as you say, a few mere strokes of paint on canvas."

"You flatter me terribly," Coxley said after a brief pause. "But perhaps— Perhaps the studio of a degenerate artist such as myself is a less than ideal destination for someone so…"

"Nothing short of a proper bacchanalian festival on the premises will put me off, Mr. Coxley, and Arthur assures me that your public image is considerably wilder than your private one."

Coxley fixed Arthur with a scrutinising look. "Has he indeed."

"Oh, for heaven's sake. If you don't want to show her your studio then don't, Jules, but if you're afraid of offending her delicate sensibilities then you needn't bother. I've already told her you have far fewer orgies, prostitutes, or indeed even lovers in your life than common talk would have her believe. She's not easily scandalised, and I doubt your paintings will be what pushes her over the edge."

Elizabeth raised her brows pointedly and took a sip of wine.

Coxley stared, his gaze flicking rapidly between Arthur and Elizabeth before he finally swallowed and dipped his head in a short nod. "Very well then. Yes, Mrs. Turtledove, I should be delighted to show you my studio, since your husband is so, ah, encouraging, shall we say, in the matter. Give me a few days to clean up the worst of the mess and then it shall be at your disposal."

"Excellent," she said brightly. "Shall we have Mrs. Patel bring out the dessert, then?"

Later that evening, as Coxley was making his way to the door, Elizabeth fetched his coat and hat and said, softly, "I really didn't intend to pressure you, Mr. Coxley. If you're more comfortable without me seeing your studio, I won't push the matter."

"Oh, not at all!" He slipped into his coat and donned his hat at a rakish angle, smiling up at her. "It's just so rare that a man is keen to push his wife toward me in such a manner; I admit I was taken aback."

"I think you'll find that I'm walking entirely of my own volition, Mr. Coxley."

He touched the brim of his hat. "Of course. Excuse me."

As he reached for the door handle, a flicker of paper darted through the gap under the door, sliding onto the floor tiles. Coxley knelt to retrieve it, glanced at the address, and handed it to Elizabeth with a smile.

"For you, my dear."

Elizabeth accepted the note. It was just a little thing, of medium-thick cardstock folded in half to hide its contents, with her name typed on the front. There was no indication of either the subject matter or the sender. Expecting some belated congratulatory note for her wedding, she flipped it open without bothering to see Coxley off first.

To Elizabeth Leicester, née Turtledove: I have it on good authority that writing to you will ensure that M. Hayes also sees this message.

Elizabeth's heart dropped as if into a lake of ice.

I know who you are, and if you want your identity to remain secret, you will oblige me in my demands. The sum of your last twelve months of royalties, which I have reason to believe amounts to £3,614, must be left in an unmarked briefcase at the furthermost left pillar of the Temple of Bellona at Kew Gardens, off the Camellia Walk, at 1:00 p.m. this Saturday. You will do this if you wish to keep the identity of M. Hayes and your own reputation intact. Taking this letter to the police will guarantee that your identity will be publicised within twenty-four hours. Your clients, friends, and family deserve to know the depth of your deceit and the truth of your duplicitous nature. Do not test me.

Holding her breath, she read it again, skimming for any sign that it was a terrible joke, but found nothing. Pushing past Coxley, she flung open the door to step outside, looking around for whomever had delivered the note.

The street was empty.

"Is something wrong?" Coxley asked cautiously.

Returning inside and shutting the door behind her, she exhaled hard and gathered her resolve. This was fine. There was no situation she couldn't manage.

Coxley watched her with some degree of trepidation. "Should I call for Arthur?"

"No." Checking over her shoulder to ensure that Arthur was still engaged in helping Mrs. Patel clear the table, she took a step closer to Coxley, holding the note between two fingers like it was poisonous. In an undertone, she said, "Tell me you had nothing to do with this."

Curious, Coxley took the note, and with every line he read, his eyes grew wider. "No, this isn't my doing."

Elizabeth ground her teeth. "You can understand my suspicion when you threatened to do almost exactly this back in the spring. You could have delivered this note yourself by some sleight of hand."

"I do understand your suspicion and I don't blame you for it in the least, but I swear, this has nothing to do with me. What would be the point of it? Then, I wanted to end your engagement. Now, you're on your honeymoon and I thought I had made it clear that I left such animosity behind me."

"Maybe it's precisely because I'm on my honeymoon that you've chosen this moment to resurrect that animosity."

"What can I do to prove that my intentions towards you are good?"

Arthur chose that moment to rejoin them, drying his hands on his trousers after helping Mrs. Patel corral the dishes into the kitchen. He took one look at the two of them and said, "What happened?"

Coxley thrust the note at him. "This isn't me."

As Arthur read it, his brows furrowed. "Oh, Beth. What a mess."

"It came under the door as I was seeing Mr. Coxley out."

"And you think Jules is behind it?"

"I'm not," Coxley insisted. "I know with my history it's all too easy to paint me as the villain, but Arthur, I wouldn't. Not now, not after you've invited me into your home like this."

Elizabeth folded her arms and shifted her weight from one foot to the other, uncomfortable and uncertain.

"I gave you a painting," Coxley pleaded.

Elizabeth didn't want to believe he was capable of blackmail. She saw nothing he could gain from such a move except the satisfaction of indulging in his spite, and she no longer thought he was an inherently spiteful person. When he had been trying to pull her away from Arthur, she had seen him at his worst. Perhaps she had never seen him at his best, but his average demeanour, when he wasn't feeling backed into a corner, didn't seem remotely hateful.

"If you aren't responsible for it, then who?" she asked.

"As I told you that day in the park, I never shared your identity with anyone else after I learned it. There was only the investigator whom I had hired to dig into the matter. John Johnson."

She knew the name from the papers; John Johnson was enjoying a moment of minor celebrity status in London at that time, liaising with Scotland Yard on a string of high-profile jewel robberies.

"And if he talked?" Elizabeth demanded.

Coxley hesitated. "He seemed a consummate professional the entire time he was working for me, but I suppose that's no guarantee."

"It could be someone at your publishing house," Arthur suggested, still frowning at the note as if he could force it to give up its secrets by the sheer strength of his disapproval. "Some people there know your real name. They have to, in order for you to legally sign their contracts and for them to pay you. Some disgruntled employee, current or former, perhaps."

"That's possible," Elizabeth allowed, relieved at having options besides the man standing in front of her. "I'll make some inquiries and see if I can't uncover anything."

"Then, you believe me?" Coxley asked.

Arthur joined him in looking to Elizabeth for her verdict, both wearing expressions of tentative hope.

"I want to give you the benefit of the doubt."

"Let me prove myself to you," he said immediately.

"You have been," she said, frustration bleeding into her tone. "For the past three months you've been proving yourself admirably, and I don't want to throw aside the trust we've built unless I'm faced with indisputable evidence, which this... It doesn't do you any favours, but it's hardly solid proof of guilt, either."

"It's a wretched coincidence," Coxley agreed with a twist of his mouth. "You go to your publisher and I'll hunt down that investigator to see what he has to say on it."

"Whatever you need of me, Beth, just say the word."

Elizabeth leaned gratefully into Arthur's shoulder. "Moral support is always appreciated."

Coxley cleared his throat. "Until this is settled and the perpetrator is revealed, perhaps it's best if I keep my distance. For your peace of mind."

Arthur made a small, involuntary noise at the back of his throat before quickly smothering it.

"No," Elizabeth said slowly. "I'll not ostracise you without proof of guilt."

Pulling away from Arthur, she took Coxley's hands in hers and looked him in the eye, willing him to show her the man Arthur had always believed him to be: steadfast and worthy of years-long loyalty. Coxley met her gaze unflinchingly, dark-eyed and awaiting judgement.

"I want your friendship, Mr. Coxley, just as Arthur has it," she said quietly, searching his expression.

He didn't blink. "You have it," he said simply.

She didn't turn to see what Arthur's face was doing. Instead, she stepped back to hold Coxley at arm's length. "Then let's end the evening on a brighter note. The matter of blackmail will keep till morning, during business hours. We had a lovely dinner and I don't want it ruined with melodrama and accusations." She squeezed Coxley's hands in silent apology. "What do you say?"

Arthur came up behind her to put his hands on her shoulders. "We should make a habit of this," he agreed. "Not the blackmail, but the dinner. It was good to see you again, Jules. Especially with all of us as friends."

Coxley visibly pulled himself together. "It was, and we should." To Elizabeth he added, "Until then, do drop by the studio. Arthur, you're invited as well, of course, though I remember your comments from last time about the state of the place, and I can tell you right now that it will be in no better shape. Plan accordingly." And then, doffing his hat, he swung the door open and disappeared into the night.

Elizabeth heaved a sigh, braced herself, and turned to face Arthur with what she hoped was a look of optimism. Arthur was still holding the blackmail note.

"It's not him," Arthur said with quiet confidence.

"I don't think it is," she agreed. "I'll admit that my immediate reaction was suspicion, but I think anyone in my position would feel the same. But it was knee-jerk only, not genuine."

"Between the three of us, we'll find out who's behind it. Nothing needs to progress beyond this single note."

"Everything will be fine," Elizabeth said firmly. "I'm not losing my pen name because of this, and I'm certainly not giving up my royalties. But I meant it when I said it could wait until the morning. There's nothing to be done overnight, and I refuse to waste it fretting over something as ridiculous as this."

Arthur planted a kiss on her forehead. "You have people in your corner, and this will get dealt with. I promise."

"I know. In the meantime, please get that thing out of my sight."

Arthur obligingly hid the note in his pocket.

Elizabeth forced a smile until she meant it. "Now: shall we have seconds of dessert and decide where to hang Coxley's orchid?"

Arthur dragged one hand over his face. "Right. Yes. You don't really want it in the sitting room, do you?"

She shrugged. "I think it'll prove a lovely conversation piece."

CHAPTER NINE

IN WHICH A SHRUBBERY MAKES FOR AN INEFFECTUAL HIDING PLACE

Saturday afternoon was hot and bright, and Elizabeth and Arthur were spending it hiding in a bush. The bush itself was pleasant enough, with sweetly-perfumed flowers and an accompaniment of friendly bees, but Elizabeth couldn't help but feel that her time would be better spent doing literally anything else. The bees made Arthur nervous, though Elizabeth rather liked their clumsy company.

Across the path stood the Temple of Bellona, which was a square, white, eighteenth-century construction of no significant size with four pillars at its front, between which was nestled a bench which would have been a much nicer place to sit and while away the hours. The temple was surrounded on both sides and around the back by a great many shrubs and trees, creating a wall of impenetrable greenery.

The briefcase demanded by their blackmailer sat hidden under one of those shrubs by the temple's furthermost left pillar, as instructed. When Elizabeth and Arthur first arrived, they had briefly debated whether the blackmailer meant the left side of the pillar when one stood facing the temple, or when one sat on the bench facing out with the temple at their back. They had settled on placing the case to the left when they stood looking at it, assuming that if they were wrong, surely the blackmailer would check the right as well.

That had been at twelve-thirty. It was now quarter after one, fifteen minutes past the appointed time, and their blackmailer had yet to make an appearance.

Of course, the briefcase was not actually full of cash, or indeed, anything at all. It was one of Arthur's older cases that he had carried to and from work for many years, and was now too scuffed up to be of any use to him in a professional capacity. He had replaced it with a newer model some months earlier but hadn't got around to disposing of the old one, and had eagerly volunteered it for the day's task, not minding in the least if it got stolen in the process.

Unfortunately, so far it seemed likely he would be bringing it back home with him.

"You would think that someone looking to steal three thousand pounds would be more punctual about the thing," Arthur commented.

"Three thousand, six hundred and fourteen," Elizabeth said, glaring at the spot where the briefcase lay hidden as if she could force her antagonist to materialise out of thin air. "It's a good thing we brought sandwiches."

"Not the most ideal spot for a picnic, but I suppose I've been in worse." Arthur rummaged through the basket sitting in the bush alongside them. "Would you prefer egg or roast beef?"

"One of each, I suppose. Who knows how much longer we'll be here."

"They're only fifteen minutes late," Arthur said, trying to sound minimally judgemental. As a habitually punctual man, that was difficult for him.

"We'll give them until two o' clock," Elizabeth said decisively, biting into the first sandwich Arthur offered. "Imagine not showing up to your own blackmail appointment! Whoever this person is, I'm losing respect for them by the minute."

Arthur made a disgruntled sound of agreement.

Elizabeth had met with her publisher the day before, and they had assured her that none of their people could possibly be behind this, while in the same breath promising to investigate. Furthermore, they said they would begin distancing Elizabeth from the name of M. Hayes as a precaution, with the idea that should her blackmailer go public, 'Elizabeth Leicester' would merely be one identity in a swirling sea of rumours, and hardly the most scandalous or interesting choice. Thus, she could easily deny everything if she so wished. Elizabeth appreciated their proactive approach to the problem, even if they hadn't been able to definitively point to her blackmailer and solve the problem entirely.

A shadow fell over their shrubbery and Elizabeth looked up with some trepidation to find Aaliyah and Jasmine, arm in arm, staring down at them. Aaliyah looked endlessly amused; Jasmine, ever so slightly concerned.

"Fancy meeting you here," said Aaliyah. "I hope we're not interrupting anything too private."

"Not at all," said Elizabeth, trying to look composed as she combed loose leaves and petals from her hair.

"Are you doing some sort of research for your next book?" Jasmine asked, giving her a graceful out.

"As a matter of fact," Elizabeth said. "We're." She cleared her throat. "Spying," she finished, hoping that sounded at least somewhat dignified.

Arthur winced but nodded along.

"Spying!" Aaliyah sounded thrilled. "On whom?"

"I probably shouldn't say. I don't suppose you've seen any suspicious-looking characters on your walk, have you?"

"Other than you two, you mean?"

"We saw Mr. Coxley on our way through the Palm House," Jasmine offered.

"And he was acting rather suspicious, now that you ask. He kept looking around like he expected he was being followed. He said hello to us but insisted that he couldn't stop to chat."

"It's not him," Arthur said to Elizabeth in an undertone. "He must be here for the same reason we are."

Elizabeth sighed. "What a waste."

"It's a nice day for it," Jasmine said with a shrug. "You couldn't ask for better weather to sit in the park."

"I've just never sat in the park quite so literally before," Elizabeth groused.

"Well, we'll leave you to it, then," Aaliyah said. "I don't suppose you have a description of this person you're supposed to be spying on, in case we see them this afternoon?"

Elizabeth shook her head, feeling foolish and frustrated.

"Right, of course not. Shall we check in with you on our way back?"

"I should hope we won't be staying that long," Elizabeth said dejectedly.

Aaliyah and Jasmine said their goodbyes and continued on their way. After they took their leave, time slowed to a crawl. Elizabeth split her attention between Arthur's pocket watch, which she knew to be accurate because he maintained it meticulously, and the hidden briefcase. Though the Camellia Walk was decently populated with pedestrians enjoying their weekend stroll, no one else stopped to notice them until one thirty-five. They had finished their sandwiches and were working their way through a little box of jam cookies that Mrs. Patel had snuck into the basket without Elizabeth noticing. The bees were particularly interested in the jam, and kept bumping into Elizabeth's fingers as she tried to eat, which caused Arthur to flinch on her behalf every time. Elizabeth was thus distracted when Alphonse and his companion stumbled upon her hiding place.

"Oh, hello," said Alphonse, blinking down at them in surprise. "Odd place for a picnic, what?"

"Please pretend you don't know we're here," Elizabeth begged without much hope. "We're hiding."

"Oh, right, as you say." Alphonse agreeably turned towards his companion as if they had stopped to chat with no notice of the bush at all. "Have you met my cousin Morgan?"

Morgan Hollyhock was slightly less blonde than Alphonse, and his demeanor somewhat more restrained. Overall, he looked like a broader, more squared-off, desaturated version of his cousin. The family resemblance was striking.

"The Leicesters, is it?" Morgan Hollyhock asked, examining the sky. "We've met briefly once or twice."

"Yes, I believe we have," Elizabeth said, trying to behave as if nothing were amiss.

"Sorry to interrupt you," Morgan said to the clouds, determinedly not looking at Elizabeth or Arthur. "Alphonse, let's give them some privacy and be on our way."

"Oh, we're not doing anything like that," Arthur said quickly. "We'd appreciate you not drawing attention to us, but we're not doing anything indecent in here."

Morgan cleared his throat in obvious disbelief, his hands in his pockets and his gaze fixed firmly on the heavens.

"What are you doing, if you don't mind my asking?" Alphonse was desperately trying to avoid looking at them, shuffling in place as he tried and failed to copy Morgan's casual demeanour.

Elizabeth couldn't think of a single good answer for him that wouldn't invite a whole host of questions. "It's a secret," she said helplessly.

Alphonse inched closer to their bush. "Did you know Jules Coxley is hiding in a shrub much like this one on the other side of that little white place?" he said in a conspiratorial tone. "We passed him not ten minutes ago. I didn't stop to say hello because I assumed he was busy, you know, doing painterly things, working in his sketchbook or what have you. Artists are odd birds, I always thought, so I didn't pay him much mind. Besides which, Morgan was telling me a ripping story about that jewel thief who's been going around London, and it was absolutely fascinating stuff that I didn't want to interrupt. So, I just pretended not to notice the old thing hunkered down there. But now, with you two in such a similar spot, I have to ask. Is it a game or something? Are the gardens full of people hiding out in the trees and whatnot? I've fallen into my fair share of hedges and tripped over no small number of shrubberies, I don't mind saying, and none of them were an awfully comfortable way to spend the time. Do you need a hand getting out?"

"He's hiding on just the other side of this temple, you say?" Arthur asked.

Alphonse nodded emphatically.

"That must rule him out as our suspect, then, don't you think?" Arthur said to Elizabeth.

"Unless he knows we're here and he's waiting for us to leave before he makes his move," she countered. "Not that I think it has to be him," she added.

"Whoever our suspect is, if they know we're here, they only have to bide their time until we give up and move on."

"But wouldn't they expect us to collect the briefcase on our way home?" Arthur asked.

Elizabeth let loose a sound of inarticulate frustration. "I don't know! I don't think our blackmailer is particularly clever—certainly not as clever as they think they are. I don't see any point in trying to guess their next move as if they're some genius chess master. In actuality, I suspect they have far more in common with those sorts who sit down at the board for the first time and win through the sheer bewildering randomness of their moves."

Alphonse had given up any pretence of pretending they weren't there and was watching their conversation with avid interest.

"You think they're going to win, then?" Arthur asked.

"Certainly not! Whoever they are, I think they're an idiot. That alone should be enough to rule out Coxley's involvement." Crumbling the last bite of her cookie to the ground as a gift for the bees, Elizabeth packed up the picnic basket with an air of finality.

Alphonse took his cue and tripped over his own feet in his hurry to back away from the bush. "It was good seeing you both, but we're off to meet the wife for lunch, so we'd better hop to it. Well, I say the wife. Jasmine will be there too. And Jacobi, I should imagine. I'll say hello to them for you, shall I?"

"Please do," Arthur said, rescuing his pocket watch from Elizabeth before it could get packed in the basket with the leftovers.

"Righto then, toodles! Now, Morgan, what you were saying about this jewel thief—"

"This is ridiculous," Elizabeth declared the moment Alphonse and his cousin were out of earshot. "Whoever it is we're waiting for would have shown up by now. I'm going to get to Coxley."

Standing, she brushed herself off and went marching across the walkway and over the temple's neatly-manicured lawn. Circling around it, she forged a path through the least dense bit of greenery and found Coxley sitting by the back corner. He blinked up at her owlishly, or rather, sheepishly.

"Arthur and I are going home," she told him. "Would you like to come with us, or are you going to stay?"

"You haven't seen anyone?" he asked.

"We've seen plenty of people and plenty of people have seen us, but no one came poking around the temple looking for our ransom package. In fact, no one has so much as spared the temple a second glance."

"And you don't think I'm the person you're looking for?" he asked cagily.

"I like to think you would have been smarter about this whole thing, or at least more inventive with it. I can't think of any good reason why you would spend your afternoon sitting in a shrubbery if you were the real blackmailer, whether you had written off today's collection attempt or not. And it has been a complete write-off. A waste of time for us and the blackmailer both."

When she offered Coxley a hand up, he seemed distracted as he took it, brushing loose soil from the seat of his trousers with his other hand as he stood.

"I'm not convinced it was a total waste," he said, releasing her fingers after a moment's delay. "I arrived just after noon, and I saw John Johnson by the Brentford Gate entrance as I was coming in."

"Your private investigator," Elizabeth said slowly.

"I don't think it's a coincidence that he should be here just when you're expecting your villain to appear."

"How did he seem? Did you speak to him?"

"Focused, and no. I followed him at a distance down the Riverside Walk hoping he'd give himself away, but he must have noticed me after him, because he led me into the Princess of Wales Conservatory. He's clearly used to being tailed, because he shook me off in what I must admit was embarrassingly little time. I scoured the place trying to find him again, but it was no good. With the drop-off to occur at one, I elected to set up camp here and try to catch him—or whomever—in the act."

"You knew Arthur and I were staking out the site ourselves. Why didn't you sit with us?"

"I wasn't sure whether you trusted me," he replied, not meeting her eye.

"So, you thought hiding out opposite us would be less suspicious?"

"I had hoped you wouldn't notice."

She narrowed her eyes, looking him up and down. "I might have to take back what I said about you being too clever to be the blackmailer."

"Fair enough."

He offered her his elbow as they made their way back down the temple's lawn to meet Arthur as he emerged from his shrubbery. Elizabeth paused to swipe the briefcase from its hiding place as they passed.

"Hello, old boy," Arthur said as he dusted himself free of leaves. "See anything interesting from your vantage point?"

"A great many ants, but no criminal activity to speak of."

"Ah, we had bees on our side."

"I think I would have preferred bees," said Coxley, handing Elizabeth off to her husband.

"Then you'll know where to sit next time," Elizabeth returned. "Assuming there is a next time, of course. I think it would be too much to hope that our blackmailer got cold feet today and has given up on the whole endeavour." Shaking her head, she resolved to set their entire day thus far behind her. "What are you doing this afternoon?" she asked, forcing some brightness into her voice. "Arthur and I haven't got any particular plans, but you're welcome to join us in whatever we end up doing."

"I'm hard-pressed to refuse such an invitation, but unfortunately, duty calls. I've neglected my work for too long today already, and I should get back to my studio."

"That's a shame," said Arthur. "Mrs. Patel was upset when you left the other evening without her noticing. She had a fresh-baked loaf of turmeric bread set aside for you to take home. We found it in the bread box the next morning with a note attached. It seems she's convinced you don't eat enough."

Coxley scoffed and waved him away, though Elizabeth could tell he was secretly pleased at the housekeeper's concern.

"Speaking of your studio, I thought I might drop by sometime next week if that's at all convenient," Elizabeth said. "Unless you've changed your mind and would like to retract your invitation?"

Coxley looked more like he had expected her to change her mind, but he quickly rallied. "Not at all. Come by any day after Monday and I'll be more than happy to show you around. Until then." Turning towards the path, he paused, one hand slightly raised. "Oh, my dear, you have a bee in your hair."

Elizabeth went very still. She had no particular fear of bees, or indeed of any insect, but neither did she want to be stung in or around her face. "Would you mind…?"

Coxley looked to Arthur expectantly.

Arthur grimaced. "Would you do it, chap? You know how I am with stinging things."

"I can do it myself," Elizabeth said, carefully raising both hands, though she didn't dare start patting down her hair for fear of aggravating the creature.

"Nonsense, I can do it," Coxley said. "If you'll allow me."

"Please do."

Coxley came in close and, with both hands, gently scooped the bee into one cupped palm. His hands were steady, but the little callouses on his fingers where he had held his pencils and brushes for so many years rasped her hair and made Elizabeth shiver. Stepping back to a polite distance, Coxley slowly opened his hands and nudged the bee onto the top of the shrubbery, encouraging it to walk away.

"Easy," he proclaimed with a smile.

"I haven't got any, have I?" Arthur asked anxiously.

"You've got a giant one just under your nose."

One hand flew reflexively to his face before he caught on and scowled.

"Your moustache is fine, darling," Elizabeth said, pressing herself to his side as Coxley laughed and set off down Camellia Walk. "It's most becoming and not at all full of bees."

"Yes, thank you," Arthur grumbled, but he was smiling as he dropped a quick kiss to her hair where the bee had been nestled.

"Let's go home and try to salvage the remains of the day," she suggested. "If nothing else, I'm taking comfort in the fact that our wretched blackmailer wasted as much of their time today as they wasted of ours."

CHAPTER TEN

ON THE NATURE OF THE ARTIST AND HIS STUDIO

On Tuesday, Elizabeth took an extended lunch break to visit Coxley's studio, which was perched on the third and top floor of an elegantly shabby building in the bohemian core, nestled amid what Elizabeth guessed must be private rooms rather than businesses. The building's interior was dark, its wallpaper neglected and floors scuffed from years of traffic and little upkeep, but it held a certain charm.

Upon reaching the third floor, she traipsed down the corridor, its old wood creaking underfoot with every step, until she reached the door at the end of the hall, bearing a weathered brass number thirty-seven. The door had been dark originally, but had since been littered either by accident or by design with a great many streaks and spatters of colour, most of them coming away in flakes. She only hesitated a second before giving the wood a firm rap, then smoothed out her hair and stepped back to wait.

A moment later, footsteps sounded from the other side of the door, followed by a brief scuffle as if something were being hastily shoved back into place. When the door finally opened, Coxley greeted her with a bright, if self-conscious smile.

"Mrs. Turtledove! Right on time. Please, come through." He stepped aside, holding the door wide as he swept her in with a bow. He was in a white shirt with his sleeves rolled to the elbows, his waistcoat rumpled and his tie absent entirely.

The studio was surprisingly spacious. Situated at the end of the hall, the entire north wall was windowed: great, arcing things overlooking the streets below as a king might overlook his land. The remaining walls were papered from floor to ceiling in drawings. There were life-size figure drawings scrawled in charcoal on thin newsprint, hasty portraits inked on cardboard, watercolour studies and messy acrylic palettes and swashes of oils and gauche and pastel. Every medium under the sun was represented in some way or another, large or small, and that was to say nothing of the paintings themselves.

"Feel free to look around," said Coxley, as if he didn't care in the slightest, though he was watching her as keenly as a hawk. "Mi casa et su casa, of course."

"Thank you," she said, somewhat breathlessly.

She hadn't been prepared for the sheer magnitude of the art. There was a world of difference between being told someone was a talented artist, and feeling it pulsing around you like a living, breathing creature. Elizabeth pressed one hand to her chest, her heart thrumming in wordless excitement as she stepped further into the room.

In its centre stood a platform the width and breadth of an adult man, though only a few feet in height, with a raised seat in the middle and draped in a careless white sheet. It was cluttered with myriad miscellaneous objects: a vase of flowers, a handful of discarded costume jewellery, an assortment of potted plants, and a silk robe that had seen better days.

"My model-stand." Coxley remained by the door, hanging back as Elizabeth wandered through his space. "For when I have live models, which is often enough. It's on wheels, you see, so I may move it around to catch the best light."

Elizabeth nudged the stand with one toe, and though it was solidly constructed and very heavy, it gave way an inch under her push. "How useful."

"Indeed."

"Though, it doesn't look very comfortable."

Coxley's lips quirked upwards. "Perhaps not, but my models are well compensated for it. Besides which, it's only used for my shorter studies. For longer sittings— portraits and the like—I have..." He waved to the far wall where an assortment of furniture had been shoved, presumably to clear a space for Elizabeth's visit. There was a handsome wingback armchair and a low French chaise, alongside a collection of cushions, poufs, and ottomans.

"Do you paint many portraits, Mr. Coxley? Or do you favour erotic flowers?"

"Portraits keep the bills paid," he said cheerfully, his hands in his pockets. "And you know what people are like: they catch a whiff of scandal and suddenly it's all the rage to have your picture done by the local eccentric."

"Is that how it works?"

"You're here, aren't you?"

She hummed and paced the length of the studio to examine its contents in closer detail. Beneath the smaller eastern windows stood rows upon rows of canvases, all stacked against one another with only the outermost layer showing their faces. They came in all dimensions: some were as long as Elizabeth was tall, others great square things, and still more were small and neat, the least of which she could hold in the palm of her hand. And, most impressively, they were all complete.

"More flowers," she observed. "So, you don't only paint them to get a reaction from people."

The first row was of gardens and bouquet arrangements and fields, wild tangles of colour and leaves swashed across the canvases in bright, bold strokes, the paint so thick in places that it rose off the surface in swirls and ridges. She extended one finger and traced the curve of a rose, careful not to touch the paint itself.

"These are exquisite." But not the stuff of scandals. She rested her hand atop the largest canvas. "May I look through the rest?"

"Please do. It's why you're here, after all."

"Do you have a favourite?"

"Of my flowers, you mean? I'm particularly proud of those snapdragons to your right: an underrated flower when it comes to art, I find. They're sold to a Mrs. Hollyhock—your friend Alphonse's mother, as a matter of fact, so you likely know her. I need to get them finished and delivered before her party at the end of August."

"Are they not finished? I thought they looked done."

"I want to fuss with them a little longer." He flapped a hand at the snapdragons. "Plenty of time!"

"And this one?" She tapped the uppermost edge of a tall, narrow piece depicting a flower so phallic that it brought an immediate blush to her cheeks, though she ignored the sensation. "I suppose I should be thankful you didn't choose this as a wedding present instead."

"Ah yes, the violet man-eater! A tropical pitcher plant of the *Sarracenia* family. I may have exaggerated a few of its… assets. Ahem."

"Yes. Men often do, I find."

A flush rose to his cheeks in turn, and she bit her lip to hide her smile as she turned back to the rows of canvases. Affecting a careless tone, she said, "That is rather more in line with what I expected from you, in all truth. Snapdragons and roses are lovely, of course— and you really do paint them so beautifully—but I had been led to expect art of the more, shall we say, salacious? nature."

"Surely your dear husband wouldn't have sent you here alone if that were the case."

She teased the largest canvas forward to reveal the next row. "You and I are the two people in the world who know Arthur best. Of course he would send me here alone, and with his blessing."

Coxley edged closer. "To what end?"

"To assuage my curiosity, and that I might learn something new," she said simply. "And that you and I might understand each other a little better, since it's been determined that we're both here to stay."

"It's hardly appropriate."

"You know as well as I that Arthur tests the bounds of propriety often enough; it's why you have been such fast friends. No proper gentleman would put up with you, I think. So, is it such a stretch that I should lack some level of propriety as well?"

She moved the first row of canvases out of the way and there, buried so shallowly as to not be hidden at all, were the paintings she had expected. Men and women stretched naked over the canvases, and other figures too, androgynous in their beauty, neither wholly male nor female. Slender youths and curved royalty and warriors boasting muscles rippling with power. There were portraits and Grecian scenes and, even further back, paintings of wild, erotic daydreams: a woman entangled in passionate embrace with a swan, with a white bull—a man and a woman entwined on the chaise she recognised from across the room, their mouths pink from kisses, and other places pink too, besides—women spread amid platters of fruit, oranges split open with their juices dripping sweet and sticky onto the table—men sprawled amid beds of wildflowers, their gazes dark and heavy and so terribly inviting—those sleek androgynous figures wrapped up in one another so closely that she had to lean in to determine where one body ended and the other began.

Her head spun at the sight of so much skin, muscles and tendons so delicately rendered with so fine a brush, as if they were alive and breathing in the room with her. Pale skin painted pink and blushing; bronze skin burnished gold; dark skin so rich and brown it glowed, and all of it infused with a heady, intoxicating vitality that sent a rush of heat coiling through her. He made every face, every gender and every body type seem enviable, no matter their age, weight, or shape, and she was struck by the sudden fantasy of seeing her own body portrayed with such reverence. Aaliyah's desire to see herself as a goddess in Coxley's style now seemed so much more understandable.

Dropping her hand from the canvases, she let them fall back into place as she stepped away. She had no trouble believing the rumours that Coxley enchanted his paintings. Whether he trapped his sitters' souls in them or mesmerised his viewers; both seemed equally plausible. The paint was so lively, invoking such intense emotions—it was easy to understand why someone might wish to blame magic for their reaction to such art.

"Ah," said Coxley. "Yes. I imagine…" He coughed softly, almost apologetically, if she didn't know better. "I imagine those are more what you expected."

"Not precisely," she said faintly, running her hands over her dress to hide how affected she was. "I had expected something more vulgar, perhaps."

"You wouldn't call those vulgar?"

She could call them a thousand things, but vulgar, never. "They're striking," she said instead. "Your mastery of colour and composition are remarkable. Anyone who would dismiss such things on account of the subject matter must be blind to all things in art, and therefore not worth listening to."

"Oh." He wore his surprise openly, a pleased smile on his lips, and she preened a little to have caught him off guard. "You know something of art, Mrs. Turtledove."

"I know good art when I see it," she allowed with a shrug, "just as I know, ah…"

"Pornography?" he offered.

"Rather. Will you tell me your favourite now that I've seen the rest?"

He studied her for a moment before relaxing, his whole body loosening in an easy shrug as he crossed the room to join her and sift through the canvases. "I wasn't lying; I am partial to the snapdragons. But of the more risqué matter, perhaps this one."

He shifted the other canvases away to reveal a large painting near the wall. The background was a haze of blues and greens crowding in from around the edges, but the figure at the forefront was all gold. It was a portrait of a young man, naked to the waist, with curling russet hair and a map of freckles across his nose and shoulders. He stared out from the canvas with a piercing, cool green gaze, his jaw as square and his muscles as firm as any Greek hero of old, and in his arms, he held a magnificent black rooster, its feathers all a-shimmer with iridescent green. The painting wasn't especially more skilled than any of the others, the subject matter not particularly different, but there was something in the golden youth's gaze that gave pause—some intensity, as if he knew he were being watched and dared any of the viewers to judge him. Elizabeth drew closer until she could see the individual brush strokes, but they did nothing to break the illusion of life.

"He's captivating," she said softly. "All innuendo aside, of course. Was the model someone you knew personally?"

"Not as such. He was on loan from a brothel, as a matter of fact."

"Do you find many of your models in such places?"

"A fair few," he admitted. "They're always willing, and of course they lack any hesitation when it comes to undressing, which is extremely helpful in my line of work. Not that I haven't had the frequent gentleman—or lady—eager to strip down for a session or two."

"Curious to get closer to their local eccentric, as you said."

"Yes, precisely. Your friend Miss Kaddour, for instance."

"Mrs," Elizabeth corrected automatically.

"Yes, of course. Tell me: do all the married women you know have husbands so keen on throwing their wives in my path?"

"Why? Would you prefer our husbands threw themselves into your path once in a while?"

They stared at each other for a heartbeat before Elizabeth dropped her gaze, an unspoken admission that neither of them was ready to discuss such things in the open.

Coxley stepped back and gestured to the rest of the studio. "Please feel free to continue your investigation, though I doubt I have any secrets more scandalous than what you've already uncovered."

"I expected more, I must admit." She glanced around. The light from the north windows slanted in, pooling in large, buttery rectangles over the floor. "Do you keep your sketches organised, or is it just what's pinned to the walls? I've always been fascinated by artists' sketches, perhaps even more so than their finished works. Something of the soul shows through clearest there, I find."

Coxley watched her with raised brows. "Are you an artist, Mrs. Turtledove?"

"I dabbled in watercolour at school, and I have my sketches and patterns for my dresses, but nothing serious."

"It's just that the way you speak, you seem to boast such an understanding of it. Art and artists alike."

"Besides fashion, painting and writing seem to have much in common. But here, now, I'm merely an appreciative spectator."

"Indeed." He cleared his throat. "In any case, yes, I do keep sketchbooks. They're... well, they're somewhere." He went striding off across the room, stopping at various tables and desks to examine their clutter until he finally landed on a stack of books he must have deemed safe enough, and waved her over. "Some of my earlier work," he offered, handing her a small brown book with a soft leather cover. "And here, my current sketchbook." He patted a larger, less-worn volume on the desktop. "Peruse away. I need to check on something to see how it's drying, if you don't mind?"

"No, please, don't mind me."

She thumbed through the older book, skimming the pages without intent at first. The sketches were a mix of pencil, charcoal, and ink, and some pages even featured a splash of paint here and there, though that seemed largely accidental. They danced back and forth between figure studies, anatomical studies, and portraits, many of which Elizabeth assumed to be more of his sex workers, their bodies wanton within the book's covers. The lines were cruder than what she saw on display in the studio; the dates scrawled haphazardly in the sketchbook's corners put it a decade back, before the war. The skill was, even then, undeniable, but the drawings lacked the flair and confidence evident in his contemporary work. Toned down too was the raw sensuality: though the bodies were more often naked than not, the poses were far less suggestive, the eroticism stripped back into something passably appropriate. It was the work of a talented student, but no master. She had almost flipped the book shut, intending to reach for the contemporary collection instead, when a portrait toward the back caught her eye and gave her pause.

Arthur, sketched in gentle graphite, stared back at her from the paper. He was missing his familiar moustache and he looked altogether more youthful than the man she knew, but it was him, without a doubt. His gaze was softly amused, as if he had agreed to the study against his better judgement; a smile lurked at the corners of his mouth, though he did not break. It was a look she knew well, at once fond and exasperated, and to see it here, captured years before she had ever met him, made the breath catch in her throat for a second. Without thinking, she brushed her thumb over his face, tracing the line of his jaw, down his throat to where it disappeared under his collar, which then faded away off the edge of the page altogether.

Holding her breath, she flipped to the next page, and the next, all the way to the end of the book, and Arthur after Arthur flickered past her fingers. Some sketches were scant lines, caught as if in passing as Arthur walked by. Others were rendered in such careful detail that they must have taken hours, unless Coxley had drawn him from memory. Elizabeth didn't know which possibility was more intoxicating: that Arthur had agreed to sit for so long, baring himself to the glittering scrutiny of Coxley's attention—and Elizabeth knew Coxley was like a magpie in that regard, fixated, unrelenting, and keen to pick a subject apart down to its smallest components—or that Coxley knew him so intimately that he didn't need Arthur in front of him to draw him down to the finest line.

"Still entertaining yourself, I hope, Mrs. Turtledove?" Coxley called from across the room, where he seemed dissatisfied with the process of some painting or other.

"Call me Elizabeth, please," she murmured distractedly.

"Only if you call me Jules. Or Coxley, if you like. I don't mind either way so long as you drop the 'mister.' It makes me feel terribly respectable."

"Oh, we can't have that."

He ambled back to her, his hands in his pockets, and she snapped the sketchbook shut and set it aside. Seeing those portraits of Arthur somehow seemed more intimate than seeing Coxley's full paintings in all their erotic glory. Those were designed for public consumption, after all, but the sketches— Stumbling upon those felt as if she had come across his diary, where he had written his thoughts plain for all to see.

But Arthur is my husband, she thought—only that didn't seem to matter. He had been Coxley's friend first, after all; they had lived together for years before she had even been a thought in Arthur's mind. And though she had never once considered that their relationship had been anything more than two friends sharing rooms, seeing Coxley's sketches forced her to reconsider that notion.

Arthur would have told her when she had asked him that night on their honeymoon. He had always been scrupulously honest about his past loves, as she had always been with him.

But that didn't mean Coxley didn't harbour feelings.

"You seem deep in thought," Coxley observed. "I didn't realise my works were so philosophical."

"Ah, no. I'm afraid my mind wandered. Come, why don't you show me more of your process? How do you take a sketch to a finished painting? I'm quite curious, I must say."

"Then I shall indulge you."

He offered her his arm, launching into an explanation of his own creative genius, though behind his smile and his cascade of words, he still seemed to be waiting for something. For her to judge him, perhaps, and find him wanting. She tightened her grip on his arm and stepped closer to his side, keeping her gaze focused on the work in question even when he flashed a startled glance her way.

"You are a man of many layers," she said amicably as her visit wound to its end. "I've quite enjoyed the opportunity to peel some of them back today."

"Likewise," he said, watching her with a bemused expression. "I've quite enjoyed the company. You're welcome to return another day, and that is not an invitation I offer often, or lightly."

"Perhaps I might see you in action next time," she suggested.

"Maybe not while my brothel models are sitting," he replied drily, but she merely arched a brow.

"No? It's not like I haven't seen it all before, but I would hate to offend your delicate sensibilities."

"I—"

She laughed at his expression. "Don't fret, Coxley. I won't do anything to make you uncomfortable." She patted his arm as he sputtered. "In the meantime, do come for dinner again. Arthur misses you, though he won't come out and say so."

Something flickered over Coxley's face but it was gone before she could parse it. He merely nodded. "I wouldn't turn down Mrs. Patel's recipes for the world. Cooking for one does quickly grow tiresome, you know."

She swallowed a pang of sympathy in order to keep her voice light. "I can imagine. Mrs. Patel cooks food to spare, so don't be shy. She'd be all too delighted to send you home with a plate, if you asked."

He tipped his head to one side in consideration before finally nodding his assent. "I'll send word in the next day or two. It was lovely to see you, my dear."

"And I you." She leaned in and pressed a friendly kiss to his cheek without stopping to consider it, darting back before he had time to protest. She smiled as if she hadn't noticed the way his eyes were round in shock. "Goodbye, Coxley. Till next time."

"Goodbye, Elizabeth," he said faintly, one hand pressed to his cheek as she turned to exit the studio with the firm click-clack of her heels on the floor, which sounded much surer of themselves than she felt.

◆ ◆ ◆

"Arthur, darling."

That night they were in bed together, comfortably undressed, with the bedside lamp still on. Arthur was propped up against the pillows, a book balanced on his chest, though he wasn't really reading it anymore. Elizabeth could tell that his eyes had stopped tracking the words a page ago, his lids growing heavy as he fought off the grasp of sleep.

"Mm?"

"Did you ever model for Coxley?"

He set the book aside, turning to face her with his chin cupped in one hand. "Why? Did you find some obscure painting in his studio that he said was me? One of his erotic nudes, perhaps?"

"Nothing like that. He just seems like he would draw anything if it sat still long enough, and you lived with him for years, so I wondered."

She was content to lay there in the lazy warmth and study how the lamplight glowed over Arthur's face, turning him gold. It caught the auburn of his hair most beautifully, burning it rich brown and red, and his freckles disappeared in the dim lighting, the smooth, strong line of his jaw softening into gentle shadows. He could be an oil painting all on his own, even the cool blues and greens of his eyes melting into gold and grey.

The image of the golden youth with the bird rose up in her mind's eye. He shared certain similarities with Arthur, to be sure, but the details were just different enough…

"He never painted me," Arthur said, "though I sat for plenty of sketches over the years. Figure drawings, even, though I kept my clothes on for it."

"He never used those sketches for anything after?"

"Like an underpainting? Not that I know of, though I wouldn't put it past him. The number of times I caught him sketching me or using me for some reference without my being aware of it—he's insatiable, you know."

"And that didn't bother you?"

"You get used to it. And trying to deter the behaviour is like trying to herd cats. Or one cat, anyway. A very large, very vocal cat. He'll do what he likes. I've always found it easiest to just go along with it."

"A very talented cat," Elizabeth pointed out.

Arthur snorted. "Yes, that too. That's why he gets away with so much."

She reached over to curl her fingers through his hair. "Would you let him paint you, if he asked?"

"I suppose." He caught her fingers and kissed them. "He never did, though. He always had plenty of models coming and going; there didn't seem to be any need for me."

Playfully, she poked one finger through the curl of his moustache. "I'd like to model for him, I think."

"Oh? Why am I not surprised?"

"I like him better than I thought I would," she admitted. "You were right about him being far less of a cad than he'd have people believe."

"And what manner of modelling would you do?"

She bit her lip and looked away to keep from laughing, but he laughed first.

"I think this is where I'm supposed to step in and say *no, absolutely not, no wife of mine is going to show her body off to another man*—but you know I won't."

Leaning in, she pressed a kiss to his jaw. "No, I know you won't say anything of the sort," she murmured.

"Though I probably ought to, for all our sakes."

"Probably, but where's the fun in that?"

He caught her by the shoulders, pushing her back just far enough to meet her eye. "Promise me you'll keep it tasteful? Or at least, if not, promise it won't be publicly displayed?"

"I will do my best to preserve your reputation of a man in control of his wife, dearest."

"It's not so much that. I just shudder to think what your mother will say."

Elizabeth laughed and kissed him properly. "I won't let it come to that. Whatever happens, I'll make sure you're not caught in the crossfire of any in-laws." Nestling against his chest, she lay her head on his shoulder and pulled the duvet up over her arms. "I love you. You know that, don't you?"

"I do." He dropped a kiss to the top of her head, buried in her hair. "And I love you, too."

CHAPTER ELEVEN

IN WHICH A PROPOSITION IS MADE OVER DINNER

Coxley apparently took Elizabeth's invitation to visit more often to mean *come over any time, whenever you like, with or without telling us beforehand*, though Elizabeth couldn't say she actually minded, and Arthur's complaints held no heat. For her part, Mrs. Patel was growing accustomed to his habits of wandering in and out of the house, and barely batted an eye. If anything, she seemed pleased at the increased opportunities to foist more food on him.

"Dinner is orange-ginger chicken on rice, Mr. Coxley," she said as he flung his coat over the rack in the entranceway. "I assume you're staying."

"Yes, thank you, Mrs. Patel. And dessert?"

"We have berry tarts for dessert," said Elizabeth, sweeping in from the dining room to greet him, "and stop bothering Mrs. Patel. She's terribly busy. Now, come through—your timing is excellent, though I suspect you didn't mean it to be."

"I meant to arrive an hour ago," Coxley said cheerfully, "but I managed to upset a great deal of paint all over myself shortly before leaving."

Looking closely, she could see some still clinging to his wrists, barely hidden by his shirtsleeves. "Well, dinner is almost ready, so you're in luck. Though Arthur and I have nearly finished the wine ourselves."

"You have another bottle, surely."

"Oh, undoubtedly. Shall we?"

Taking his arm, she tugged him to the dining room, where Arthur was already seated at the table contemplating his drink.

"Ah, there you are," he said, glancing up as they entered. "I was beginning to think you'd somehow got lost on the way over."

"Not at all, old boy. I could find my way here in my sleep, at this point. I can't count the number of times I've come here to eat. Which reminds me: I really ought to repay the favour of so many dinners."

"You don't have a cook," Arthur pointed out, "and even if you did, Mrs. Patel would be better. Besides which, I'm willing to bet anything that you've been living in your studio since I moved out."

Coxley threw himself into his chair with a dramatic sigh. "It's terribly inconvenient, screening for new flatmates, you know. A most tedious process."

"Well, last time you tried it you got me, so it can't be all that bad."

"No, but look how that turned out! You tossed me aside at the first opportunity—no offense intended, my dear," he added, turning to Elizabeth as she sat down, arranging her dress over her knees. "You make a lovely wife for him, and I continue to wish you both all the happiness in the world."

"Thank you," she said mildly. "But surely Arthur isn't the pinnacle of companionship. No offense, darling."

Arthur raised his glass in a silent toast.

"There's nothing wrong with living at the studio," Coxley countered. "It saves me a great deal of time from having to commute back and forth, for one thing, and besides, there's a bed. What more does one need?"

"There is no bed," Elizabeth said disapprovingly. "There's a chaise, and I can't imagine it does your back any favours, sleeping on that, night after night."

He waved her off. "Nonsense. I'm not so old or delicate as that."

Before Elizabeth could argue the point, Mrs. Patel brought in dinner. Despite Elizabeth and Arthur's protests, she insisted on serving them at the table as if they couldn't carry their own plates to and from the kitchen. Arthur said he felt uncomfortable treating her as serving staff on top of a housekeeper and cook, but Elizabeth was of the belief that Mrs. Patel could, and would, run the house however she pleased, and if that included table service, so be it. They would simply have to keep raising her wages to match her services, which, Elizabeth supposed, may have been Mrs. Patel's intention all along. Well: the more power to her, then.

The dishes were beautiful, as always. The chicken sat glazed in a thick orange-ginger sauce atop a bed of rice and gently cooked greens, seasoned to perfection. Mrs. Patel was unapologetic in her use of Indian spices, and though it had taken some getting used to, Elizabeth was privately determined to pay her whatever wage necessary to keep her on indefinitely.

"If it tastes half as good as it looks then you've outdone yourself, Mrs. Patel," Coxley announced, studying the dish intently as he nudged at the greens with his fork. The rusty orange colour of the fowl complimented the vegetables nicely from an artistic perspective which he seemed to appreciate.

"There is enough for seconds, should you enjoy it, Mr. Coxley," said Mrs. Patel. "And thirds."

"I'm sure I will, but I don't know if I can manage thirds if I want to leave room for dessert."

She tutted. "I'll pack some up to take home with you, then."

"But first, another bottle of white, if you would, Mrs. Patel?" Elizabeth requested, pouring the last of their current bottle into Coxley's glass.

Once the wine was brought and everyone topped up, Elizabeth allowed them to get ten minutes into their meal—as delicious as Coxley had guessed, of course, the ginger adding a lovely sharp bite to the chicken— before clearing her throat.

"Coxley," she said, her fingers curled lightly around the stem of her glass. "Is there any particular project you're working on at the moment?"

"I'm putting the finishing touches on a portrait of a young man with a horse," Coxley offered, spearing a portion of chicken on his fork. "For a private client who was very particular as to the nature of the youth's—ahem—physical endowments." He took a bite, chewing thoughtfully for a moment. "The horse's too, for that matter."

"I don't believe I saw that one."

"No, I had it put aside to let it dry in peace. Not that you would have disturbed it, of course, but one can never be too careful when bringing new people around."

"I understand completely. And what of your future plans, once the boy and his horse are finished?"

Coxley set his fork down and levelled her with a look. "My dear, if there's something in particular you want to ask—"

"I believe," Arthur cut in smoothly, "that my wife has a proposition for you."

"Oh, indeed?"

"As a matter of fact, yes. I should like to commission a portrait, if you have the time."

"A portrait? I should be delighted. Of yourself?"

"Yes, I think so. Paid, of course."

Coxley immediately shook his head. "No, I couldn't possibly. You're good friends, and I—"

"Have just told us you're living out of your studio," Arthur said. "We're paying you, Jules." He took a sip of wine. "Besides which, you haven't heard what Elizabeth's going to ask for."

Coxley glanced back at her. "A portrait. Something big? Complicated?"

"A full-body portrait," Elizabeth confirmed, her heart fluttering as she said it aloud. She had already discussed it at length with Arthur, naturally, and was entirely committed to her course, but it was something else to set it in action. "You're to name the same price you would to any of your other clients, and Arthur will tell me if you're undercharging. What I have in mind is rather large, and I imagine quite time consuming, and I insist you're fairly compensated for it."

Interest sparked in Coxley's eyes, and he leaned in just a little over his plate. "And what precisely did you have in mind?"

"Well, Arthur and I were talking, and we thought—"

"Ah," Arthur interrupted, holding up one finger. "Credit where it's due, dearest: this was entirely your idea."

"Fine. I thought, then, that I should like a painting of myself on that chaise for which you've abandoned your bed. With an assortment of flowers, too, since you paint them so nicely."

Coxley looked back and forth between them, his gaze flickeringly fast. "On the chaise," he repeated. "Yes, of course. Might I suggest you wear green? You look lovely in it, and with the flowers—"

"I wasn't planning on wearing anything, actually." Her cheeks flooded with heat and she dabbed at her mouth with her napkin to stall for time, but didn't back down.

Coxley stared at her, and then at Arthur. "Er," he said finally. "Arthur, old chap. Dear boy. Did you— Are you—"

Arthur raised both hands. "Steering clear of the matter. She has my blessing—you both do—but that's the extent of my involvement, thank you."

"You're alright with your wife wanting to pose in the nude? On my chaise? Where I sleep?"

"I didn't know you were sleeping there when I decided it," Elizabeth pointed out. "You can drape something over the cushions, surely."

"That's not the point!" Coxley was looking as flushed as Elizabeth felt, which she found gratifying.

"Then what exactly is your objection? You paint nudes all the time. If I wanted myself painted in a fancy dress, there are a dozen artists who could serve. But I know you can do justice to the body as well, and I find that far more interesting."

"You can turn her down," Arthur said, pointing at Coxley with a forkful of greens. "You're not actually obliged to take the commission just because we're friends."

"Oh, certainly," Elizabeth agreed. "If it makes you uncomfortable…"

As predicted, Coxley bristled at the suggestion. "My comfort won't be a problem, I assure you. I'm just trying to work out why it doesn't make *you* uncomfortable."

Elizabeth exchanged a look with Arthur. He hadn't tried to talk her out of it, but merely sighed and laughed into her shoulder, pressing her down into the pillows, his eyes bright with helpless affection.

She shrugged. "We're all adults. What we do behind closed doors is our own business, surely."

Coxley flinched back imperceptibly, as if she weren't speaking about portraiture at all, and she bit her tongue. Arthur too looked at her strangely, just for a second, and she dropped her gaze to the tablecloth.

"We are," Coxley finally said. "And I would be delighted to paint you, in whatever state of undress you choose." He glanced at Arthur, who was determinedly focused on clearing his plate.

"Excellent," Elizabeth said.

"Give me a week to finish my current project and get my schedule in order?" Coxley coughed, dropping his fork onto his plate with a clang. He clumsily fumbled it back into his hand again. "After that, I'll be entirely at your disposal."

"I look forward to it."

Dessert brought berry tarts: little open-faced pastries baked to a perfect golden brown, with clumps of sugar clinging to the crust, and filled with sweet berries that bled purple with every bite. Elizabeth watched Coxley as they ate: how his eyes lit up, sparks dancing in their depths when he landed on some topic of interest, and how he talked with his hands, and how the berries stained his lips dark before he licked the juice away.

How he was utterly, helplessly unsubtle in how he looked at Arthur, his heart written plainly on his face. He looked how Elizabeth felt when she looked at Arthur, and how Arthur had looked back at her on their wedding day. She took a bite of her tart as she considered the situation, letting the berries burst sweetly over her tongue. Arthur didn't know about Coxley's feelings for him, of that she was sure. He was gently oblivious to such things, she had learned first-hand during their courtship. No matter how obvious she tried to be in her affections for him, he had needed her to spell it out.

"Arthur, for heaven's sake," she had finally said after their sixth date, "I like you very much, and I wish you would hurry up and take me to bed already."

The startled look in his eyes gave way to delight and he had pressed in close, dipped her, and kissed her as thoroughly as she could have wished.

Clearly, no such conversation had ever occurred between him and Coxley. But she suspected that if Coxley had said those words to him first, Arthur would have complied. There was an energy between them she couldn't ignore. It spoke to years of friendship, to be sure, but there was an undercurrent of longing on both sides she couldn't be imagining. Coxley's portraits of Arthur looked like how a lover might draw his beloved, with compulsive repetition, like he couldn't shake Arthur from his mind.

And sometimes, when Arthur looked at Coxley, it was like the rest of the world ceased to exit, his whole focus narrowed to his friend. Seeing them together, Elizabeth quietly marvelled that she had ever won Arthur for herself.

That he truly loved her, she had no doubt. But she suspected that he loved Coxley just as much, and

Coxley him in return, and the only reason she and Arthur were together now was that she had come out and actually told Arthur of her love.

She plucked a fat cherry from her tart and sucked on it contemplatively. Coxley was recounting some dubious adventure that had resulted in his first hiring of a boy from a brothel to model for his paintings, and Arthur was watching him with fond amusement. He had doubtless heard the tale before—Elizabeth recognised his expression from their wedding planning, when she had gone over the same details day after day and he had patiently nodded along—but his interest never wavered.

"Not that my reputation was pristine beforehand," Coxley concluded, "but it was that brothel that drove the nail in the coffin, I believe."

Arthur snorted. "I'm sure you would have managed to drag your name through the mud just fine without ever visiting a brothel."

"I was of the impression a great number of gentlemen visit the brothels," Elizabeth agreed. "Most manage some measure of discretion."

Coxley rolled his eyes and flicked their words away with his fork like swatting flies. "Oh, but where's the fun in that?"

And Elizabeth had to agree, though she didn't say as much out loud.

CHAPTER TWELVE

AN ESCALATING SENSE OF INCOMPETENCE

Elizabeth was visiting Alphonse and Jacobi at their home while Jasmine was at work and Aaliyah was out for lunch with her father. She had timed her visit so she could speak with the two men privately, not daring to hold the conversation in a public place, and hoping for a little more delicacy than Aaliyah generally had the patience for. It was a comfortably overcast afternoon in late June and they were ensconced in the back garden, with a little patio table holding their tea, which Jacobi had meticulously served as if he were still a butler and not an equal partner in the household.

"I wanted to ask you about a somewhat delicate matter," Elizabeth began.

"Righto," Alphonse returned cheerfully.

Though no one could ask for a better disposition, Alphonse was sorely lacking in the department of self-preservation, a fact that Elizabeth had no intention of using to her own advantage. She was, however, grateful that it made her line of questioning so much easier to bring up. Jacobi was another matter, keeping his cards so close to the chest that few people even knew what game he was playing, never mind what hand he held. But Elizabeth had his trust, and so long as she wasn't careless with it or with Alphonse, Jacobi was likely to help her, if perhaps not in so open and eager a manner as his partner.

"You see, I have a friend whom I suspect is in a position similar to yours, or at least, how yours used to be. I've broached the subject with him and he didn't shy away from it, but neither does he seem particularly interested in exploring his options."

Alphonse nodded politely, looking like he had no idea what she was talking about.

"He's attracted to men," she clarified.

"Oh! Yes, I do see how that would relate to us, rather. What about it?"

"Well, he happens to be happily married—not like you and Aaliyah, but properly married—and I worry that he's boxed away this whole other half of himself without ever taking the opportunity to explore it. It's not that I think his marriage will suffer, I only wonder if he might come to regret such lost chances."

"With all due respect," said Jacobi, "are you quite sure it's your responsibility to ask such questions on his behalf?"

Elizabeth thumbed her wedding ring, spinning it around her finger in short, fidgety movements. Jacobi caught it immediately, his expression smoothing over.

"I see," he said.

"See what, old chap?" Alphonse asked.

"It's Arthur," Elizabeth said, trying not to feel guilty at sharing her husband's secret even with two friends who must surely be sympathetic.

"Well, did he tell you he had any regrets?" Alphonse asked. "Because I must say, he's positively radiating wedded bliss these days."

"I don't doubt his happiness, and I don't believe he's mourning any lost love from his past. It's just—" She swallowed, realising all too abruptly that she had little way forward without divulging the whole story. "Well, it's Mr. Coxley."

"Ah," said Jacobi.

"Ah?" asked Alphonse.

"I think he's in love with Arthur, and I think the only reason Arthur is with me now instead of him is that Coxley never said anything."

"This is approaching the edges of gossip, Mrs. Leicester," Jacobi said in gentle admonishment.

"This is a friend unburdening herself from a matter of the heart!" Alphonse countered. "Who can possibly advise her in this manner if not us?"

"I don't mean to gossip and I certainly don't mean for a single word of this to escape this garden. But I must admit that solving this problem—in as much as there is any problem to be solved—is rather outside my lived experience, and I don't know who better to ask than you."

"If Arthur's situation is anything like mine was," Alphonse said, "then perhaps you merely need Aaliyah to bully him into a realisation of his own feelings. I'd been pining after Jacobi for years without properly noticing it, and she only had to take one look at me to figure it out."

"Unless your real concern is whether a man who harbours such inclinations towards his fellows is capable of finding fulfilment with a woman alone," Jacobi said.

"I want him to be happy. With me, certainly, but also to be as happy as possible. And if that means finding some additional source of happiness outside our marriage…"

"But he hasn't said anything about actually wanting to stray beyond the marriage bed," Jacobi clarified. "You're merely inferring this from a conversation in which he confided to being attracted to men."

"Yes," Elizabeth admitted.

Jacobi looked mildly disapproving.

"Say that you told him to go for it," Alphonse said. "To make a move on Coxley. What do you think he'd do?"

"Arthur?"

"Either of them."

"I think Arthur would deny everything, to both of us, in order to keep from upsetting the equilibrium of his marriage and his friendship. And as for Coxley." Elizabeth bit her lip. "I think he would be terribly hurt by such a denial, yet unable to communicate that hurt without admitting his own feelings. It would make a terrible mess, I'm afraid, and I don't want to be responsible for that kind of carnage."

"Shall we set Aaliyah on them, then?" Alphonse suggested.

"I'm not sure the blunt-force approach is what's called for here." Elizabeth looked back and forth between the two men. "Do you think I'm right, though? Even if you disagree with my notion of pushing Arthur towards this, do you think I'm right in seeing this mutual yearning between them?"

Alphonse looked expectantly at Jacobi.

"I really couldn't say anything in terms of absolutes," Jacobi said apologetically. "Though I can confirm that Mr. Coxley does, on occasion, frequent certain gentlemen's clubs that cater to such a crowd. Of course, such could be a coincidence, considering Mr. Coxley's social eccentricities."

"But you suspect," Elizabeth said.

"If you're asking if we can recognise one of our own, I must regretfully inform you that we do not in fact all share some common pheromone allowing us to unerringly hone in one another."

"I can tell you straight up that I'm absolute rubbish at recognising any such thing," Alphonse confirmed. "Imagine if I had a single ounce of that ability! I'd have seen right through Jacobi on day one and saved us all those years of tiptoeing around each other." He shook his head mournfully. "What a waste."

There was a flurry of activity from within the house heralding Aaliyah's return from her lunch date, and a moment later she came through the back door to join them.

"Hello," Aaliyah said cheerfully, dropping into one of the empty chairs and crossing one knee over the other. "What are we talking about?"

Alphonse looked at Elizabeth, who sighed. Perhaps she had wrung as much delicacy as could be had from the conversation and it was time to embrace Aaliyah's battering-ram approach to navigating relationships.

"Do you think Arthur and Coxley are in love?"

"Yes," Aaliyah said immediately. "Absolutely, without question. Why? Has one of them finally done something about it?"

Elizabeth groaned. "How long have you known?"

"Oh, since forever," she said dismissively. "Did you only figure it out recently?"

"Yes, rather."

"Poor thing. How are you taking it?"

"She's taking an admirably goal-oriented approach," Jacobi said.

"Are you really?" Aaliyah asked delightedly. "You want to set them up together?"

"I mean, I want to give them the option."

"And you don't think that will backfire terribly?"

"I don't know. It's a pressing concern, certainly."

"Who else knows?" Aaliyah asked.

"Outside of this garden? No one."

"Let's keep it that way. We'll get Jasmine in on it, of course, but other than her— Alphonse? Not a word of this to anyone, not even a hint."

Alphonse mimed sealing his lips shut.

"We can have this sorted before the end of the summer," Aaliyah said confidently. "The Hollyhock garden party: that's the deadline."

"There's no need to rush anything," Elizabeth said. "Neither of them are going anywhere, after all."

"The end of the summer is taking it slow," Aaliyah said. "If I wanted to rush things, I could have them in each other's arms by the end of the week. You know how I work."

Alphonse nodded emphatically.

"Well," said Elizabeth, "I suppose I'll have no shortage of opportunity to work on them. I may have a commissioned a portrait."

Aaliyah leaned all the way across the table. "Have you? Tell me everything. Has he started yet?"

"No, it's only just been put in motion. It was a bit impulsive. I went to his studio out of curiosity and wanting to know him better, and then I couldn't get the idea out of my head."

"Did I make it sound so appealing that you signed up without even seeing how he did mine?" Aaliyah asked, laughing.

"I saw his other work, but yes, it was you who piqued my interest originally. I can't blame you entirely, as much as I might like to."

Aaliyah pushed her chair back and leapt to her feet, taking Elizabeth by the wrist to drag her up too. "You have to come and see it. It's so impressive, and funny in its own way, of course, having this enormous Renaissance-looking thing hanging so casually in the house. Come on, come and see."

She led Elizabeth through the house to her office where, as promised, the painting hung behind her desk. It was five feet tall and three feet wide, displayed in a dark gold baroque frame like something in a museum. Aaliyah was the undisputed focal point, with a dark wilderness of trees at her back and a host of hounds in front. She was bare-breasted, a circlet in her hair, holding a bow and arrow in one hand and the reins of her horse in the other, with her horse being a beautiful Arabian specimen with an arched neck and flowing mane. The hounds were lively and bright-eyed, seeming ready to rush out of the frame, but Aaliyah was poised and still, her dark eyes gazing triumphantly out at the viewer.

Elizabeth stood with one hand over her mouth, as entranced by the painting's beauty as she was by her friend's boldness.

"Do you like it?" Aaliyah asked smugly, like she already knew the answer.

"It's stunning. If he does half as good a job on mine, I should be delighted."

"He doesn't strike me as the type to half-arse any work. I'm sure it will be gorgeous. What did you ask for, though? Are you going to be a goddess too, bare in all your glory?" Aaliyah teased.

"We haven't discussed the details yet, but your guess might be closer than you realise," Elizabeth admitted.

"When I saw the way he paints bodies, I couldn't help myself. I might like something a little subtler than what you went for, but I understand the appeal entirely."

Aaliyah laughed, astonished and delighted, and threw one arm around Elizabeth's shoulders. "You won't regret it," she promised. "It was a fantastic experience, and of course the finished artwork is worth any amount of time and money. Also, this gives you the perfect opportunity to orchestrate something between Coxley and Arthur. Can you convince Arthur to get his portrait done with you? Or better yet, alone?"

"I really don't know. He's never been interested before, and while he's certainly happy to support me in this, I'm not sure he would ever go for it himself."

"Do you think you could use your alone time with Coxley to weasel a confession out of him? Get him to open up to you and admit his feelings for Arthur?"

"This isn't an undercover spy operation," Elizabeth protested. "The last thing I want to do is make either of them uncomfortable."

Aaliyah rolled her eyes. "Fine. Speaking of spies, though, are you ever going to tell me what you and Arthur were doing that day in the bushes in Kew Gardens? Was it about Coxley after all?"

"No, although it turns out he was there for the same reason we were." Elizabeth glanced around to ensure Alphonse wasn't in the vicinity before dropping her voice to a whisper. "I'm being blackmailed," she confided, leaning close to murmur directly in Aaliyah's ear. "Someone has found out my pen name and is trying to extract payment from me in exchange for their silence. We were hoping to catch them that day in Kew Gardens when they came to collect their ransom, but they never showed."

Aaliyah pulled back to stare at Elizabeth, wide-eyed with her mouth dropped open. "What an ordeal! Is this ongoing?"

"We haven't heard from them since, but it's certainly not resolved. I'm not entirely sure what to do. Obviously, I'm not going to give them any money, but…"

"What you need to do is work out their identity before they can expose yours. What if you hire someone to take care of it for you?"

"There's a chance that the blackmailer is actually a private investigator. Which would slightly complicate the matter, I think."

"Is there anything I can do to help?"

Elizabeth paused for a second to properly consider her options. "You said that Alphonse is a fan of M. Hayes?"

"She's one of his favourites," Aaliyah confirmed.

"And he's one of the most social people I know," Elizabeth mused. "What would be helpful is if you could get him to spread certain rumours about M. Hayes' identity. There are a few beginning to circulate that he might have already heard. The more outlandish, the better. Anything to make me sound like the least interesting outcome, should the real name go public."

Aaliyah grinned. "That is absolutely something we can do. Alphonse will believe anything, and he'll have a brilliantly good time doing it."

"Thank you. I know it's not much, but I think it will help."

Aaliyah wrapped her in a hug, which Elizabeth returned gratefully.

"When you find out who it is, don't hesitate to set me on them," Aaliyah said, her chin hooked firmly over Elizabeth's shoulder. "By the time I'm done with them, they won't be in any state to blackmail anyone ever again."

"I appreciate that, though you might have to wait in line behind Arthur and Coxley."

"Let us deal with them in turns," she suggested. "And then you can step in at the end to finish them off."

"That sounds excellent to me."

◆ ◆ ◆

When Elizabeth returned home late that afternoon, there was another note from her blackmailer waiting for her under the door. Like the first, it was typed on thick cardstock and hand-delivered, bearing neither stamp nor return address. Unlike the first, she couldn't muster any particular alarm at its presence. The novelty of being blackmailed had worn off, and though she still found it frustrating, she was more fed up with the affair than threatened by it.

To Mrs. Leicester, read the note: *As you have failed to meet my demands, you leave me no choice but to follow through on my word. Your identity will be publicised and your career ruined by summer's end. The people in your life will thank me for revealing your true nature: that of a self-obsessed liar who thinks herself cleverer than she really is, and a woman with an unfaithful, nymphomaniacal mind, as made evident by the repulsively salacious matter of your books. I will give you one last chance to save yourself and realise the severity of your situation. Bring the £3,614 to the Temple of Bellona, as specified in my last letter, at 7 p.m. on this Friday, and you will be spared.*

"Well, I'm not going to do that," Elizabeth declared.

"What's that?" Arthur called from the sitting room.

"Another blackmail note. Whoever our mystery blackmailer is, they're a complete coward. Not only do they conceal their identity while blustering about revealing mine, they haven't even got the nerve to follow through on their own threat." Going to the sitting room, Elizabeth waved the note in amused disgust. "They're giving me a generous second chance to hand over all my money. If I refuse again, do you think I'll be offered a third?"

"Is that a risk you're comfortable taking?" Arthur asked as she sat down beside him on the settee.

"I would rather risk their good will running dry than risk losing such a percentage of my savings, yes. My publisher has already begun spreading rumours that the author isn't English at all, but French, or Italian, or even American, and is in fact an established literary presence in one of those other countries, and is merely using this pen name to have a little fun on the side. I'm told gossip is already circling as to who this famous author might be, writing steamy romance novels under an alter ego. If our blackmailer does claim me as the authoress, people will likely dismiss me in favour of some more exciting option."

"Do you want to go back to Kew Gardens this Friday to see if they show up this time?"

"Certainly not. Look at this: *'as you have failed to meet my demands.'* We were there, the briefcase was there—unless they could somehow tell that it was empty and we were lying in wait, they're the one who failed to fulfill their end of the arrangement."

"They seem to hold an awfully personal grudge against you," Arthur noted. "Or against your writing, at least." He tapped the card with a wrinkled nose. "*'A self-obsessed liar who thinks herself cleverer than she really is, and a woman with an unfaithful, nymphomaniacal mind.'* I rather think I should pop them one for daring to speak so badly of my wife, should they ever show their face."

"Yes, they do seem awfully keen on putting me in my place," Elizabeth agreed. It left a bad taste in her mouth, but she was far more annoyed than afraid. "What an absolutely ridiculous person. I'm not going to waste my Friday evening playing along with their little farce. Let them stew in it."

With that, she tossed the letter aside, and when Friday evening rolled in, she spent it with her friends, passing around a very nice bottle of wine. Whoever her blackmailer was, she hoped they were having a miserable time lurking around Kew Gardens, perhaps being bitten by angry ants. It would serve them right.

CHAPTER THIRTEEN

ON THE INTIMICACIES INHERENT TO PORTRAITURE

One week later, Elizabeth returned to Coxley's studio for her first sitting. He opened the door to greet her, froze, and then looked down the hall over her shoulder with a faint air of desperation.

"Are you expecting someone else?" she asked lightly.

"I, ah— I had assumed Arthur would be accompanying you."

"What on earth for? He's not modelling for you, and he can't paint."

"No, of course not. Why would he come? People's wives get naked in the company of other men all the time." He opened the door wider, dipping his chin as he ushered her in. "Please: make yourself comfortable."

She stepped inside, her heels clicking smartly against the floor. She had in fact asked Arthur if he wanted to join her, or to commission his own portrait, as Aaliyah has suggested. But he had pointed out that his work wouldn't think it a valid reason to grant him the day off, even if it was a Friday. Elizabeth didn't mind. She didn't think she could convince them to simultaneously admit their love for each other, not when they had lived together for so many years without ever managing it. Coxley alone, she might have a better chance, and even besides that, she was intensely curious about him and his painting process. Whether he was in love with her husband, or Arthur in love with him, she would have wanted her portrait done regardless.

Turning, she faced him with a bright smile to mask her nervousness. "So? Shall we get right to it?"

"You seem very sure of yourself. Why don't we start with you explaining what exactly it is you want this portrait to be?"

"Of course."

She made her way to the chaise: no longer shoved off to one side, but brought front and centre, replacing the raised platform. Undoing her coat, she shrugged out of it and dropped it over the cushions. The early morning light slanted delicately through the windows, lighting the room in pale, warm yellow. Coxley hadn't cleaned the studio as scrupulously this time; canvases were propped up in multiple places against the walls, and his easel stood opposite the chaise with a sheet of sketching paper pinned to it. His gaze followed her as she moved; even when she couldn't see him, she could feel his eyes on her, warming her from the inside out with the attention. Imagining that same gaze on her with no clothes between them—she blushed, then immediately tamped it down. Taking a steadying breath, she turned to face him, hoping he wouldn't notice the splash of colour on her cheeks.

"Elizabeth."

But of course he had. She cleared her throat. "For the portrait: I was thinking of something like the Venus of Urbino, or Manet's Olympia, you know? Though perhaps somewhat more modest, so as not to cause too much of a scandal."

Coxley looked incredulous. "I'm afraid there's no escaping the scandal of it, my dear. Not unless you hide the painting away forever."

"I trust you to make it tasteful," she said firmly. "I'm not afraid of a little nudity, and I have faith that you can work the colours and shadows to your advantage. As for the rest, I thought I might hold some flowers." She coughed. "Strategically."

"I can do whatever you wish," he said carefully, "but there will always be those who say you look like a common courtesan pretending to be a queen. I need you to understand what exactly it is you're getting into."

"I understand perfectly. And your concern is touching, Coxley, it really is. But I'm not a fool." She smiled. "I know what I want. And if that's what they'll say, let them. You can paint me in a crown."

Coxley barked out a laugh. Finally shutting the door to his studio, he spread his arms wide. "Alright. If you want to be Venus, then Venus you shall be. Sit, sit. Get comfortable. Though do keep your clothes on for the time being, if you don't mind. I'm not quite ready yet."

She sank down onto the chaise. It was no bed, but more comfortable than she had expected. Of course, if she was to spend hours on it at a time, as previous models had done, a semblance of comfort was really the least it could offer.

"Arthur told me you often did preliminary studies," she said. "Of the face and form, to familiarise yourself with the subject?"

Coxley was fussing with something at his easel, the details of which were blocked to her. "No need. I am more than familiar with you, my dear."

Her blush returned and she nodded. "Good."

"No: we can jump right in."

But he stayed hidden behind his easel, busying himself with something invisible for several uninterrupted minutes, until she decided that he wasn't actually doing anything but stalling for time.

"I know you've seen all manner of bodies in the nude," she teased, "and I've certainly been naked myself, before—in company, even."

"My goodness, the scandal."

"I am married, Coxley," she said gently, and then in a burst of daring added, "but even if I weren't, why, I've hardly lived as a nun."

"Oh, you wouldn't believe what some of those nuns get up to," he replied, leaning to one side of the easel and flashing a smile, finally seeming to relax.

"Coxley."

"Elizabeth?"

"Are you quite ready?"

He cleared his throat before finally stepping out from behind his shield. "Yes, of course. Here, let me draw the privacy screen."

It seemed ridiculous to have her remove her clothes behind a screen only to lay herself out nude on the chaise after, but she bit her tongue. Coxley pulled the screen into position, its silk panels as paint-splashed as everything else in the studio, before draping a robe overtop of it and retreating to his easel once more. Elizabeth allowed him his retreat, putting the screen between them before beginning to undress.

Coxley looked away as if the screen didn't afford her enough protection; as if the act of shedding her clothes was somehow more intimate than the following nudity. She let her dress pool to the floor, tulle rustling around her ankles, before stepping out of her chemise to sit on the chaise, removing her shoes and unrolling her stockings. She watched Coxley's silhouette through the screen as she did it: how his shoulders tensed under his waistcoat with every sound, and how his fingers twitched restlessly at his sides. But he never turned around to look, not even to sneak a glance out of the corner of his eye. It was chivalrous in a way, but ultimately ridiculous, given the circumstance. She sat down on the chaise, crossed her legs at the knee, and folded her hands in her lap.

"I'm not sure how you're going to paint me if you never turn around," she said softly, and watched the tremor that ran up his spine at the sound of her voice.

It was a remarkable thing, to have that kind of power over a man. Arthur was the same, though far less shy about hiding it. Coxley hesitated a moment longer before finally turning, his features schooled in an expression of careful coolness, but she saw his breath stutter for a second before he recovered.

"Quite right," he said, his voice almost at its normal pitch. It might have fooled her if she weren't paying such close attention. As it was, everything about him showed his tension, as if he were frightened of her—or of his reaction to her. It was at once electrifying and unnerving, and she determined to set him at ease as quickly as possible, for both their sakes.

"You look like you expect me to eat you alive. If you're having second thoughts, I can put my dress back on and leave right now, no damage done."

"No, my dear, no second thoughts. I apologise." He shook his head. "I was distracted. Terribly unprofessional. Let's try that again." He caught up his sketchbook and a pencil, all business, and abandoned the shield of his easel to approach her, his mouth set in a determined line. "If you would lay down? You said Venus, Olympia, so if you set your head at this end and your feet up here—" He directed her with sweeping gestures of his pencil and she obliged, stretching out lengthways along the chaise. "Good. Now, for the cushions…"

He fetched them from their far-flung places around the room and carried them back in his arms, stacked high and tucked under his chin. They varied in colour from red to gold to green to violet, all of them rich and plump, though somewhat shabby from years of use.

Some were tasselled, others embroidered, and still more sequined, and he dropped the lot of them on her lap.

"Here. If you would lean forward, these two will go behind your back to keep you propped up more comfortably, and this one, under your elbow—yes, just so—and these, under your feet, to give your legs that elevation." He stepped back a pace to regard her pose with a critical eye, one hand under his chin. "Hm. Lean back? Get comfortable. You're going to be here a while, after all."

She settled in among the cushions, adjusting them until she could lounge back and have it feel natural.

"Good. Now, may I?" He held out the hand without the pencil, awaiting permission to proceed.

"Please, if something needs adjusting, don't hesitate to correct it. I would have you treat me the same as you would any other model. I trust that you know what you're doing."

"My prostitutes, you mean? I can't see Arthur being too happy about that."

"I don't believe you actually slept with any of them. Not at the same time you hired them to model, anyway."

"No?"

"No. I think you take your work far too seriously for that. I wouldn't be here, otherwise."

He stared at her for a moment, his eyes dark. "You are so far from what I expected," he murmured. "Very well: you are one of my models."

Stepping closer, he slid his pencil between his lips to hold it out of the way as he arranged her into the precise pose he wished to paint. Her elbows, he adjusted to rest against the cushions just so. Her hands, he placed with surgical precision, one against the chaise and the other laying demurely against one thigh. Her knees, he crooked up, angled gently and folded to one side to rest against the back of the chaise, and her feet he positioned carefully at the far end. His touches were light but steady, his hands warm and dry and unafraid of her skin. Elizabeth kept her breathing steady and prayed her body would do nothing to betray her. The situation was unavoidably intimate, his every touch sending little shivers of electricity through her nerves, yet he remained as professional as anyone could wish.

That made it worse, somehow.

"Now, turn your head in this direction." He pointed and she turned to follow his finger. "And your chin—tilt it upwards? Yes, just so." His fingers grazed her chin, adjusting the angle of her neck until she was perfectly where he wanted her. "Good."

Abruptly, he left her side, striding back to his waiting easel, and there he folded his arms, narrowed his eyes, and studied her.

He didn't look at her with a lover's gaze, but as a scientist might study his subject. She breathed in through her nose and out through parted lips, carefully and evenly. What did he see when he looked at her body? Did he see, as she did, the little roll where her stomach folded, and the same pale expanse of flank and thigh? Did he think her hips too narrow and her breasts too small, as she sometimes wondered? The flat garcon look was in vogue at the moment, but far from universally beloved.

Men did not, in her experience, judge women's forms when they were naked in bed together, being preoccupied with better things. But she had never laid herself bare in such a way, inviting—indeed, requiring—such scrutiny. A blush began in her cheeks, fanning over her face and down her throat to spread warmly and mortifyingly over her chest, impossible to hide.

"Relax," Coxley said, or perhaps ordered. "You're holding yourself far too stiffly. You will be here for at least an hour at a time, likely for several hours a day, for several days. You must relax. It's painful to look at you like this."

Taking a deep breath, she exhaled slowly and consciously forced her body to let go. Her muscles loosened in increments, sinking into the cushions bit by bit until, finally, everything settled and she found his eyes again.

"Much better. Are you comfortable?"

"I think so."

"And you can hold that position?"

She considered herself. "Yes, it should do."

"Then let's begin."

He began not with the canvas, as she had expected, but with charcoal and paper, mapping her likeness across a double spread of pages in his sketchbook.

"To catch the shadows before the sun shifts too far," he explained as he worked. "And here, see?" He turned the book around to show her. "This is how the flowers will lay, when we get to that stage."

In the drawing, she lay sprawled with easy comfort, exuding a dignity in repose that Elizabeth didn't think she matched in real life. In the hand that lay against her hip was a loose bouquet of flowers. They were scribbled in without much detail, but even from such a quick sketch, she could see how they were arranged so that the flower heads rested against her chest, covering her breasts, and the stems and leaves came down to sit between her thighs. Suggestive still, but no longer strictly naked.

"When will you add the flowers?"

"Not until much later," he said, returning his attention to the drawing and blocking in the shadows. "I will paint you first, in your entirety, then add the flowers after. You must paint in layers, you see, for the thing to work as a whole." He glanced up. "Do you wish to see it in stages, or would you prefer to only see the finished piece?"

She imagined a canvas featuring her own naked body, pale and pink, lounging like some decadent queen of the ancient world. "The finished piece, if you please," she said, her mouth dry.

As Coxley delved deeper into his work, dabbing swatches of experimental colours in his sketchbook, Elizabeth began to relax properly. Coxley made easy conversation in between long minutes of intense silence as he problem-solved, and gradually, Elizabeth forgot that she was naked. The sun was warm enough to keep her comfortable, and Coxley treated her no differently than he would if she were clothed. She had hoped her nakedness would be empowering; she had expected it to be awkward. Instead, halfway through her first sitting, she found it to be entirely casual. Perhaps that was the best option of the three.

Once Coxley began work on the canvas, he said conversationally, "Now, why don't you tell me why you're really here?"

She blinked. "I'm sorry?"

"Flattered as I am by your appreciation for my work, I can't help but suspect you have some ulterior motive. You could have as easily commissioned a clothed portrait, or even some nice, un-erotic flowers to hang in your sitting room. Is it boredom driving you to manufacture some sense of scandal in your life? I know it's not out of unfaithfulness."

"No, it's not." It was difficult to navigate a sensitive conversation without being allowed to move, but she was determined to try. "I genuinely do want this portrait from you because I admire your talent with a brush. And Aaliyah made the experience sound so appealing, never mind the end result. As for the potential scandal, I've never been as well-behaved as some would like. But you're really reading far too much into this. Can't I want a painting from the finest artist I've ever met without there being some overarching plot in play?"

He paused for a moment to consider her. "No," he finally said. "I don't believe you can."

She blew out her breath. "I suppose if I must be assigned an ulterior motive, I'd like the opportunity to talk to you about Arthur."

"You're married to him. What could I possibly tell you that you don't already know?"

"You told me once that I didn't know Arthur well enough to marry him."

"Lies and inaccuracies, obviously. I stand corrected."

"There's no denying that you've known him for much longer than I have. And I'm not fishing for secrets," she added. "We tell each other everything. I'm just curious about how you would describe him, and his life. An alternative perspective, I suppose. He says you never painted him."

"That's correct."

"But you've drawn him plenty of times."

"Certainly. I draw anyone and everyone who crosses my path."

"Did you ever ask to paint him?"

"I never thought he'd be much interested."

"I hardly think he'd refuse you anything," Elizabeth pointed out. "Did you never want to paint him?"

"Is this a roundabout way of telling me that you want a painting of your husband to match yours?" Coxley asked, looking at her from around the edge of his canvas. "Because you can just come out and say so, if you do."

"Not at all. I'm just curious about what it was like when you lived together."

"I'm sure it couldn't have been awfully different from what it's like living with him now. He's still the same man, after all."

"Yes," Elizabeth agreed, "but I'm not you."

"An astute observation."

Elizabeth gave it up as a lost cause, and when Coxley made to change the subject, she allowed it. She would have the opportunity at each subsequent sitting to ask him about Arthur again, after all.

So it went for the next two weeks, with Elizabeth going to his studio to catch the late morning light whenever she could, fitting it in around her seamstressing and the daily hour she dedicated to drafting that wretched book, the soul of which was still eluding her.

"Perhaps it doesn't need a soul," Elizabeth said. She was over for dinner with her friends, and she bemoaned the state of her writing as they waited for Alphonse and Jacobi to arrive from whatever social event had delayed them. It was Jasmine's turn to cook, and the Caribbean dishes smelled sweet and hot on the stove, lending a decadent, sultry air to the mid-July night. "Perhaps I'll finally write a book so uninspired that it will put an end to my entire career, never mind the efforts of that damned blackmailer. They want royalties from me? They can have pennies. And I won't ever have to go through the trouble of writing another romance again."

"It would solve a few of your problems," Aaliyah agreed, "but it's a bit overdramatic, isn't it?"

"Have you heard from your blackmailer again?" Jasmine asked.

"No, though I expect I will soon enough, seeing as I ignored their second deadline. I've been expecting a third note under my door for weeks. I have to say, I'm a little surprised it hasn't come by now."

"Maybe they're too busy plotting how to expose you," Aaliyah said. "What will you do if your pen name does get burned?"

"Deny everything, wait for the fuss to blow over, and then make a new one, I suppose," Elizabeth said. "I do enjoy my privacy, but it's hardly the end of the world. I doubt I would lose many of my clients from my day-job, if any at all. As for the rest of it." She shrugged. "Maybe it would be a good excuse to quit the romance scene altogether. This current book has been such a struggle; I wonder if I've lost my spark. Perhaps it's time to try an entirely different genre, like... thrillers, or mysteries, or something. They're popular at the moment, and I'd enjoy the change of pace."

"Aaliyah is right," Jasmine said. "Quitting romance entirely might be a little overdramatic."

The sound of the front door swinging open interrupted them.

"Who's being overdramatic?" Alphonse called. "Sorry we're late, by the way; we got caught up in a thing with a man and a dog. Anyway! I say, it smells awfully good in here, what?"

"Elizabeth is being overdramatic because she's trying to manage too many things at once," Aaliyah informed her husband as he came traipsing into the kitchen, Jacobi a sleek shadow at his heels.

"Sounds to me like you need a holiday," Alphonse said.

"I just had my honeymoon last month."

"I mean a real holiday! You didn't even leave the city. You ought to go somewhere abroad where you can sit on a beach, soak up the sun, and have someone waiting on you hand and foot for a month or two until you feel like yourself again. No cooking, no housekeeping, no business to run or clients to manage with all their dresses and charms. Spain, maybe, or somewhere in the tropics, what? That's what the doctors are always suggesting for people who need a little pick-me-up: somewhere bright and balmy."

Elizabeth had to admit, a holiday did hold a certain appeal. As they dished up and found their seats at the table, she said, "Unfortunately, Arthur and I have obligations we can't just drop whenever the whim strikes us. I have three separate clients waiting on dresses right now, to say nothing of Arthur's work at the firm, where they're heaping ever more responsibilities on him—"

"Ugh," said Alphonse, "right, yes, I'd forgotten you were all so respectably employed. That does throw a wrench in things."

"Besides which," Elizabeth added, "Arthur and I couldn't possibly disappear on holiday for months at a time. I fear he and Coxley would be quite lost without each other, and I'd feel terribly guilty separating them for so long."

Aaliyah pulled her chair in and poured the wine, bright-eyed with a devilish grin. "Speaking of: I've thought of a way to get them together."

Elizabeth perked up. "Do tell, because these painting sessions with Coxley are getting me nowhere. He insists on changing the subject the second I start prodding too closely at his feelings for Arthur, or vice versa."

"It's simple. I propose you get them both drunk, preferably in a state of undress, introduce the subject of Arthur's sexuality, then step back and let the scene run its course." She spread her hands, looking pleased with herself. "It's foolproof."

"You don't think Arthur's loyalty to me might prove an obstacle?" Elizabeth asked doubtfully.

"An obstacle to be cleared after the fact. All you need is for Coxley to confess his feelings. You may reassure them both of your blessing after."

"Hm." Elizabeth turned to the others. "I don't suppose she workshopped this with any of you?"

"It's subtler than what she did for me," Alphonse offered.

"She has a very good track record of getting what she wants," Jasmine said lightly. "Who are we to doubt her in this?"

"And you?" Elizabeth asked Jacobi, who was perhaps the sole voice of reason in the room.

"Normally, I would hesitate to interfere in such matters," Jacobi said. "Their hearts are no one's business but their own."

"But then I reminded him that some people really can't get anywhere on their own without the occasional nudge—or rather, hard shove, as the case may be—from outside sources," Alphonse said.

"Which is a truth to which I must concede," Jacobi concluded.

Elizabeth sat back. "Well then. I suppose I'll have to concoct some plan to get them drunk, chatty, and in the nude."

CHAPTER FOURTEEN

IN WHICH MAGIC, AND THE LOSS THEREOF, IS REVEALED

The next day at the studio, Elizabeth had only been sitting for half an hour before the increasingly dark sky opened up and let loose a torrent of heavy rain: the kind of summer storm that turned the clouds black and sent the wind whipping through the treetops. Marvellous to observe, but hardly conducive to painting by natural light. Coxley muttered a curse and waved for Elizabeth to abandon her pose.

"It's no good. The sun's gone, so I'm fetching lunch and a bottle of something good," Coxley announced. "I assume you have no objections?"

"Food and drink sounds lovely," Elizabeth agreed, sitting up and shrugging into her silk robe. Or rather, Coxley's silk robe.

"Preferences?" Coxley asked, donning his hat and coat in a flurry as he headed for the door.

"Whatever you're having."

"Excellent. Back in a dash."

Assuming their light would be lost whether the rain cleared or not, Elizabeth took her time getting dressed again. She always dressed lightly for her studio appointments, as she spent so little time wearing any clothes at all, and thus preferred an outfit she could slip in and out of in a wink.

When she was fully dressed and still had a few minutes before Coxley's estimated return, her gaze was drawn as if magnetically to the easel. The canvas stood with its back to her, hiding Coxley's work-in-progress, and the temptation to walk over and steal a glimpse of the wet paint was suddenly overpowering. She had told him in the beginning that she didn't want to see the piece until it was done, out of a fear of self-consciousness if she saw her body painted as some unfinished thing. But now, having laid herself bare near daily for weeks, that fear seemed as pale and inconsequential as morning mist. Coxley would indulge her if she changed her mind; she was sure he would be delighted to show her his progress every single day and explain it in detail if she asked. But she was only tempted because she was alone. She wanted to sneak over to the canvas and stare at it uninterrupted until she recognised herself in the strokes Coxley had laid down.

Steeling herself, her heart beating unaccountably fast considering this was such a small decision in the grand scheme of things, she stood up—

And Coxley returned through the door carrying two brown paper bags and a bottle of red wine.

"I hope I didn't keep you waiting long," he said, striding over to thrust all three items into her arms so he could shed his dripping coat and hat, dropping them over an empty easel in the corner like it was a hat stand.

"Not at all," she replied. The impulse to steal a look fled in company. "I was just stretching my legs. Where shall I put these so we can eat?"

"Throw them on the model stand; I'll drag some cushions over and we can sit on the floor. But I haven't got any plates, and I doubt I have a cup that I haven't yet contaminated with paint water. I hope you don't mind drinking from the bottle."

"Not at all. This style of lunch is very reminiscent of my university days, I must say."

"Youth: a charming time. Eating with our hands and passing the bottle around like a bunch of animals. I remember those days well." He presented her with a passably plump cushion, inviting her to make herself comfortable, which she did.

When they were both seated and deep in their sandwiches, the wine open and flowing freely between them, Coxley turned to her and asked, quite apropos of nothing, "What colour is your magic? I mean incorporate that into the palette, if it's at all flattering."

Brushing a scattering of crumbs from her mouth, she replied, "Blue. Sky blue."

Coxley tsk'd. "Unhelpful. Let me see it."

Elizabeth took another bite of her sandwich before setting it aside to indulge Coxley's curiosity. Raising her right hand, she waved her fingers and let a little shimmer of magic out unformed. It was her magic in its most natural and uncontrolled state, and it danced as light as a butterfly through the air before dissipating like summer mist at dawn. She rarely let her magic out in such a way; it was considered unpractised and a bit childish to be so uncontrolled, with polite society preferring to keep all magic confined within the bounds of known spells and theorems. It was only children, radicals, and the uneducated who let their magic out unchecked and pushed back against England's magic regulations—or at least, so it was said.

Behind closed doors, everyone had tried it once or twice, just to see what it was like. There wasn't a soul in Great Britain who didn't know the colour of their own magic. Spells and incantations often lent their own colour to it—illumination spells leaned to white or a warm, pale yellow, and incendiary spells were usually red and gold like fire, for example—but everyone had a specific colour that their individual magic tended towards. Not so very long ago, scientists and philosophers considered it the colour of one's soul.

Sky blue was the closest approximation Elizabeth had for her own colour. It wasn't exact, because like the sky itself, her magic held a number of colours all at once. Sometimes it looked more like the silvery blue of a rain shower, and sometimes it held a glint of yellow like a sunbeam alongside the blue, both colours mingling together, mixing yet held separate without ever turning to green.

'Behind closed doors' was key, though. In Elizabeth's adult life, the only other person to whom she had shown her unformed magic was Arthur, and that had only been the once. Yet, there was no hesitation in showing Coxley, when he asked. There was nothing illicit to it, after all, and it only made sense that he should see that part of her when he had seen the rest of her naked already.

"Again, if you please," Coxley requested.

Cupping her hands, Elizabeth let her magic fill them like a pool of water, spilling crystalline over her fingers to cascade like liquid diamonds to the floor. Her magic evaporated before hitting the floorboards, a never-ending stream running from her hands like a park fountain. Coxley leaned in, utterly entranced, his elbows braced against his knees and his nose mere inches from her fingers as he studied the infinite colours held within what she called sky blue.

"Beautiful," he breathed. "Not at all what I had imagined for your palette, but more fool I for not asking sooner."

"What colours were you planning to paint me in?" she asked.

"I had thought to paint you in the height of summer's golds: bronze and amber and sienna, with the flowers dusky red and aubergine."

"There's no reason you shouldn't."

He shook his head. "No, no. Having seen this, I couldn't possibly paint you in anything else. It's no matter; so many of the colours are yet to be determined on the canvas. This is no setback. Rather than the decadence of August or September I will paint you as the month of June, in brilliant full bloom."

Elizabeth's mouth went dry at the passion in his voice. "I'd like that very much," she managed. Closing her palms, she swallowed up her magic and collected herself. "And yours? What colour is that?"

"Ah, of course. Turnaround is fair play."

Standing with a flourish like a street performer, Coxley fanned his magic out between his hands like a peacock displaying his tail. He had none of Elizabeth's compunctions about keeping his magic politely contained to a small space. Instead, he let it spread like a wild thing, a broad swath of rich forest green that ran the width of his studio from window to wall, as if the room had been filled with a tangle of old-growth jungle. It was the colour of violet leaves or wet fern fronds, glinting here and there with gold like glimpses of a sunrise through a shrouded canopy. It spread in twists and swirls like vines exploring the limits of their world, approaching Elizabeth with creeping tendrils which, when she held out one hand, curled around her fingertip with the lightest of touches as if in greeting.

Shocked at the touch of another person's magic, she pulled back, though she couldn't hide her delighted smile. "This is magnificent! Do you always let it out in such a display?"

"Any opportunity to show off," he assured her with a smirk. Holding his arms wide, he invited his magic back into himself, where it folded up like a flower closing for the night and tucked itself neatly into his chest to disappear.

"Magnificent," she repeated. "But you don't need me to feed your ego." Picking up the wine again, she saw no better opportunity to ask about the more arcane rumours surrounding his art. "Tell me," she said casually, "do you use it in your work?"

"Hardly at all," he replied, rejoining her on the floor to resume their lunch. "I used to dabble in all manner of experimental things when I was starting, but I've found it far more satisfying to keep my magic and my art practices separate. They each require their own kind of dedication, you see. Mixing the two, I fear, would lead to less impressive results from either." He took a bite of his sandwich, then added, "But I assume what you mean to ask is, do I use magic to bewitch my audience and steal people's souls." He polished off the end of the crust, taking his time as she waited expectantly for his answer. "I do not," he finally said.

"But you don't discourage the rumours."

"Oh, not at all. They bring a startling amount of business. If people want to believe me some wicked sorcerer out of a fairy tale, I'm more than happy to let them, so long as it keeps my paintings selling." Leaning over, he held out one hand for the wine, which she relinquished. "But you never believed such things, did you?" he asked, his gaze glittering.

"No. Although," she admitted, "I can understand where people get the idea. I feel I could lose myself in your art."

He took a swig, smiling around the bottle. "Does it feel like I'm stealing your soul?" he teased.

"I don't know what you'd do with it if you were. Mine or any other."

"Eat them, I suppose." He shrugged. "The old stories are always going on about eternal youth or whatnot, though it's usually soul-stealing just for the sake of it. Like collecting butterflies."

"Well, it's just as well you're not taking mine. Arthur would be upset about it, I imagine."

"Of course. I wouldn't want to step on his toes. Surely your husband has the right of first refusal, if your soul is being offered up at all." He took another drink before passing the bottle back again. "But no. I hesitate to call my art mundane in any sense of the word, but technically: yes, it's entirely mundane. There's not a drop of magic in it. I want to master the art of painting on its own terms. Magic is its own practice."

"I understand what you mean. Magicking up new colours or bringing your paintings to life—"

"An entirely different hobby from painting," he agreed. "Which is not to say I've never tried either."

"Perhaps some other time you might show me such attempts," she suggested.

"Certainly not before your portrait is finished. I don't want anything distracting me from achieving perfection."

Elizabeth held up one hand in acquiescence as she held the last of her sandwich in the other. "Far be it from I to stand between you and your calling. I only ask that you keep me in mind as an interested party should you ever want to experiment with such things again."

"Of course. I will admit, it's tempting to have such a willing audience. I never made a habit of showing off my magical experiments to Arthur, but you use magic in your sewing, do you not? I caught a glimmer of it in your wedding dress, I believe."

"Yes, I did weave a handful of charms into it," Elizabeth said around the last bite of her lunch. "I have a fair few clients who make special requests for spells to be sewn into the hems or the beading. Little charms like that, for luck or health or prosperity, or minor glamours to flatter their figures or attract the right sort of attention. That kind of thing. I don't do it often for my own clothes, outside of those for special occasions, but it's a popular request. And, of course, I can charge quite a bit more for those services, which does make the practice more appealing."

"Naturally. It's difficult to live on artistry alone, more's the pity."

Elizabeth took another drink. "Maybe there's some spell I can weave on the finished painting so my mother never notices my nudity when she looks at it."

Coxley snorted. "A good use of your talents, to be sure."

Elizabeth was approaching the edges of tipsiness and had no intention of crossing that line, especially as it was barely noon, but it felt good to drink in Coxley's company, with the conversation so light and easy between them.

Without thinking of any ulterior motive at all, she asked, "What colour would you paint Arthur in?"

"Hm? Oh—I forgot you've never seen his. In any case: I wouldn't. It would be in poor taste, which I know is rich, coming from me. But I wouldn't do that to him."

As none of that made any sense to her, Elizabeth assumed Coxley had misheard her in some way. "Theoretically, if Arthur had magic, I mean," she clarified.

Coxley looked at her strangely. "Arthur *had* magic."

They stared at each other for a beat.

"He told you—" Coxley abruptly shook his head. "Never mind. My mistake. The wine went to my head and I misunderstood—"

Elizabeth laid one hand on Coxley's arm, on the brink of something tremulous and aching. "What do you mean, he had magic? He doesn't now. Did something happen?"

Gently, he removed her hand from his person. "That's not my story to tell. I shouldn't have said anything."

"Well, it's too late now to pretend you didn't." She tried to keep her voice steady and almost succeeded. "Either Arthur has been hiding his magic the whole time I've known him, or something happened to prevent him from practising." Both options made her feel hollowed out and sick.

"Whatever he told you, I'm sure he had good reason for it."

"I'm sure he did. And he has the right to his secrets." But it had never occurred to her to keep a single secret from him, so the thought that he was hiding something left her lost and unsure how to proceed.

Coxley must have seen that loss in her expression, because he took pity on her. With a sigh, dragging one hand through his already unkempt hair, he said, "It was the war."

Elizabeth's stomach dropped, like missing a step in the stairs.

"We knew each other as boys, and he had magic then. Whatever it was they did to him in the army, when he came out the other side of it, he couldn't conjure so much as a spark."

"Do you know—" Elizabeth's voice broke and she had to swallow the ache in her throat before trying again. "Do you know what happened to him?"

Coxley shrugged, not meeting her searching gaze. "The same thing that happened to every other soldier, more or less. If you want to know, you'll have to ask him. But I doubt he'll want to talk about it." His eyes finally found hers. "Not even to you," he said quietly, but without malice.

"No. No, I don't expect he will."

They sat in silence for a moment as Elizabeth mulled over this revelation, that her husband was not all he had told her. For him to have confessed with relative ease his past dalliances with men, yet hidden the loss of his magic which she had never known or seen, suggested that the latter was a source of far greater shame. And for him to hold such pain without allowing her to share that burden made her hurt for him.

"Thank you for telling me," she finally said. "I hope you don't think that you've betrayed his trust by doing it."

Coxley's mouth twisted to one side. "I slipped up. As you said, I could hardly take it back once it was out."

"I'll handle the matter with the care it deserves."

"I know you'd never intentionally hurt him."

"But unintentionally?"

"You're not infallible," he said gently.

"Obviously not." She looked for answers in the bottle of wine. Finding none, she asked, "Is this what you meant all those months ago, when you said I didn't know enough about Arthur to properly take care of him?"

Coxley didn't answer. The silence stretched until Elizabeth thought he wouldn't answer at all.

"Arthur was one of the lucky ones," he finally said, his tone forcibly light. "He escaped unscathed, at least physically, but he didn't come home the same man as when he left. None of us did, I suppose, but some were better at hiding the invisible damage than others. He was in the infantry. A miracle he came back at all, really. Most of his fellows didn't. They had them using his magic for the offence, you see. It was brutal, by all accounts. And by the time they were done with him, he simply had nothing more to give." He glanced at her. "He didn't tell me this. Not in so many words, at least. But having known him before, and knowing where he served, I had enough of the pieces to put it together." His brow crumpled. "Though, on a selfish level, perhaps it would have been easier not knowing," he added in a lower voice. "He had such a gift, before they leeched it out of him. It's hard, knowing everything he's lost."

"Is that why he kept it from me? To save me that hardship?"

"I would assume so. Or maybe he didn't want you to look at him and see that lost potential. To think of him as half the man he once was."

"I would never."

Coxley's dark gaze cut across to her. "His parents do. They mourned him like he was dead, when he first returned. His father served higher up; you've seen his medals. He thought Arthur should have been stronger. That he would have kept his magic, if he had been."

"That's why he's not as close with them," she realised.

"If you must tell him that you know the truth—and I assume you feel you must—then please make it out like I was drunker than I am. We'll blame the wine for my clumsy tongue." They hadn't even finished the bottle between them. "I really didn't know you were in the dark."

"It's not your fault. I'm sure he won't hold it against you."

Coxley sighed, thumbing at his frayed shirt cuff where it was unbuttoned and loose.

"Would you tell me one more thing?" Elizabeth asked softly.

"Hm?"

"What colour was it?"

"Amber," Coxley replied wistfully. "Like sunlight glancing through bottled honey."

CHAPTER FIFTEEN

WHEREIN THE VILLAIN IS EXPOSED, TO MUCH DISGUST AND DISAPPOINTMENT

Coxley walked her home that afternoon when the rain had lightened to showers, the sun peeking through the clouds like a bride stealing glances through her veil. Elizabeth was lost in thought for much of the walk, constantly straying from under Coxley's umbrella to be caught in the raindrops, only for him to tug her back into shelter by the elbow. She barely noticed either the water or his efforts to keep her dry.

Arthur had kept a secret from her. He had his reasons for it, and she didn't begrudge him his privacy. What distressed her was deciding how to approach it now that she knew. Should she pretend otherwise? That seemed dishonest, and besides, Coxley knew that she knew. She disliked the thought of the two of them pretending to Arthur that nothing had changed. But if she was to broach the subject, how to do it without upsetting him? Because it was an upsetting topic, no doubt. The mere thought of losing her magic introduced a coil of anxiety in her stomach, and couple that with his time in the war—

"Elizabeth."

She blinked, coming back to herself in time to realise that she had walked straight past her house.

"Oh, how silly. I was more distracted than I thought."

"Rather," he agreed, still holding the umbrella for her with a faint line of concern etched in his forehead.

Climbing the front steps, she asked, "Will you come in for a cup of tea and dry off?"

The offer was genuine, but she also wanted a buffer between herself and Arthur for a few minutes, until she could pull herself together and look at him without imagining honey-amber magic in his veins.

"I'll drop in to say hello, but I won't be staying. I have some errands to run, and if you reel me in with tea, Mrs. Patel will trap me with supper, and then the whole evening will be gone, I'm afraid."

"Fair enough," she conceded.

But when she entered the house, she found not the calm teatime atmosphere she had expected, but Arthur anxiously pacing the rooms waiting for her, a tell-tale cardstock note in one hand. With a pinched face, he handed it to her without a word. When she had read it, she passed it to Coxley.

"An ultimatum," she said.

To Mrs. Leicester, Coxley read aloud. *You have exhausted my patience. After giving you so many chances, I have no choice now but to follow through with that which I promised: the exposure of your identity.* Coxley paused. "You didn't get a third letter before this one, did you?"

"Maybe they left it on the front step and it got lost," Arthur offered.

"Or they lost count," Elizabeth suggested. "Perhaps they're blackmailing so many people at once, they can't keep track of how many letters they've sent to each one."

Taking the card from Coxley, Arthur examined it with furrowed brows.

"I can't quite put my finger on it, but I would swear I've seen this exact cardstock before," he mused.

To Elizabeth's untrained eye, it looked no different than any other mid- to high-quality cardstock used by important businesses and self-important individuals around London. But Arthur was much more familiar with such details as a result of his job. Every lawyer that passed through the firm where he worked had their own particular preferences for their business cards, and Arthur had developed an eye for them.

"The little embossment at the bottom here, on the back: the card was put into the typewriter backwards. Normally the embossment would be on the front, like a signature. I don't recognise it, so I can say with certainty that you're not being blackmailed by one of my firm's lawyers. I'm sure I've seen it somewhere, though." He tapped the paper's edge against his chin, frowning furiously in concentration.

"Where else do you see such paper besides at work?" Elizabeth asked.

"Maybe when I was living with Coxley?" Arthur passed the card back to him. "But you don't paint on stuff like this, do you?"

"Sometimes I'll scribble ink drawings on cardstock, but I would never buy embossed paper." Coxley squinted at the embossment, which meant nothing to Elizabeth, and then his face cleared and he straightened up, triumphant. "You did see it at my flat," he announced. "This was the cardstock private investigator John Johnson was using when I first met him. By the time I hired him to find M. Hayes' identity he had changed it, but he'd already left a calling card with me. He must have had sheets of this original stuff leftover that he wanted to use up, and had been using his new stock for long enough that he didn't think anyone would connect this to him." Scoffing, Coxley flicked the card from his fingers and it fluttered anticlimactically to the floor.

"Unfortunately, there's not much accomplishment in finding out his identity," Elizabeth said. "Listen to the rest of it." Retrieving the card from the floor, she read, *You will meet me by the Temple of Bellona at 8:30 a.m. on the first Monday in August, from which point we will go together to your bank where you will withdraw your royalties and give them to me. This price, both social and monetary, is a fitting punishment for the lewd rot you take such pride in publishing. It is women like you—with equal blame laid on your husband, who has proven himself utterly incapable of controlling you—who give these modern times a bad name, and who will be ultimately responsible for bringing fair London to her knees.*

She finished it with a shake of her head and a bad taste in her mouth. "He might not have signed his name, but I'd certainly know who he was by the end of that encounter."

"That's daylight robbery!" Arthur objected. "In what world does he imagine he could get away with it?"

"I don't think he does," Elizabeth said slowly. "The way he talks about my writing and my career... I don't think he cares about my money at all. I think he wants to put me in my place. He wants me to refuse him so he can publicly humiliate me."

"Damn the man!" Coxley swore. "If he thinks he can ruin anyone's career faster and more effectively than I can, he's going to be in for a very rude awakening."

"Yes, but will ruining his career accomplish anything besides revenge?" Elizabeth asked. "He can still expose me whether he's been discredited as an investigator or not."

"I'd like to see him try to expose anything by the time I'm done with him."

"God knows I don't doubt your abilities, Jules, but Elizabeth is right," Arthur said. "We have to think of the most practical way to approach this. We can take it to the police—"

"With whom he works with on a regular basis," Coxley interjected with a sneer.

"I'm going to deal with it," Elizabeth said firmly. "If he wants to meet me face to face then that is exactly what he's going to get. But he's not going to get any satisfaction out of the encounter, and he's certainly not going to get a single penny of my royalties. I'll burn that pen name to the ground before I let him for one moment try to hold it over me."

"Don't," Coxley said. "Let me get to him before you make any drastic decisions."

"I don't want this escalating beyond what it already is. I will handle him. If you want to help me, you'll finish my painting so I'll have something to look forward to when this is all over. That's the only role I want you to take."

"I can help more than that," Coxley protested. "I can ruin the man's entire life in a matter of a few short days if I try."

"The way you tried to ruin mine?" Elizabeth asked.

"Hardly. Attempting to cut short an engagement isn't at all on the same level as what I want to do here."

"He could do it," Arthur confirmed softly to Elizabeth. "He's made few true enemies in his life, but those he has, he has managed more ruthlessly than he ever attempted with you. If you let him, you can rest assured that Mr. Johnson will never trouble us again."

"And what kind of businesswoman would I be if I let men steamroll over every obstacle and inconvenience in my path?"

"I'm not offering this as a man trying to come to your rescue," Coxley said, "but as a friend trying to make amends for my own involvement in this whole mess. And as a friend on its own merit. Arthur knows I'd offer the same to him, if the occasion arose."

"No. And that is my final answer. I will not have you starting fights with this wretch on my account. I'll meet him, I'll finish him myself, and then I'll put this whole thing behind me and move on with or without my pen name. To be quite honest, I might be glad to be rid of it."

"Your publisher," Arthur began.

"Will support whatever decision I make, or I will leave them to find one that does. My books are in high demand under the Hayes name. With the correct marketing, any future books can find just as much success under any other name I choose. Mr. Johnson cannot dictate my future any more than he can dictate where my money goes. Now: let's drop this."

Coxley looked unhappy, but he gave a nod of agreement.

"Mrs. Patel is starting supper," Arthur offered uncertainly in the silence that followed, "if anyone's hungry."

"I've never been less hungry," Elizabeth said, tired to her bones, "but I ought to eat. I suspect I'll need something stronger than our usual wine, though."

"I'll fetch something," Arthur promised, pressing a kiss to her temple. "Jules? Are you staying?"

"I can't," he said shortly. "I hadn't meant to stay as long as this, in fact. Have a drink for me, if you please, and Elizabeth? Try not to make any rash decisions regarding your career, my dear. You've had a trying day."

And with that, he departed back into the late afternoon showers, his umbrella flaring overhead.

◆ ◆ ◆

July turned to August, and Coxley disappeared for ten consecutive days, declining invitations and apparently not so much as stepping out from his studio.

"Is he sulking because I asked him not to go for Mr. Johnson's throat?" Elizabeth asked over dinner on the tenth day. She hadn't realised how accustomed she'd become to Coxley's presence in their home, but it was undeniable: she missed him when he suddenly wasn't there anymore.

"He gets like this," Arthur said, seemingly unconcerned. "You told him to finish your portrait. Painting is an immersive experience, according to him. He'll resurface when the project is done."

"I didn't mean 'finish my portrait to the exclusion of all else.' Does he do this every time?"

"Only with the pieces that get under his skin. I must say, I prefer the experience from this side of things. Actually living with it is exhausting." At Elizabeth's enquiring look, he continued. "At his worst, it's an obsession. He forgoes sleep, forgets to eat..." Arthur rubbed his hand over the back of his neck. "Sometimes I would go out to stay with other friends when he got like that," he admitted.

"What, you left him there to forget to sleep or eat by himself?"

"I tried to help, in the beginning, before I really understood it. But I'm not his keeper, Elizabeth, and he doesn't want me to be. As you say: we're all adults here."

"I suppose." Giving up on clearing the end of her plate, Elizabeth folded her hands on the table before her and asked, "Did you think adulthood would be very different from what it is? As a girl, I always thought that married couples and grown-ups working professional careers must be so serious and put together. But it's all a bit silly, isn't it? We still have our petty schoolyard squabbles, our personal grudges, the hobbies we stay up late pursuing long after we're meant to go to bed because we never seem to have enough hours in the day to do everything we want to do. I'm still writing the same silly little stories I used to scribble in the backs of my school notebooks, and all children love to draw; Coxley just never stopped. The only difference now is that we get paid for it."

"I remember when I realised that most adults were making everything up as they went along," Arthur said. "It was a bit crushing, really. But now here we are, doing the exact same thing. It keeps me from feeling too much of an imposter, at least, knowing that everyone else is pretending to have it together as much as I am."

"Bumbling along in the dark is one thing," Elizabeth agreed. "It's the people making actively malicious, asinine choices that I take issue with."

"Johnson, you mean."

"Yes, him, that absolute toad of a man. I'm meeting him tomorrow and I can't say I'm looking forward to it whatsoever."

"Did you mean it when you said you would be relieved to see the pen name go?" Arthur asked.

"I think so. I've had a good run with it, but I've been hitting a wall for so many months now; starting fresh with a new name and a new genre does hold a certain appeal. Killing this one off doesn't have to mean the end of my career. It could mean the start of a new one."

"I just don't want you to be making this decision out of frustration. You've struggled with your current book, but that won't last forever. And if you do kill this pen name, whether because Johnson forces your hand or of your own volition, you won't be able to easily bring it back to life if you change your mind."

"I haven't decided anything. I'm only weighing my options right now. And if I give my pen name too much weight, that gives Johnson leverage over me, and I won't allow that. If I have to lose it, better to throw it out with my own hands, I think."

"You'll do whatever you think is best, but I wish you would let me come along with you to this confrontation. With what little we know of Johnson's character, I'm really not at all comfortable with you going to meet him alone. If he's willing to blackmail a woman, who knows what else he's capable of?"

"I agree, but you mustn't take time off work for something so tedious. Don't worry; I'm bringing Aaliyah and Jasmine along, and they will be more than capable of leaping to my defence should things turn nasty. Or, rather, nastier than they already are."

◆ ◆ ◆

The next morning, Elizabeth met her friends at Kew Gardens and together they marched down the Camellia Walk to the Temple of Bellona, where she stationed them out of sight within the greenery. With Aaliyah and Jasmine lying in wait, Elizabeth sat down on the bench between the temple's pillars to wait for her blackmailer to arrive. She was incandescent with rage, and would have much rather spent her time pacing up and down the paths, but she was determined to look composed and unruffled by his ludicrous demands. Therefore, she sat, and only her white-knuckled hands clenched tightly in her lap gave away the magnitude of her stress. She was dressed to the nines, wearing her newest dress, her eyes and lips painted, and her hair twisted in a chic knot at the back of her neck, willing her sharp looks to give her the strength needed to get through this meeting and come out on top.

A low, whistling birdcall sounded from the trees as Aaliyah warned Elizabeth of her blackmailer's approach. Elizabeth stood, her spine ramrod straight, and fixed the man with a freezing stare as he walked up the path towards the temple. Not giving him the chance to take control of the situation, she strode right up to him, intercepting him halfway across the lawn.

"Mr. Johnson," Elizabeth said coldly. "The famous private investigator. The papers make you out to be quite the celebrity."

John Johnson was a staunch, middle-aged man with a bristling moustache and a face like a bulldog, though he had none of the good-naturedness inherent to the breed. Though broad-shouldered, he was quite stocky, and had to glare up at her to meet her eye, which no doubt contributed to his temper. Elizabeth, who had been tall all her life, found there was a common subset of men who felt emasculated by her height, and made every attempt to drag her down to their level. Mr. Johnson, she suspected, was one such man. He looked vaguely familiar, which she put down to having seen his photo at some point, though for some reason she thought he hadn't had the whiskers then. It bothered her, the feeling that she had seen him somewhere else before, like a word caught on the tip of her tongue.

"My celebrity status is exaggerated," he said shortly. "And we are not here to discuss my business, Mrs. Leicester."

"Are we not? What business are we to discuss, then?"

Johnson looked around sharply as if expecting her to have planted spies in the bushes. Which, of course, she had, but he wouldn't find them unless he went around beating the greenery with his stick. When he moved he didn't seem as old as he'd appeared at first sight; he was only a few years older than her, she realised, with his prematurely-greying bristles giving him the illusion of those extra years.

"Wait a minute," she said. "I know you, don't I?"

"What?" he snapped.

"John Johnson. The name didn't mean anything to me when I heard it or when I read about you in the papers, but now that I see your face—did we go to school together? You were a year or two ahead of me, maybe."

"It's a small world, Mrs. Leicester," he said, seemingly annoyed at her admitted lack of recognition.

The pieces slid into place.

"I *do* remember," she said. "In my final year, you kept coming back to loiter around the school campus, even though you'd already graduated. You were a bit infatuated with me, weren't you? You asked me out at least once, if I recall correctly."

"*If you recall*," he repeated slowly, his face reddening. "Five times I asked you out, three when we were in school together, and twice more after I graduated. I came back specifically for you, even though you had shot me down at every previous attempt. As if you were getting any better offers from those simpering, spotty-faced boys who fawned over you on a daily basis! I came all the way back there just for you, hoping that you would see me more favourably once I was in university. But you never looked twice at me, ignoring my superiority over all those worthless boys you favoured, deliberately snubbing me like the vain, self-obsessed little vixen you were—"

"Yes," Elizabeth interrupted, "I'm remembering now why I tried so hard to forget about you."

He sputtered, spit flecking his lips like a rabid dog.

"It's a shame you had to go dredging it all back up," she continued. "I much preferred you as an obscure footnote from my school days. So, this is about revenge, is it? A chance to get back at the girl who rejected you half a lifetime ago?" She shook her head. "You must be terribly disappointed in the experience so far."

His mouth worked soundlessly for a few seconds before he managed to bite out, "Let's not waste any more time. You know why we're here. Have you finally decided to stop playing around and agree to my terms?"

"Your terms in which I buy your silence with royalty payments from my books whose pen name you will agree to keep secret provided the payments are to your liking? But why should I trust that you will be satisfied with that money? What's to stop you, an evident con man and scum of the worst calibre, from continually demanding more and more from me in exchange for your silence?"

"Don't test my patience, Mrs. Leicester," Johnson snapped. "You have nothing to bargain with."

"I have everything to bargain with," she corrected him. "You want my money. I haven't given it to you yet; if I continue to refuse, what can you possibly do to get it from me? Rob me outright? If you expose my pen name, I'll have nothing to lose *but* my money. Why should I give it to you then?" She smiled. Even in the early August heat, it felt frosty. "We are at an impasse, Mr. Johnson, and I have written vastly more competent villains than you. You are far from the mastermind you hope to be, and a third-rate blackmailer at best."

Johnson had gone beetroot-red with impotent fury, his moustache bristling like a catfish's whiskers. "Mrs. Leicester, if you think for one minute—"

"Out of the two of us," she interrupted, "I seem to be the only one capable of any thought at all. Please don't embarrass yourself further. If you agree here and now to let the matter drop, then I will drop it on my end as well, and let that be the end of it."

"Stop talking like you're in control of the situation!"

"I think you'll find that I am. You see, I'm quite prepared for you to expose my pen name. I don't particularly mind in the least. However, I very much doubt that you are prepared for me to take action against you."

"What action? I've worked alongside the police for years. They'll never take your side against my good word."

"Oh, I wasn't planning to go to the police." This was the only part of the confrontation in which she really had to bluff, as she had no idea what Coxley intended to do to the man. Squaring her shoulders, she didn't let the unknown slow her down. "I have a friend, you see, one with whom I believe you are already acquainted. And he is very keen to get his claws in you."

"His claws," Johnson repeated. "Are you threatening me? Is that supposed to scare me?"

"It should worry you a little bit. Because I really don't think you're as prepared to lose your investigative career as I am to lose my pen name."

"I could have made you a respectable woman," Johnson seethed. "Instead, look at you, ruining yourself, surrounded by these weak, enabling, so-called friends and that utterly useless man you call a husband."

"Yes, I'm ruining myself so badly writing these salacious books, that you want to steal all the money they've earned for me. You're clearly a jealous man, Mr.

Johnson, but I can't tell whether you're more jealous of my success or of my useless husband, who makes me very happy, by the way. It's not a flattering look for you at all."

There was a sound from the trees behind them that might have been a snort of laughter or might have been a very sarcastic-sounding bird.

"I don't think we have anything more to say to each other," Elizabeth said, before Johnson could take a stick to those bushes after all. "As you can imagine, I'm terribly busy. I have a business to manage, a house to keep up, and a husband to satisfy. Therefore, I would appreciate it if you never contacted me again, either by letter or any other manner. Good day to you."

With a firm nod, she crossed her arms and glared at him as he worked his mouth open and shut like a flabbergasted fish, lost for words in the face of her audacity. Finally, as her glare only intensified, he puffed himself up and declared, stabbing one stubby finger in her direction: "This won't be the last you hear of me, Mrs. Leicester!"

She allowed herself the satisfaction of a tiny sneer—no more than the slightest curling of her lip—as he turned and blustered away, huffing and cursing to himself with every step.

As soon as he was out of range, Aaliyah and Jasmine darted from their hiding place to join Elizabeth at her side. Elizabeth paced in a tight circle, clenching and unclenching her fists as she walked, trying to calm down. She hadn't noticed her surging adrenaline, but now that the confrontation was over, the excess rushed through her with such force that her knees threatened to buckle.

"You held yourself together admirably," Aaliyah said.

"Are you alright?" Jasmine asked.

"That was actually incredibly satisfying," Elizabeth said, still pacing. "I'm fine. It went better than I'd hoped, to be honest. It was encouraging to know you were within reach, though, should things have gone south."

"You're shaking," Jasmine noted.

Elizabeth glanced down, taking stock of herself. She was indeed trembling, like a tiny lapdog intent on taking down a foe ten times her size.

"I wish you had called on us," Aaliyah said. "What a bastard! He held a grudge against you for what, ten years? Longer? All because you wouldn't go out with him in school? Small wonder; if he was even half as insufferably entitled as he is now, he's lucky you didn't slap him in front of the entire assembly the first time he tried to talk to you. I would have hit him just now if you'd asked. Hell, I'll run after him and do more than hit him if you want."

"Let's not do anything that might encourage him to press charges," Jasmine said sensibly. "Elizabeth, are you sure you don't want to sit down for a minute?"

"I'm afraid if I sit down my legs will go all watery and I won't get up again," Elizabeth admitted.

Aaliyah clapped her on the back before giving her a brusque rub between the shoulders, as one might thump a horse that needed encouragement. "No sitting," she agreed. "What you need is a stiff drink."

"It's barely nine a.m.," Jasmine objected.

Aaliyah shrugged. "Sometimes it's called for."

"No, Jasmine is right. I should go to work and get on with my day. I don't want to give him the satisfaction of driving me to day-drinking or feeling rattled or anything at all. He's not worth it."

Aaliyah glanced down the path like she was debating whether to catch up to Johnson after all. Elizabeth wasn't given to violence, but she didn't feel inclined to intervene, either.

"I think going about business as usual is for the best," Jasmine said, before Aaliyah could commit to her course of vengeance. "You should drop in on Arthur first, though. He'll be fretting over you. We'll get a cab and drop you off." She nudged Aaliyah. "Won't we?"

"Right. Yes," Aaliyah agreed reluctantly. "We'll let the bastard go and deal with him later."

"Soon," Elizabeth promised. "He won't last the rest of the month."

♦ ♦ ♦

Elizabeth didn't make a habit of interrupting Arthur at work, but she only needed to steal him for a second. When there seemed to be a lull in activity, she waved at him through the window, and he slipped away from his desk to join her outside the firm to the side of the building's front steps.

"How did it go?" Arthur asked. "I can't tell from your expression whether I should be relieved or anxious."

"A bit of both, most likely," Elizabeth said, stepping into his arms for a quick hug. "Things are about to blow up; it's only a question of whether he exposes my pen name or we set Coxley on him first."

"What do you want to do?" Arthur asked, tucking her hair behind her ear.

"I rather want to let Coxley have a go at him," she admitted. "Did you know Johnson and I went to school together? He's been carrying a miserable little torch for me all these years. I spurned him, apparently, and he's never moved on from it."

Arthur groaned. "Oh, he's one of *those.*"

"He had nothing but terrible things to say about you, my darling. Apparently, you've failed to mould me into the proper woman that he would have done."

"Does he even know me? I don't think we've ever met."

"You haven't, no, but I don't think that particularly matters to him. No husband of mine could ever measure up to his potential, you see."

"So, since he can't have you, he's going to take all your money and publicly humiliate you," Arthur said, "as… punishment?"

Elizabeth rested her forehead against Arthur's shoulder. "Aaliyah wanted to punch him."

"I rather think you should have let her."

Lifting her face, Elizabeth met Arthur's eyes. "You promise Coxley can take him apart, given the opportunity? I still want to handle him myself, and I have a plan to do it, but I wouldn't be opposed to a little extra help."

Arthur's arms tightened around her, protective and reassuring. "Jules is more than capable," he promised, "and he would be absolutely thrilled if we asked him."

CHAPTER SIXTEEN

THE LONG-AWAITED GARDEN PARTY

Elizabeth spent the rest of the week high-strung and tense, waiting to see whether Johnson would make his move before she had the chance to make hers. She intended to expose him to as many people as she could, which meant the Hollyhock garden party at the end of the month. If all went according to plan, she would deliver him a social blow from which he couldn't possibly recover, discrediting him both professionally and personally. She suspected that he intended the same for her. Exposing her pen name in the papers would reach a far wider audience, but he wouldn't be able to see her reaction to it, and if she knew anything of his character, he would want to see her face when her life came crumbling down around her.

Of course, there was a chance that she had misread him and he would be so furious from their meeting that he would want to destroy her immediately, public spectacle be damned. She didn't think it likely, but neither could she entirely discount the possibility. However, as the first week of August crept into the second and then the third, she felt increasingly confident that they both meant to strike at the same moment.

Yet it wasn't a confidence on which she'd bet her livelihood, so she spent the days before the party an anxious mess, growing increasingly frustrated when she couldn't control her nerves. Arthur stayed by her side as much as he was able, solidly reassuring. Coxley, she only saw once, when he briefly stopped by the house before disappearing again.

"When you say you can destroy him, can you guarantee that it will be done safely?" she asked. "I mean, in a way that won't reflect badly on us, or give him some excuse to pursue the matter legally. I want him left in tatters, but not if it's going to bring us down with him."

"There's always some risk involved in confronting such a miserable excuse for a man," Coxley said. "He takes great pride in his reputation, so we must expect him to fight for it. Of course, that only makes it all the more satisfying when we do succeed in tearing him down."

Elizabeth bit her lip, not wholly reassured.

"Don't worry, my dear! You look like I intend to challenge him to pistols at dawn. My attack will be entirely verbal, in plain view of a dozen witnesses. Any retaliation he attempts will only make him look worse.

No matter how he tries to expose or humiliate you, you've done nothing wrong, whereas you have his blackmail letters to prove him a criminal. His career won't survive the night."

"Just be careful. Don't do anything too drastic that I wouldn't do."

"Come now," he said with a crooked smile. "What am I here for if not to do exactly that?"

◆ ◆ ◆

The party took place on the last Saturday of August— not summer's end in a technical sense, though it did feel like they were sending off the season with one last huzzah. Alphonse's mother, Estellabeth Hollyhock, was famous in certain circles for her grand dinners and soirees, and her summer garden party was always highly anticipated among those expecting to receive invitations. The guests were generally from old money, or enjoying a moment of local fame, or otherwise socially relevant.

Elizabeth and Arthur likely wouldn't have been invited if they weren't friends with Aaliyah, and if poor Alphonse, who was easily intimidated by his mother, hadn't begged them to come in order to lend him moral support. Coxley, Elizabeth thought, would likely have been invited on his own merit, seeing as the Hollyhock matriarch had been enough intrigued by him to commission a painting. The three of them arrived together, dolled up as if they were going to a wedding all over again. Elizabeth had made herself a brand-new dress for the occasion: dark green and shimmering with gold, with a few good-luck charms sewn in amongst the beading. She never bothered with such things in her day-to-day wardrobe, but she had the feeling she might need them that night. Arthur wore his finest summer suit, a warm-toned light beige, while Coxley, ever the rogue, was all in black, though neater and sharper than usual.

Alphonse greeted them at the door, where he was apparently already hiding from his mother.

"It's not as bad as it used to be," he confided in them, taking their coats as they entered the grand old manor of the Hollyhock Estate. "Not now that I'm married off the way she wanted, but old habits, what? She turns that look on me and I quake whether I've done anything wrong or not, so I do awfully appreciate your being here to insulate me from some of the old maternal wrath."

"We're happy to be here, chap," Arthur assured him with a clap on the shoulder. "You give Jules the word and he'll be delighted to draw her attention. Even without you giving the word, I dare say."

"Fear not, Mr. Hollyhock," Coxley told him. "Something tells me there shall be no shortage of drama this evening to keep your dear mother's gaze fixed firmly elsewhere."

"Oh?" Alphonse leaned in, intrigued. "What's that, then?"

"A surprise, dear boy! Where's the fun in spoiling it before half the guests have even arrived?"

"Righto, fair enough." Alphonse turned to Elizabeth and Arthur. "Are you two in on this surprise, or should I be worried?"

"We're not entirely sure, to be honest," Arthur admitted.

"But we have an inkling," Elizabeth added, with a deliberate look at Coxley.

He offered a cheerful wink, giving nothing away.

"Well then," Alphonse said, "I'll just have to wait and see. Till then, I'd best find my wife before my mother starts questioning why I'm not being a dutiful host, glued to her side. Toodles for now!"

Though Elizabeth's party was by no means the first to arrive, they were earlier than many of the other expected guests. With Arthur by her side and Coxley slinking ahead to do reconnaissance, Elizabeth slipped through the house, maintaining a cheerful air as she greeted all she passed, while keeping a wary eye out for Johnson.

"He's not here yet," Coxley said in a low voice, returning to her side. "In any case, I wouldn't think him likely to start spreading rumours before the dinner itself. He seems the type to want a captive audience."

"Are you sure you won't tell us what you have planned for him?" Arthur asked.

Coxley patted his arm. If the gesture was meant to be comforting, it was undermined by the devilish glint in Coxley's eye. "Best to catch you unawareness," he promised.

"You joked about challenging him to a duel, but you're not planning to simply shoot him at the dinner table, are you?" Elizabeth asked, only half in jest.

"Metaphorical bloodshed only, I assure you."

"There you are!" Aaliyah called.

She waved to them from outside, wearing a tiny black dress that showed a remarkable amount of leg, and that Mrs. Hollyhock had surely tried to talk her out of. She had apparently lost Alphonse again; he was perhaps hiding in the coat room. The great French doors that separated the rose garden from the main room where the party was hosted had been propped open to let the summer breeze waft through the house, carrying with it the delicate perfume of so many carefully-tended blooms. As more guests trickled in, they began to move outside to the gardens, and Elizabeth allowed the house's natural currents to usher her through those doors and into the warm evening air.

The event wasn't called a garden party for nothing. Mrs. Hollyhock took great pride in her landscaping, cultivating all manner of flowers so that, at the height of summer, her estate was a veritable tapestry of petals and blooms. The rose section of the garden that framed the French doors boasted thick, leafy bushes that grew as tall as Elizabeth herself, exploding in so many flowers that they seemed more pink than green.

Aaliyah gestured for her to come over, and, bemused, Elizabeth parted from Arthur and Coxley to join her friend. Before Elizabeth could say hello, Aaliyah dragged her deeper into the garden, away from the other guests, to sequester her in a private alcove made of multicoloured hydrangeas so enormous that Elizabeth felt she might disappear into them entirely.

"Alphonse suggested that Coxley is plotting something tonight," Aaliyah said. "Is that to do with Johnson's blackmail scheme?"

"Yes, but before you start prying for details, I don't know exactly what he's going to do," Elizabeth said.

"That's fine. To be honest, I'm not terribly worried about it. Johnson is an idiot and I doubt he'll survive the night, especially if you have his blackmail letters with you."

"We do," Elizabeth confirmed. "But why did you pull me into the hydrangeas if you're not concerned about the blackmail plot?"

"I would have pulled Arthur and Coxley in too, if I wanted to talk about that," Aaliyah said dismissively. "Don't get me wrong, I'm glad you have it under control, but I'm much more interested in whether you're planning to get the two of them together tonight."

Elizabeth blanched. "I don't have a plan," she admitted. "Not for tonight or any other time. I've had so much on my mind lately that I haven't give any further thought as to how to make that happen."

She still hadn't talked to Arthur about his lost magic. Every time she tried to broach the subject, the words caught in her throat and refused to come out. Because she couldn't figure out how to talk to him about it, talking to him about anything else suddenly seemed equally difficult. Suggesting that he was in love with his best friend was a delicate subject to begin with. At least the blackmail problem gave her a valid distraction and kept them both busy.

"Do you want me to orchestrate something?" Aaliyah asked bluntly. "Or have you changed your mind about the whole thing? No one would blame you if you had. It's a bold move, pushing your partner into someone else's arms."

Before Elizabeth could deny that, Jasmine came through the hydrangeas, unerringly honing in on Aaliyah's location as if they were all standing out in plain sight.

"Johnson is here with his wife," she said in a low voice. "Hello, Elizabeth," she added, more brightly.

"He's married? God, that poor woman. Unless we think she's in on it?"

"I can't imagine she'd be pleased that he's still simmering with resentment over your schoolgirl rejection of him," Aaliyah said. "I'm sure you'll get a read on her soon enough."

Elizabeth took a deep breath, and it only shook a little on the exhale. "Alright. I'm ready. Aaliyah... don't do anything about Arthur and Coxley yet. I think there will be enough going on this evening without complicating things."

"Fine. If you change your mind, just give the word. In the meantime—" Aaliyah threw one arm around Elizabeth's shoulders, tugging her into a tight sideways hug— "I can't wait to see what Coxley does to Johnson. This is going to make for spectacular entertainment."

◆ ◆ ◆

By eight o'clock, everyone had arrived and was seated for dinner, with the food beginning to roll out. Whatever the room's original purpose, it had been cleared to make space for a table of incredible length to seat everyone. Mrs. Hollyhock was at its head, with Alphonse and Aaliyah at her right hand, and Jasmine, Elizabeth, and Arthur seated next to them. On Mrs. Hollyhock's immediate left sat Mr. Johnson and his wife and then Coxley, presumably as her most interesting and recognisable guests. Next to Coxley, directly across from Elizabeth, sat a strikingly pretty dark-skinned Indian girl who bore more than a passing resemblance to Mrs. Patel. Next to her, across from Arthur, was Alphonse's cousin Morgan Hollyhock, whom Elizabeth and Arthur had met in Kew Gardens while hiding in a shrub. The rest of the table was filled with family friends, socialites, and local politicians, none of whom Elizabeth knew personally.

Nor was she interested in getting to know them. No: for the moment, her interest was fixed on Mrs. Johnson, sitting between Coxley and her blackmailer. Mrs. Johnson looked younger than her husband, or perhaps more accurately, she looked her proper age while he looked older. She was a pretty blonde whose makeup regrettably did nothing to hide the dark rings under her eyes, which could speak to either sleepless nights spent blackmailing writers, or to her exasperation with being married to such a beast. Her dress was more modest than the current trend, making her look drab and dowdy, the cut and colour failing to flatter either her face or figure. Elizabeth itched to redesign it for her, but held her tongue until it became clear whether the woman was conspiring alongside her husband, or merely under his thumb.

However, Elizabeth didn't have the chance to interrogate her, as Coxley was intent on monopolising the woman's conversation. Every time Johnson got caught up in talking to his hostess, Coxley leaned in to strike up something with his wife, to Johnson's obviously increasing annoyance. When Elizabeth shot Coxley an inquiring glance, he merely winked at her and sidled closer to Mrs. Johnson, who seemed quietly delighted by the attention.

So, difficult as it was, Elizabeth practiced patience.

Her side of the table sat facing the open French doors and the gardens beyond, and whenever Johnson tried to catch her eye, staring meanly, Elizabeth studied the roses. Although she very much wanted to snap at him, pick a fight and force their confrontation into the open to get it over with, she bided her time. The food was good, the conversation lively, and the roses beautiful. It was easy enough to avoid interacting with Johnson for the time being. If she moved too soon, she risked upsetting whatever Coxley had planned.

It will be over soon enough, she promised herself. The evening crawled by at a glacial pace, but that was only because she was so anxious. The longer she had to wait, the more tightly her stomach twisted, making it harder to eat. Thankfully, the wine still went down easily, and though she tried to pace herself, she couldn't resist an extra drink for courage. Any other time, she would be enjoying the party immensely, and with every passing minute, she resented Johnson all the more for ruining it.

Still: she made it all the way through the main course without acting on her hatred for the man, or indeed, without even letting it show too obviously on her face. Her friends could tell, of course; she wasn't so good an actress as that, and besides which, they already knew. But she liked to think she could successfully hide it from her hostess, and those sitting nearby who weren't in on the drama. She wasn't as outgoing as she would normally be at a dinner party, so it was unsurprising that it took until dessert for the young Indian woman sitting across from her to strike up a conversation.

"Elizabeth Leicester," she said, her voice smooth and musical. "I'm Deepa. We have a mutual friend in Mr. Coxley, and, of course, you know my mother."

Elizabeth hesitated a second before asking, "Are you Mrs. Patel's daughter?" She hardly wanted to assume that every Indian woman in London must be related, but the family resemblance was strong. When Deepa nodded, Elizabeth broke into a relieved smile. "She's mentioned you, but she does keep to herself much of the time. She says you're quite busy these days—I never expected to meet you like this, I must say."

"Yes, my mother and I move in different social circles," Deepa agreed wryly. "She has little patience for social politics, even if she were to be invited. And of course," she added in a conspiratorial tone, "no one else knows my mother is a housekeeper. Coxley and I have told everyone I come from a line of maharajas."

"Never mind your lineage," Aaliyah interjected. "You're Coxley's Lady Godiva, aren't you?"

Jasmine looked at Deepa consideringly. Meanwhile, at the mention of his name, Coxley broke off his conversation with Mrs. Johnson to turn and pay attention.

"I am that model," Deepa confirmed with a pleased smile. "I have him to thank for my current popularity, including this dinner invitation, I expect."

It was small wonder that her portrait had captured Aaliyah's attention. She was slender, her eyes large and liquid black, framed with the kind of lashes to make anyone jealous, and her hair, which she wore piled at the back of her head, shot through with ropes of pearls, was thick and glossy.

"I'm confident that a woman with your drive would have found herself climbing the social ladder with or without me," Coxley put in.

"Oh, yes, I'm sure my looks have nothing to do with it."

"I do find that drive and beauty work best hand in hand," he allowed.

"Speaking of beauty," Deepa said, turning back to Elizabeth, "I've passed your shop once or twice, and I must say, I'm altogether entranced by your designs."

"Thank you," Elizabeth said, one hand over her chest. "I'm flattered."

"It's not empty flattery," Deepa corrected with a smile. "I want one. They are bespoke, are they not?

Let's make an appointment. I would love to go over everything in so much detail with you."

"Of course," Elizabeth stammered. "Let's reconnect after the party."

Deepa inclined her head. "Yes, let's. It's no good discussing business at the dinner table. But let me just ask: you use magic in your fashion, don't you? The dress you're wearing tonight—it's stunning, by the way, absolutely eye-catching—have you sewn charms into the beading?"

"Yes, I often add charms to my dresses. Some women request more complicated magic, of course. Why? What do you have in mind for yourself?"

"I would be a fool to turn down good luck, but I was also thinking of something to attract a little extra attention," Deepa confided. "I know there are women who use glamours to shape their figures or make themselves look more beautiful, but I have no interest in that."

"You hardly need it," Elizabeth agreed.

"Thank you." Deepa preened. "But I would like a dress that keeps all eyes on me, even in the most extravagant of crowds and busiest of parties. Can you do something like that?"

"I think you could wear the plainest dress in the world and still draw all eyes to you," Coxley said smoothly with a smile.

On Coxley's far side, Johnson sniffed: just once, in order to draw attention to himself and demonstrate his disdain. "In my opinion, it's unbecoming for a young woman to use her looks to such an advantage," he said.

"A country's moral compass may be judged by its women's actions, I think."

In between him and Coxley, Mrs. Johnson seemed to barely hold back a sigh.

Not a co-blackmailer, Elizabeth was willing to bet.

"And what is the proper action for a young woman such as myself?" Deepa asked. "In your opinion."

"I'm sure it's not my business to dictate your life," he returned, doing just that, "but I should think that the most respectable course of action for any young woman is to find herself a good husband capable of providing for her, and settling down," he said with a short nod. "Take my Grace, for example. No one will ever take her for one of those uncivilised flapper girls, and that's as it should be."

Mrs. Johnson—Grace—took a long-suffering draught of her wine.

"When you say 'providing for her,'" said Aaliyah, "do you think that we shouldn't be expected to provide for ourselves?"

"I think that this rush for independence is hasty and ill-considered."

"He's certainly not suggesting that all women belong in the home," Coxley said with a laugh. "Why, just look at our current company. We're surrounded by women more than capable of providing for themselves with or without any husband attached to them. Aaliyah is inheriting her father's business, Miss Bailey is an artist and an entrepreneur, Mrs. Leicester a seamstress, and of course Miss Patel is only just beginning to explore all that London has to offer. That Mr. Johnson's wife is herself a homemaker is no more than coincidence, I'm sure. After all, some women are perfectly happy in that position. You're happy, aren't you, Grace?"

"I never imagined a better life for myself than cleaning up after my husband and cooking him three square meals a day," said Grace.

Johnson whipped his head to the side to glare at her so sharply, Elizabeth could almost hear his neck crack at the movement. Grace finished her wine and held out her glass for Coxley to top her up, smiling blandly at the party as she pointedly ignored her husband and his blatant outrage. Judging by his reaction to her words, Elizabeth guessed they were out of character for her. And judging by Grace's apparent familiarity with Coxley, they had been acquainted prior to the party. Her skin prickled with curiosity. That Grace had a part to play in Coxley's plan of taking Johnson down a peg, she had no doubt.

"And then there's our esteemed hostess herself," Coxley continued, turning to raise his glass to Mrs. Hollyhock. "The respected matriarch of this vast estate who has managed it successfully for so many years without a single man's interference. Mr. Johnson, you wouldn't be suggesting that she needs a husband to provide for her, would you?"

Johnson was tight-lipped as Mrs. Hollyhock regarded him with a cool, appraising gaze.

"No," she said slowly, "he wouldn't be suggesting *that*."

Johnson swallowed his wine inelegantly, presumably to avoid digging himself into a hole and letting the gathering know exactly what he thought of women.

But Mrs. Hollyhock was disinterested in forcing him into such a hole, either because she didn't like the look of baiting her guests, or because she wanted to avoid any politically inflammatory topics at her party. Instead, she changed the subject entirely. "Tell us, Mr. Johnson: are there any especially exciting cases you can share? Assuming you won't be breaking client confidentiality, of course."

"Oh, I'm sure client confidentiality has a little leeway," Coxley said, "doesn't it, Mr. Johnson?"

"I assure you, I take my clients' privacy very seriously," Johnson said, his tone of utmost self-importance. "But yes, there is one recent case I'd be glad to share."

"Is it about that jewel thief?" Alphonse asked, leaning in excitedly.

"No, it's—"

"Because Morgan was telling me the most incredible things about that one, weren't you, Morgan?"

"Nothing that can't be read in the papers," Morgan offered with a shrug, more focussed on his dessert than the conversation. "But I imagine Mr. Johnson here could add some colourful anecdotes, seeing as he's the one investigating it."

"Yes," Johnson began, "but the case I mean to talk about is—"

"Limited anecdotes, I should think," Aaliyah interrupted as if Johnson had never spoken, "seeing as the thief remains at large."

"Their steals have been getting bolder and more expensive every time, haven't they?" Jasmine asked.

"Tell me," said Coxley, "do you feel you're closing in on the culprit, or are they leading you on as much of a wild goose chase as the papers make it seem?"

"That is an ongoing police investigation," Johnson said loudly, "and not something on which I can comment at this time!"

Deepa nudged Elizabeth's foot under the table, winking and rolling her eyes theatrically. Elizabeth hid her smile behind her fork. Gratifying as it was to watch everyone needle the man, she sensed that things were about to kick off, and her nerves were strung taut enough to snap.

Alphonse huffed, visibly disappointed by Johnson's refusal to discuss the matter. "Bother. I'm quite invested in the story, I don't mind saying."

"I'll keep you up to date on it," Morgan promised him.

"There's not much to tell besides what anyone can read," Grace said carelessly, and was immediately rewarded by Coxley pressing his shoulder to hers with a crooked grin.

Elizabeth stared, as fascinated by Grace's behaviour as Johnson was enraged. However long Grace and Coxley had known each other, she seemed firmly on his side versus her husband's. If Coxley could somehow convince the woman to publicly leave her husband that very evening—

"The case I would like to share with you," Johnson boomed, his voice pitched to bowl over any further derailments but also to carry the considerable length of the table. "I assume most of those present this evening are at least passingly familiar with the writing of one M. Hayes?"

"The romance novelist?" Mrs. Hollyhock asked.

"I know those books!" Alphonse piped in. "Ripping good stories, those."

"I've read several at Alphonse's insistence," Aaliyah said. "Isn't there a rumour going around that the author has been arrested for something in France?"

"A rumour with no weight to it," Johnson said, "as I will prove to you shortly."

"How could she be arrested in France?" Jasmine asked. "I heard she was a former German spy writing undercover for the English market. Can Germans be arrested on French soil?"

"You're both wrong, surely," Alphonse said. "I would put money on her being American."

Johnson cleared his throat. "If I may lay the matter to rest most definitively—"

"American," Mrs. Hollyhock repeated, frowning faintly at her son. "Do you think so?"

"Yes, absolutely! It's in the attitude of the thing, you see. She might be writing about English dukes and duchesses and whatnot, but the sense of adventure is all awfully American, isn't it? I was debating just this with Jacobi back when her last book came out, me assuming of course that she must be English, what with all her books being in England, et cetera, but then Jacobi suggested this American alternative—far more persuasively than I can argue it here, I must say—and I was altogether persuaded by the notion. It does make sense, doesn't it?"

"As much sense as any other nationality, I suppose," Aaliyah agreed.

"She is English," Johnson began impatiently, only for Mrs. Hollyhock to interrupt him.

"I had considered that M. Hayes' attitude towards propriety is rather more American than English," she said thoughtfully. "She must certainly be one of this younger generation, in any case."

"How so?" Elizabeth asked, despite her determination to stay out of the conversation.

"It's the way she writes magic, in my opinion," said Mrs. Hollyhock. "A proper English novel always ought to be very clear about the morals of magic use. I know it's in fashion to bend such rules nowadays, but not so long ago it would have been unthinkable to show a serving girl wielding the kind of magic shown in— What was the name of that book?"

"*The Duke's Forbidden Passion*?" Alphonse suggested.

"No, the one where he's courting the kitchen girl."

"*The Earl's Lost Love*?"

"No, it was a maid in that one."

"*The Highlander's Secret Affair*!"

"That's the one, thank you. Now, in this book, the girl is born of very common parents and never revealed to be the lost heir to any titles or fortune, yet she commands this power that far outstrips the lord's own. Now," she added, holding up one hand to forestall any protests, "I understand that this is a mere fantasy meant to entertain the masses. But is it not irresponsible to put forth such ideas? Delivering them straight into the hands of those common, working class souls she is so unrealistically uplifting?"

"It's not as if Hayes is writing books on etiquette," Elizabeth objected. "Showing the lower classes using magic isn't endorsing the practice any more than writing about a lord marrying his serving girl makes it realistic. It's meant to entertain, not to radicalise."

"I agree entirely, my dear," Mrs. Hollyhock replied, "but some people do look on it quite suspiciously." She raised her thin eyebrows suggestively.

Alphonse scoffed. "Oh, come now. Who could take a silly romance novel so seriously?"

"You never know what's going to take root in the public consciousness," Mrs. Hollyhock intoned.

"I suppose you're right," Elizabeth said. "Just look at us, voting and flashing our knees in public. Who knows where we'll be another few years from now? Why, we could end up with a woman Prime Minister."

"Let's not get entirely carried away," said Mrs. Hollyhock.

"If I may," Johnson said loudly, his frustration at the conversation's detour all too obvious. "I know exactly who is behind the M. Hayes' name." That got the party's attention back where he wanted it. He smiled smugly. "In fact," he said, "she is in attendance this very night."

Elizabeth's stomach dropped. Under the table, Arthur squeezed her knee reassuringly.

"In attendance *here?*" Alphonse asked, leaning in with his elbows on the table. "Right here in this very room?"

Johnson met Elizabeth's eye and smiled meanly. Hiding her nerves, she looked back at him with utter impassivity, not letting her contempt show on her face.

"Mr. Johnson," she announced to the room at large, "is convinced that M. Hayes is none other than myself."

There was a beat of silence broken only by the thundering of Elizabeth's own heart, which she hoped no one else could hear. Johnson, she was pleased to note, had apparently not expected her to steal his spotlight in such brazen fashion.

"You," said Mrs. Hollyhock. "He has reason to believe this novelist is you?"

Elizabeth kept her gaze locked on Johnson's. "He's quite convinced of it."

Johnson drew himself up, puffed out his chest, and tried to reclaim control of the evening. "The identity of M. Hayes was a recent case of mine, and the investigation I conducted to uncover her identity left no stone unturned! I can tell you—"

"Are you sure?" Aaliyah interrupted. "Because I've known Elizabeth for years, and I can tell *you*, she's not the sort of person at all inclined to swooning romance stories."

"It's true," Arthur agreed. "I love my wife dearly, but I must say, she's altogether too pragmatic for such fantasies."

"I always thought you were a bright young woman," Mrs. Hollyhock mused, studying Elizabeth with her sharp, pale eyes. "The way you manage your business and your life. You're organised enough to add a writing career on top of that, I think."

"I'm very flattered you think so," Elizabeth said, "but I really wouldn't know where to begin."

"With a typewriter, I should think," Alphonse put in.

"I have statements from her publisher!" Johnson declared at top volume, cutting through the speculation.

"Do you," Elizabeth said.

"Providing irrefutable proof of her identity!"

"Have you got it here with you?" Arthur asked.

"I don't know what you have," Elizabeth said, calmly lying through her teeth, "but I sincerely doubt it's that."

Before Johnson could reply, Alphonse turned to Elizabeth with a hopeful, wondering expression. "Is it really you?"

"Of course she's not M. Hayes," Coxley said, speaking up for the first time since the subject had been raised. "I am."

Elizabeth stared at him as the table erupted in an outburst of exclamations.

"It's true that I hired Mr. Johnson to uncover the Hayes identity," Coxley continued, waving them all quiet, "but I only did it because I wanted to test his skill. His name had been in all the papers lauding his talent as an investigator, and I was bored, you see. How he managed to land on Mrs. Leicester, I have no idea."

"I can tell you precisely how I landed on her," Johnson began angrily, but Coxley cut him off.

"And then," Coxley went on, speaking over him, "after coming to the false conclusion that it was Mrs. Leicester behind the name, Mr. Johnson proceeded to blackmail the poor woman!"

Grace turned her full attention to Elizabeth for the first time that evening, wide-eyed and intent.

"Is that true?" Mrs. Hollyhock asked Elizabeth, frowning.

"It is," Elizabeth confirmed, glancing at Johnson, who was glaring daggers at her. "I kept it all very quiet, of course. I had no idea how to respond! But Mr. Johnson wouldn't entertain the notion that M. Hayes was anyone else but me."

"When he thought you had the time to write such books, I can't imagine," Arthur said. "Surely he's aware you have a business to manage."

"A seamstress by day and an authoress by night," Elizabeth agreed. "Does he not realise I need sleep as much as the next person?"

"I can show you the proof—" Mr. Johnson cut in.

"And I can show everyone those awful letters you sent me," Elizabeth said coldly.

"John," said Grace, her voice pitched low as if to speak with her husband privately. "Is it true that you wrote threats to Mrs. Leicester?"

"Not threats—"

"Asking for money!" Elizabeth added. She didn't have to feign her outrage. "In order to buy his silence on the matter. Arthur, darling, you haven't got one of them on hand, have you?"

Arthur made a show of checking his pockets as Mr. Johnson got redder and redder in the face. "I'm afraid not," Arthur said apologetically. "I think we left them at home, in the safe."

"Well, no matter. Mrs. Hollyhock, you may take my word on it: when I received the first one in the mail, I was absolutely shocked. Shocked, I tell you! And to come from such an esteemed man as Mr. Johnson was made out to be—well, I can only imagine what other vile habits he must be hiding, if blackmail comes so easily to him."

The whole table tittered. Johnson was approaching a purple complexion, and looked near to apoplexy.

"Mr. Johnson," said Mrs. Hollyhock sternly. "Is there anything you can say in your defence?"

"Only that Mrs. Leicester is exaggerating the matter of those letters sent," he replied from between gritted teeth, "and that my deductions were correct, and she *is* the writer behind the M. Hayes pen. If you will look at this paperwork I procured from her publisher—"

"Oh," said Arthur, reaching into the inner breast pocket of his suit, "I do have those letters on me after all."

He brought them out with a flourish, displaying them for the table before handing them to Elizabeth, who passed them to Jasmine, who gave them to Aaliyah, who sent them through Alphonse and right into Mrs. Hollyhock's waiting hand.

The entire table held its breath as she read them silently, with knitted brows.

When she was done, she slowly lowered them to her lap, her eyes pale and cold as ice.

"Well," she said. The room was so still and quiet, one could hear a pin drop. "That is most interesting."

"What do they say?" Alphonse whispered.

"Mr. Johnson," said Mrs. Hollyhock. "What do you have to say for yourself?"

Johnson's mouth opened and closed ineffectively.

"John," said Grace, her tone full of warning. "Say something, for god's sake."

Before he could find his words, Coxley cut in like a knife.

"I think you ought to apologise to the lady," Coxley said, his eyes glittering, "for all the distress you've caused her. Heaven knows I've apologised a thousand times already for it." When he glanced at Elizabeth, she could see his regret—cleverly masked now that they were in company, but present all the same, and she inclined her head in acknowledgement.

"He's covering for her," Johnson said, as if the truth of the scenario were unfurling before his very eyes. "And furthermore!" He stabbed his finger at Coxley. "They are having an affair!"

Coxley burst out laughing.

"Are they," Arthur asked flatly, sounding less amused by the accusation.

"Can a woman not even be friendly with a man without you spinning some story about it?" Elizabeth asked. "Truly, your vendetta against me is most concerning! Did you know," she asked the table, "that Mr. Johnson is convinced I once rejected him? Romantically, so he says." Catching Grace's eye, she offered an invisible wince and a silent apology.

"Is she the reason you've been so foul-tempered lately?" Grace demanded of her husband. "Have you really been scheming over this poor woman because of some perceived slight? Look at me, John!"

"I've done nothing of the sort," he snapped at her. "And I'll thank you to watch your tone when you speak to me. We'll discuss this later, at home."

"My tone is perfectly reasonable, all things considered, and I'd like to discuss it now. Have you been chasing after other women behind my back?"

"Perhaps only this one particular woman," Coxley said.

He leaned in to speak intimately in Grace's ear, his arm slung around the back of her chair in a move designed to make Johnson's blood boil. Confusingly, it also served to make Elizabeth's stomach twist in a most uncomfortable way. If Coxley was involved with this woman, it would mean all Elizabeth's efforts to get him together with Arthur would be for nothing, but that wasn't all there was to it.

She had no time to decipher her own feelings at present.

"You bare a passing resemblance to her, don't you think?" Coxley said to Grace. "He's been obsessed with her for over a decade now. Have you ever wondered why he is so insistent that you lighten your hair to blonde?"

There was a hushed intake of breath from the whole table at once as Grace turned to stare down her husband.

"A decade," she said slowly. "Did you choose me as a replacement, when you found you couldn't have her?"

"He is poisoning your mind," Johnson said, his hand shaking violently as he pointed at Grace and Coxley where they sat as a united front against him. "He's a scoundrel and a womaniser—"

"You've always been a dog, John," Grace said, making sure that all the company could hear her. "You can't blame Mr. Coxley for that. All he's done is encourage me to stop putting up with you. As for Mrs. Leicester…"

Elizabeth held her breath, waiting for Grace to come down as either her ally or another enemy.

"I'm only sorry you've had the misfortune of knowing him," Grace told her with an air of finality. To the rest of the table, she announced, "I have no doubt that Mrs. Leicester's accusations are true. I've long known that my husband has a wandering eye and a spiteful nature. He preaches the importance of women's morality, and practices none of his own."

Johnson slammed his cutlery down hard enough to rattle all the dishes in his vicinity. "You— You unfaithful— Disloyal—!"

"She does look a little dim, doesn't she?" Elizabeth said to Mrs. Hollyhock. "I hardly think it's a coincidence that the first blackmail letter arrived so shortly after my wedding. These are not the actions of a well-adjusted man."

"How dare you—" Johnson seethed, rising from his seat.

Arthur and Coxley immediately both rose to meet him, on edge and defensive.

"I think," said Mrs. Hollyhock, "that it is time for you to leave, Mr. Johnson. I must say, I'm terribly disappointed in your conduct tonight. The city's most renowned private investigator, indeed."

The vindication Elizabeth felt watching Johnson leave the room was incredible. When he was finally out of sight—escorted off the property by Mrs. Hollyhock's staff like a common vagrant—Elizabeth let out a deep breath, relief making her boneless. Arthur held her hand tightly under the table, grounding her, and if Coxley had been sitting nearer, she might have held his, too.

CHAPTER SEVENTEEN

IN WHICH CERTAIN FEELINGS ARE
BROUGHT TO LIGHT

The rest of dessert passed in a tizzy, with the letters being handed around and read aloud until even those in attendance who had initially supported Johnson or admired his work were loudly denouncing him. It was satisfying, the knowledge that his reputation would be thoroughly ruined within twenty-four hours as the gossip spread through London like a wildfire. And until then, Elizabeth was surrounded by friends, and even the guests whom she didn't know personally gathered around her in support. She knew they would have turned on her as quickly as they had on Johnson if he had got the upper hand, and they were far more interested in the scandal of the thing than in her as a person, but still, she savoured the victory.

But there were only so many times the letters could be read, and as dessert came to an end, Mrs. Hollyhock expertly shepherded the conversation to greener pastures. The table and chairs were cleared to make room for dancing, and as the night ticked closer to eleven, everyone took to the floor in a shimmer of silk, sequins, and tulle. The music started fast and jazzy, clearly influenced by Aaliyah's tastes, and the alcohol flowed liberally as people broke off into small groups and couples to swing each other around, spirits high and knees flashing. Coxley and Mrs. Johnson were conspicuously missing from the dance floor, which Elizabeth firmly told herself was none of her business, and she almost believed it.

She danced a quick foxtrot with Arthur first, before splitting off with Aaliyah, Jasmine, and Deepa, forming a group that dominated the entire floor in a loosely-coordinated Charleston. Their efforts were met with raucous applause from the onlookers, and by the time the song was finished, Elizabeth was delightfully short of breath and sweating from exertion. She spun back into Arthur's arms for another round, the music just as quick, before she had to beg off to drink some water and catch her breath. Arthur joined her, and they stood side by side with their arms around each other, tucked out of the way by the French doors as they rehydrated.

"It went well," Elizabeth said, leaning her full weigh against his side. "As well as it could have gone, I think."

"Did you know Coxley was planning to take credit for the name?" Arthur asked.

"Not at all, though in hindsight I should have seen it coming. Did you know Johnson was married, and that Coxley has been turning his wife against him all this time?"

"I hadn't a clue. Are you happy with the outcome, though?"

"It's not as if I had anything specific in mind. Coxley didn't physically fight the man or otherwise risk getting arrested, I got out of it unscathed, and you got that nice dramatic moment when you produced the letters. Everyone is on our side, sympathetic to our trials, and I don't think a single one of them suspects that Johnson was actually right about me. I consider it a grand success, all told."

"Good." He kissed her, tasting sweetly of champagne, and she was rushed back to memories of their wedding reception.

"Dance with me again?" she asked against his lips.

He laughed. "Give me another minute to recover. The Charleston is a hell of a workout, and I think your energy outmatches mine tonight."

"Fine, I'll let you rest." She gave him another peck. "Come and find me when you're ready."

She downed another drink as she weaved through the party, abandoning the crowded room to slip through the doors and into the sultry night air. There, she found Coxley amid the roses, nursing his own drink at a much slower pace. She was inordinately pleased to find him alone, though she would be hard-pressed to articulate why.

"I would have thought you'd be enjoying yourself at the centre of everyone's attention," she said. "Did it get to be too much for you?"

"It doesn't feel entirely earned," he admitted. "While I always enjoy my notoriety, and this evening went as well as one could hope, it was a bit of a mess, and I wish it hadn't happened at all. Which is a new feeling for me. Regret, you know." He lifted one shoulder in a lazy shrug as he took another sip of his drink. "But it's done, Johnson is vanquished, and you're out the other side safe and sound."

"What happened to Mrs. Johnson?" Elizabeth asked, hoping she sounded politely curious rather than invested in the answer. "You both disappeared so quickly after dessert, I assumed you had stolen away together."

"Grace said her goodbyes to the Hollyhocks and then I saw her off in a cab, as a matter of fact. She's going to stay with her parents for a time. For some unfathomable reason, she didn't feel up to any more socialising this evening." Coxley smiled into the end of his drink. "Whatever happens between the two of them, I think it's safe to say that Johnson's pride will never recover from having his wife belittle him in front of company like that. I told her I would help however I could if she chose to leave him, but who can say how things will shake out?"

"You two seemed rather cosy during dinner," Elizabeth noted.

"Yes, I made her acquaintance late last month and have spent the last several weeks convincing her that she would be better off without him. It took barely any effort at all, to be honest. She lost patience with him some time ago, I think, and she only needed a little friendly encouragement to stand up for herself."

"Just how friendly was your encouragement, exactly?"

"I'll have you know, I was a perfect gentleman. The last thing that poor woman needs right now is another man meddling in her life. I'm not pursuing her like that, and she doesn't expect me to."

"Good," Elizabeth said, without thinking.

"Good?" Coxley echoed.

It may have been Elizabeth's imagination, but he looked as invested in her reply as she had been in his.

"I mean," she said quickly, "we're going to celebrate our success when we get home, aren't we? It would be in bad taste to revel in her husband's downfall right in front of her."

Coxley's expression smoothed. "Ah, yes, of course. In that case, I'm pleased to say that you needn't worry. You have me entirely to yourself tonight. You and Arthur both," he added, correcting himself.

"Speaking of Arthur, we should head back inside before he wonders where we've got to. Will you dance with me?"

"Did you wear Arthur out already?"

"Temporarily, yes."

"Then your wish is my command." Finishing his drink, he set his glass aside on a decorative stone bench and allowed her to take his hand and guide him back inside.

"I do appreciate what you did for me tonight," she whispered in his ear as they spun into their dance, stepping in time to the jazz.

"It was the least I could do. What's one more scandal under my belt?"

"I could have weathered it, but I'm glad I don't have to. Though I should probably retire the pen name now, regardless."

"Ah, yes. I should apologise for that, as well."

She pressed one finger to his lips to hush him and he fell silent immediately, his eyes wide.

"You've apologised enough, and I've forgiven you," she said firmly. "It's not your fault things got so out of hand."

"It really is, though," he said, his lips soft as silk against the pad of her finger.

She quickly withdrew her hand, pretending not to have noticed. "Well, yes, it is entirely your fault, but if you and Johnson hadn't weaselled out M. Hayes' identity, someone else would have, eventually. And now with Johnson discredited, I only need you to keep the secret."

"I will."

"If not for my sake, then for Arthur's, I hope."

"For both of you," he promised, catching her hands and pulling back to look her in the eye. "I wouldn't hurt you any more than I'd hurt him. Not intentionally. Not now." His eyes were enormous, dark in the low glitter of the chandeliers, and earnestly fixed on hers.

"I believe you."

The song slowed and they drew off to the side, leaving the floor to more romantic couples.

"Your painting is finished, by the way," Coxley said, faux-casually.

"Is it?"

"I didn't want to tell you until this business with Johnson had been concluded, but I left it at your house earlier this evening. It's waiting for you."

"You have to come home with us," she said immediately. "I want you there when I see it for the first time."

"That's hardly necessary—"

"I insist. You should be there to see my reaction."

"But what if you're disappointed?" he teased. "How terribly awkward would it be—"

"Are you shy?" she asked incredulously.

"Not at all."

"Let me get back to Arthur and see how long he wants to stay. We don't want to be the first to leave, but I don't feel inclined to linger until the very end, either. I'd much rather see that painting than stick around for another ten dances or another circuit of gossip."

"The painting will keep as long as need be," he began, before reading something in her expression and changing course. "Although, you've had a trying evening, and I think our hostess would find you valid in wanting an early night."

"Thank you. You're welcome to stay as long as you like, of course—"

"No, no. If you want me there, I wouldn't dream of denying you."

"Excellent. Now, have you seen where Arthur went?"

"He was watching us from by the doors, last I saw," Coxley said, nodding towards the garden.

Pleased and too tipsy to consider Coxley's tone when he said he wouldn't dream of denying her, Elizabeth skipped through the French doors and into the dark once more. Her dress swished against her legs, good-luck charms glinting in the dim light. They had served her well. Perhaps she should start wearing one as a piece of permanent jewellery, though there was a chance that wearing it full-time would diminish its effects.

She found Arthur in the hydrangeas, sitting all alone on a little stone step, the distant light from the party barely reaching him. He smiled at her approach and rose to greet her, though he seemed quieter than usual. Tired, perhaps. It was past eleven now, and past their bedtime.

"My darling," she murmured.

"I saw you roped Coxley into a dance. Did you enjoy yourself?"

"Very much so."

"I'm glad," he said softly, ghosting one hand over her hair without quite touching her.

"What is it?"

"Nothing. You just looked…" He shook his head.

"How did I look?" she asked teasingly.

"Beautiful, my darling. And very happy. I'm glad you two have become friends. It was terrible having you at odds in the beginning, but now, seeing you together…"

Arthur trailed off for a second before gathering his thoughts anew. "I must admit, I do sometimes wonder what would have happened if you had met him before meeting me."

She stooped to drop both arms around his neck, pressing a kiss to his cheek before loosening her embrace and settling in at his side, nudging him until he made room for her on the step. "That we could have been friends right from the start, do you mean?"

"That you might have been wearing his ring on your finger instead of mine."

Startled, she pulled back to stare at him, but he didn't seem upset. A little wistful, perhaps, but there was nothing accusatory in his expression.

"If Mr. Johnson's accusation got to you—"

"It didn't," he said. "My darling, it didn't. I know you would never do anything of the sort." He smoothed one hand down the skin of her back where her dress was open and offered her a reassuring smile. "I'm just feeling lucky to have you, that's all."

"You do have me," she told him. "You'll have me forever. There is no world, no situation, in which you were going to be anything less than my first choice."

"As long as you're happy."

"I couldn't possibly be happier."

Arthur hummed but didn't vocally agree, and his quiet neutrality left her unsettled.

"He says my portrait is finished," she offered hesitantly. "I told him I'd like to head home sooner than later to see it. Unless you want to stay longer?"

He shook his head, patting her knee with one warm hand. "We can go whenever you like. I saw a few other couples beginning to drift away, so it won't look like we're cutting out early. Do you want to go now?"

She was brimming with anticipation to see the painting, but also anticipation of a more nameless sort that she couldn't quite put her finger on. It had something to do with the way Coxley had looked at her after their dance, which, coupled with the strange trepidation Arthur had roused in her with his quiet solitude, left her restless and cagey.

She didn't try to explain any of that. Instead, she just said, "Yes, please."

"Then we'll say our goodbyes and see how Jules has immortalised you on canvas."

They shared a cab home together. On Elizabeth's right, Coxley was tense with nervous energy in preparation for the reveal of his painting, and on her left, Arthur was quiet, sitting straight-backed with military stillness; lost in thought or bracing for something, Elizabeth wasn't sure. The energy in the cab was strange, electric and unsettled like they were all three balancing on the verge of something momentous. She was perhaps a little drunk.

By the time they got home she was practically vibrating in place, strung so tight with that strange energy that she wanted to take a hammer to the tension and shatter it like a sheet of glass.

But shattering it would take some drastic measure she wasn't sure she was prepared to enact.

As it was Saturday, not to mention after midnight, Mrs. Patel was absent from the house, leaving them alone without a buffer. And as they had come straight from a dinner party, Elizabeth could hardly stall for time by offering Coxley food or drink. She couldn't say why she wanted a buffer or an excuse to stall. She wanted to see the painting—she was dying to see it—but something told her that once it was unveiled, the tension between them would shatter after all, and it would be impossible to put all the pieces back together the way they had been before.

The painting waited for her on the dining room table, five feet long and four feet tall, wrapped in plain brown paper and tied up in twine. She had never stolen a glimpse of it in the studio; she could scarcely imagine the finished artwork, and now that it was sitting right in front of her, she found she needed to gather her courage before pulling the twine loose.

Once the twine was off, she could hardly avoid opening the rest. She stripped the paper away in long, clean lines, and when the canvas was finally revealed she stepped back to take it all in at once. Her breath caught in her throat; she raised one hand to her mouth as she sought for something to say.

Coxley had made her beautiful. Wildflowers framed her body, their petals delicate against her skin, which glowed pale gold in the sunlight. Her hair was a tumble of blonde, her gaze steady and knowing, and her body—

It wasn't that Coxley had painted over her flaws. She was recognisable from tip to toe, but it was as if he had taken her flaws and acknowledged them as a lover might, not with shame or judgment or even with gentle acceptance, but with something approaching worship. There, her knees and elbows were bony, but his brush seemed to kiss them with the paint. And there, her stomach was soft and pliant, but the brushstrokes caressed it and shaped it into something enviable.

And the flowers themselves: there were periwinkles and sky-blue forget-me-nots, wild chamomile, cornflowers and sweet pea blossoms and morning glories, flax flowers and columbines and stalks of perfect bluebells, every one of them the colour of her magic. They rested against her breasts like she was a wood nymph who had stepped out from her meadow, beautiful and unashamed of her nakedness. Like flowers were all she had ever worn. She had told him to paint her as a queen and he had given her a crown of hydrangeas, big soft clusters of blue and purple flowers like a cloud. She reclined, easy and elegant, against the chaise-lounge, which was draped in silk and taffeta. Gold foil dotted the flowers' centres like spots of pollen and shimmered in her hair and in the background. And behind her shoulders, her beloved suncatcher flowers glowed gold and green, their star-shaped petals like little clusters of stained glass.

"Oh," she finally said, a soft utterance of a single syllable. She needed to say something more—to thank him, to express the depth of her gratitude—but words failed her. Her throat worked soundlessly for a moment; all she could do was stare at the painting.

"Jules," Arthur said in a low voice. "What have you done?"

Elizabeth turned in time to see Coxley's expression slip from expectation to something blank that she couldn't recognise.

"I should go," he said.

"Wait, what—"

"No," Arthur said firmly. "He's right. He should go."

Elizabeth looked back and forth between the two of them, lost. "But I—"

"My apologies," Coxley said, nodding to her. "I…" But then he caught Arthur's gaze and ducked his head, turning away without finishing his sentence, and swept from the room and the house without another word.

Elizabeth stared after him, one hand still on the canvas, holding it in place. "What was that? Arthur? What did you say to him?"

Arthur shook his head, his mouth in a line. "I'm sorry. I should have realised." Clearing his throat, he gestured to her, and then the painting. "This wasn't a good idea," he said finally.

She laughed, more in surprise than amusement. "It's a little late for that, darling. What exactly is your objection?"

"He's gone and fallen in love with you."

Elizabeth looked at the painting and its million careful brushstrokes. In her crown of hydrangeas, tiny golden bumblebees glinted like jewels, nestled delicately among the petals. The vivid memory of Coxley's hands against her hair that day in Kew Gardens as he rescued the bee crashed into her like a wave, strong enough to rock her off course.

She looked back at Arthur. "I'm sorry. What?"

"I've seen how he looks at you," Arthur said quietly. "When he thinks you're not watching. It's not how an artist looks at his model, and it's not how a man looks at his friend's wife. Like you hung the sun and the stars and he's blind to everything else."

"No, you have it backwards," Elizabeth said confidently. "Coxley and I aren't in love; the two of you are."

They stared at each other for a second.

"Coxley and I," Arthur repeated, "are in love?"

Her words caught up to her and Elizabeth realised what she had just said. She stood perfectly still, her mind whirring as her body froze. She could hardly take back her assertion, so there was nothing else for it but to forge ahead.

"I never meant to put it so bluntly," she said, silent apologies dropping from her tongue, "but I can't have you thinking that he and I are having any kind of affair when all this time I've been trying to work out some way to get the two of you together."

"I never thought you were having an affair," Arthur said, seemingly numb. He stood as still as she, like he'd been shell-struck. "I would have said something sooner in that case. But this— How on earth can you think I'm in love with him?"

"There are so many reasons, darling. But Arthur," she said, her words beginning to trip over themselves in her haste to explain, "you mustn't think I'm angry with you for it. I'm not upset in the slightest. I want you to be happy, and if he could make you happier—"

"But I'm in love with *you*," Arthur insisted desperately.

"I know you are. I've never doubted it."

"Then how—"

"Men are perfectly capable of falling in love with their own sex. You only need look to Alphonse and Jacobi to see proof of that."

"Yes, certainly, but I'm in love with *you*," Arthur repeated, shaking off his shock to step forward and grasp her hands as if that would help him communicate the depth of his sincerity.

Elizabeth squeezed his fingers in response, trying to reassure him even as she asked, "Do you not think that you can love both men and women? Or do you not think you have the capacity to love two people equally at the same time?"

Arthur looked like the floor had dropped out from under him. "I married *you*. I gave myself, present and future, to you alone."

"But why does it have to be alone? Coxley was your best man and ring bearer. He's been your best friend and confidant for years longer than I've known you. And he loves you, Arthur. He loves you as deeply as I do, and for longer than I have. And I'm convinced that you feel the same for him, even if you don't recognise it."

Keeping hold of one of his hands, she released the other to press her palm flat to his cheek as she willed him to understand her. "You took two years to propose to me when we both knew in the first week that we were it for each other. I told you that day in Kew Gardens that I was ready to propose to you myself if you didn't go through with it already. Coxley loves you, but he can't act on that the way we did for a million different reasons. Because you're both men, because you're married, because he doesn't know if you reciprocate those feelings. But I want him to have what I have with you. Do you want that?"

Arthur opened and closed his mouth a few times before managing to get out, "When did you know?"

"The first time I went to his studio. I saw his sketchbooks full of you. Though, looking back, it would have been evident from the day I met him, if only I'd known to look for it."

"Three months, then, since you were sure. And you spent those three months trying to orchestrate some way to bring us together," Arthur said slowly.

"Yes," Elizabeth admitted.

"Yet in all that time, you never noticed that you'd fallen in love with him, too?"

"I haven't," she said automatically. "Why, we've only just become friends."

"If you're going to be the one to break it to me that I'm in love with the man, I think it's only fair that I be the one to break the same to you," Arthur said dryly.

Elizabeth took a moment to actually think it over. Once she put her mind to it, she found she didn't need much convincing. "Well. I'll be damned."

"Am I right?"

"I think you are. How did I not notice that?"

"You were distracted, I assume."

"You're not upset about it?" she asked tentatively.

"I think it would be terribly hypocritical of me if I were."

"And you're not upset with him?"

He softened. "How could I be? How could I blame anyone for falling in love with you?"

"You sent him away."

"I did." Arthur dragged one hand over his face. "I wasn't really prepared to deal with such stark evidence of his feelings for you," he confessed. "Not at my dining room table, anyway. I'll fetch him back."

He made for the door like he meant to run Coxley down in the street that very minute. Elizabeth caught his wrist as he passed her and bade him pause.

"We might want to first discuss how to approach the matter with him," she suggested.

"The matter," Arthur repeated.

She raised her eyebrows meaningfully.

"That we've all inadvertently fallen in love with one another without noticing?" he asked.

"That's easy enough to say. Though I wouldn't say none of us noticed. I'm willing to bet that he's entirely aware he's fallen in love with us, which is more than either of us can claim. It's what we plan to do about it that I think we need to map out."

"What do we plan to do about it?"

She raised her eyebrows another notch.

"Oh. Oh."

"Only if you want to," she added.

"Do you want to?"

"Yes," she replied, without hesitation. If she was less drunk, she would likely have given it more thought. But she had been so ready to push Arthur and Coxley into one another's arms when they had been the only ones in love; did adding herself to the equation change so much? She thought not. "Do you think he wants that?"

Arthur made his way back to the table, pulled out a chair, and sat down. "To be clear: are we inviting him into our bed, or into our marriage? Because those are two separate things."

Elizabeth had never thought of them as such, but perhaps a third party might consider them so. "What do you think he would want?"

"I don't know. Maybe neither."

She was sceptical of that, but then, Arthur had much more to lose than she did. "Let's assume he wants something of us. I don't think it's fair to invite him into one and not the other."

"If we plan everything out beforehand, he might enter the conversation and feel trapped by it. And you know how he lashes out when he feels trapped."

"The choice will be his. Whatever he wants; whether he wants to have the conversation at all. I just want the two of us to be very clear first about what we're offering."

Arthur looked up at her. "We're offering him everything."

Her heart skipped a beat, simultaneously thrilled and scared at the possibilities opening up before them.

Still, she tried to approach it pragmatically. "This doesn't need to happen tonight. Or overnight, or even tomorrow. It's been so sudden— We should sleep on it, talk things over in more detail, and decide for sure whether we want to go forward with it, or whether there's a chance we might regret changing things so drastically."

"Do you imagine you might regret it?" Arthur asked.

"I haven't regretted anything regarding Coxley so far," she confessed. "Not even that horrendous first meeting in that dingy little seafood restaurant that gave him food poisoning."

The corner of Arthur's mouth tugged up in a little smile. "Me neither. There have been times when I've been so fed up with him that I wanted to wring his neck, and it would be naïve to think there will never be such times again, but I've never regretted the time I spent living with him. Or letting him sketch me. Or anything of his friendship. I did briefly regret introducing him to you, but that's clearly worked itself out, thank god."

"Indeed. In that case, if we've agreed that neither of us intend to go chasing him down to discuss our feelings and invite him back to bed this instant, shall we call it a night? Because I think I passed the point a while ago where I went from pleasantly tipsy to properly drunk and exhausted, and I should very much like to get out of this dress."

"Let's sleep on it," Arthur agreed.

But as they traipsed upstairs, shedding their clothes as they went, Elizabeth somehow doubted either of them would be getting much sleep at all.

CHAPTER EIGHTEEN

AN INVITATION TO PARTAKE IN DESSERT, BED, AND MARRIAGE, IN THAT ORDER

Elizabeth hadn't felt so shy about climbing into bed with Arthur since their first time. Nothing had changed except the realisation they were both in love with their friend, but somehow, that changed everything. Elizabeth had never been less than present with Arthur, but now, she couldn't stop imagining what Coxley might be like alongside them. Whether he would split his attention evenly between them; what he would most like to do or have done to him; what his eyes would look like when they were dark with hunger. Whether Elizabeth would feel jealous, seeing Arthur with someone else for the first time. She didn't think she would, but it was likely one of those situations where she couldn't be sure until she was in it. She didn't want to be jealous, and she certainly didn't want Arthur to be.

Even assuming Coxley said yes, that he wanted to be involved with them both in equal measures, there was still so much uncertainty about that new dynamic. Elizabeth did not enjoy uncertainty. She didn't find it invigorating the way more spontaneous people did. She wanted to know exactly what she was getting into, and plan accordingly.

"You're thinking incredibly loudly," Arthur said to her.

They sat facing each other, she cross-legged in the middle of the mattress and he perched on the edge, one foot on the floor and the other tucked under him.

"I can't stop thinking about him." She toyed with one corner of the sheet. "If he were here with us right now... But that seems unfair. I don't want to fantasise about him like he's some object, not before we've talked to him, not when we have no idea whether he would even want this—"

"I'm willing to bet he does," Arthur said. "I agree with you, of course; I have no interest in fantasising about him without hashing it all out first. But I know him as well as I know you, and I really don't think he'll turn us down."

Elizabeth rolled up onto her knees to shuffle closer. Arthur positioned himself more firmly on the bed so she could sit in his lap, her thighs bracketing his with her elbows resting lightly on his shoulders.

"You should know that I asked for help in the matter of getting you and Coxley together," she told him, faintly embarrassed. "I was out of my depth and I needed advice."

Arthur briefly shut his eyes, tipping his head back in resignation. "Let me guess. Alphonse would be the most approachable and the most relevant, but I imagine the least useful. Jacobi, then. But you would never be able to keep the secret from Aaliyah, and if she knows, then Jasmine must as well. Is there anyone in our circle from whom this was kept private?"

"Other than you and Coxley?" Elizabeth ventured.

Arthur groaned.

"You know those four will be discreet, at least."

"I suppose there's that."

The way he rubbed his thumbs in slow circles against her hips, warm through her silk chemise, promised that he wasn't actually upset about it.

"On the subject of secrets," she said carefully.

He straightened, attentive, at the sudden seriousness of her tone.

"If we're inviting Coxley further into our lives, regardless of whether he accepts, I don't want there to be any walls between us going forward."

Lifting his hands from her hips to her face, he cupped one cheek as he sifted his fingers through her hair, tucking an errant curl behind her ear. "What's on your mind?" he asked softly.

She still didn't know how to broach the subject, but continuing to sit on it wasn't going to make it any easier. She'd been avoiding it for weeks already. Taking a deep breath, she willed her voice to come out steady.

"Is it true that you used to have magic?"

Arthur went very still beneath her. "Jules told you?"

"He didn't mean to. He thought I already knew."

Arthur let out all his breath. "What did he say?"

Elizabeth hesitated, carding her fingers through the short hair at the back of his head. "We were having lunch at the studio and we'd had a few drinks. We were talking about my magic; he wanted to see the colour in order to incorporate it into the art. I asked him what he imagined yours would have looked like, and we confused each other. He tried to take it back, but." She chewed on her lip for a second. "I know you don't like talking about the war, and I won't push you to. He didn't say anything more than that; only that you had it before the war, and lost it somehow during. I just don't want to pretend that I'm still in the dark about it. I don't want to keep anything from you."

Arthur's gaze wandered over her face, following the shapes of the shadows cast by the lamplight, the tumble of her hair over her shoulder, the slope of her arms around his neck. "It's not that I wanted to keep it a secret from you. But I enjoyed the fact that you didn't know me before the war. You couldn't compare me to the man I used to be." His mouth slanted into a wry smile. "Or the boy I used to be, rather. I was so young."

With a soft sound, she covered his hand with hers.

"It's true that I don't like talking about it. I think one day I'll tell you anything you want to know. But not yet." He met her eye. "Do you mind waiting?"

"You could talk to me about it tomorrow or in ten years or never at all and I would never mind," she promised.

Grateful, he pressed his face against her neck, wrapping both arms around her back so they held each other in a loose embrace.

"I did have magic," he said quietly. "But the war was a terrible thing."

"I'm so sorry," she whispered uselessly, her heart breaking.

"It's not like losing a limb. They say that maybe one day I'll be able to practice again, but no one knows for sure. Maybe it will come back, or maybe I'll be able to access what's left. Tomorrow, or in ten years, or never at all. It is what it is, and I've learned how to make do without it, for the most part."

She gathered him close and pressed her lips to his forehead. "I will be by your side regardless."

They sat like that for a moment, holding each other close, before Arthur said, his lips grazing Elizabeth's throat, "It's just as well you and your friends never worked out how to get me and Jules together. I shudder to think what Aaliyah's approach might have been."

Elizabeth smothered a laugh in Arthur's hair. "She suggested that if I could just get you both drunk and naked together, everything else would take care of itself."

"Ah, yes. Letting nature run its course."

"Something like that. I was sceptical, but I hardly had any better ideas, so yes, you should consider yourself lucky that things shook out as they did."

"I wouldn't necessarily be opposed to having a few drinks with him and losing a few layers," Arthur said, "but I would rather go into it aware of what's happening."

"I quite agree. Not that I knew how to orchestrate that in the first place. Although I'm sure Aaliyah would have made a plan, if I asked."

"I much prefer the idea of you being present for it," Arthur said, biting lightly at the side of her neck in between his words. "The three of us sharing a bottle as we get undressed, not just Jules and I."

"Me, as well," she agreed breathlessly, and then their conversation fell apart as Arthur tipped them both sideways onto the bed, his playful nips turning to kisses with more intent behind them. By the time her chemise had been rucked up out of the way, any chance of forming a coherent thought, let alone a sentence, was far out of reach, and there was no more serious talking until morning.

♦ ♦ ♦

The next day they sent a note round to Coxley inviting him over for dinner again. Elizabeth was more nervous awaiting his arrival than she had been at her own wedding, because while there were far more things that could have gone wrong during her ceremony, in no worst-case scenario had she entertained the possibility that Arthur would simply turn around and walk out of her life. Once they put their proposition to Coxley, there was a chance, however slim, that he might do just that.

It being Sunday, Mrs. Patel was off, but Elizabeth pre-emptively rang her to give her Monday off, as well. She was tentatively optimistic that Coxley might stay the night, but if he refused, she and Arthur would appreciate an extra day to nurse their rejection in private.

"Whatever happens tonight," Elizabeth said to Arthur in an undertone, as if their housekeeper could overhear them from a distance, "we should assume that Mrs. Patel is very much aware of our intentions towards Coxley."

"Should we be concerned about that?"

"We can either keep raising her pay or we can let her go, and I don't think either of us wants to do without her cooking. Assuming Coxley wants anything to do with us after tonight, of course."

"He will," Arthur said firmly, though he sounded much more confident than he looked.

At precisely eight o' clock that evening Coxley slunk inside like a dog waiting to be whipped. He only looked at Arthur askance, and he refused to look at Elizabeth at all. Which was a shame, as Elizabeth had gone to the effort of dressing up for the night, taking a leaf from Aaliyah's book and going for a short, flashy number that showed her knees and everything.

"Thank you for coming," she greeted him. "Last night was a bit of a cock-up, and I don't think any of us want to leave things as they were."

There had been some debate as to whether Arthur and Elizabeth should take more time to sit with their newfound feelings before bringing Coxley into them, but they had agreed that it would be less stressful to keep moving forward. Now that momentum had been achieved, Arthur was approaching the situation in much the same manner as Elizabeth imagined he had approached the war: with his jaw set and a determined, if somewhat panicked, look in his eye. And she was in no better state. Elizabeth would have preferred a calmer, or at least more buoyant approach, but they would have to make do with what they had.

"We're going to have a talk to set things straight, as it were," she said.

Coxley flinched imperceptibly, looking like nothing more than a man awaiting his execution.

"It's alright, Jules," Arthur said. "Really."

"Is it."

"Let's sit down," Elizabeth suggested. "Come through to the sitting room—and stop looking so apprehensive," she added. "You'd think I'd just read you your death sentence!"

She took them each by the arm and ushered them through the house, depositing them in the sitting room and shutting the door firmly behind herself. The two men immediately took up positions in opposite corners, Arthur with his arms crossed defensively, and Coxley looking surly. Elizabeth caught Arthur's eye, silently asking for assistance; he just urged her on while looking helpless and slightly terrified.

Very well, she thought. *I can handle this.*

"Right," she said aloud. "Coxley. Jules."

His gaze darted up at his given name. "Elizabeth," he said cautiously. "I should probably apologise."

"No, you shouldn't. Let's start with last night's painting reveal. Arthur is convinced it's evidence that you're in love with me. Is that true?"

Across the room, Arthur winced at her bluntness. She was perhaps taking more than just fashion advice from Aaliyah.

Coxley glanced in Arthur's direction. "Ah. I thought he might figure that out. I assure you, it was never my intent to—" He shut his mouth abruptly. "This was a terrible idea. I should go."

He made for the door like he intended to leave that very instant, regardless of the fact that he had just arrived. Elizabeth blocked his path and he retreated to the centre of the room, looking as cagey as a trapped animal.

"I'll stay?" he hazarded. "Though I really don't see how that—"

"You're in love with me," Elizabeth confirmed. "That's quite alright; no one is holding it against you." She paused, giving him the chance to respond. When he said nothing, she continued: "You're in love with me, just as you're in love with Arthur."

Coxley jerked like he'd been slapped, his eyes round and white, before stealing a panicked glance at his friend. "That's not—"

"It's alright," Arthur said, his voice somewhat hoarse. "You see, I've been reliably informed that I've been in love with you for quite some time as well."

Coxley's mouth worked silently on empty air for a beat. "Oh," he finally said. "I see."

"And I feel the same," Elizabeth added, "though I, too, needed some assistance in arriving at that conclusion. In retrospect, it's all perfectly obvious, of course, but such is the nature of hindsight. Now: would you like to confirm or deny anything?"

"I, ah, can confirm that I do harbour feelings for you both," Coxley confessed, still looking wild about the eyes. "Arthur…"

"Jules?"

"I never intended to tell you."

"I can see that. It might have saved you a lot of trouble if you had. How long was it?"

"Forever," Coxley said simply.

"And for Elizabeth?"

"Since the first or second week of painting," Coxley said. "It was inevitable, but I fought it as long as I could. I'd never have said anything, I swear, but—"

"But Arthur could tell from the painting," Elizabeth finished. "And from how you looked at me. You'd think he'd have figured out that you look at him the same way, but you know how he is." She crossed the room to take her husband's hand, leaning into his shoulder. "Perfectly oblivious to all but the most overt gestures, and even then, there's still a chance he'll miss them."

"Thank you, dear."

She kissed his cheek. "So, the question is: what are we going to do about all this?" She waited a moment, and when Coxley didn't seem inclined to voice an opinion and Arthur wasn't going to step in to lead, she said, "It seems to me that there's an obvious solution, and having seen your paintings, Coxley, I'm surprised you haven't suggested it."

"I'm not sure what you're talking about," he said carefully.

"She's talking about the three of us being together," Arthur said.

"Yes, I am," Elizabeth confirmed. "What do you think?"

"What do I *think?* I barely know where to start."

"Let me start by assuring you that Arthur and I have discussed this, and we are perfectly serious," Elizabeth said, her voice dropping in pitch as she left Arthur's side to cross to Coxley's. "And let me follow up by proving that."

Telegraphing her movements and giving him time to reject her, she placed one hand on Coxley's shoulder and the other on his chest, leaning in until she could smell the chemical burn of the paint perpetually clinging to his clothes, and pressed a kiss to his mouth. It was a firm, no-nonsense kiss: not one of magical romance, but one that straightforwardly communicated her intent, and after a second his hands came to rest at her waist, light and trembling, like he couldn't believe he was allowed to touch her. When she broke the kiss and pulled back, his eyes were dazed and his lips parted.

"Alright?" she asked softly.

He darted a glance in Arthur's direction. Arthur stared at the two of them, his pupils blown large.

"Any objections?" Elizabeth asked.

Arthur mutely shook his head.

"I regret ever underestimating you," Coxley confided, stroking his thumb over the tulle at Elizabeth's waist.

"You never will again," she promised.

"I won't." Turning to his friend, Coxley asked hopefully, "Arthur, old boy, I don't suppose that's in the cards for us as well?"

Elizabeth stepped away, leaving a clear path between the two of them, her hands clasped behind her back to curb the urge to reach out and grab hold of them both at once.

"Since forever, you said," Arthur mused, head ducked almost shyly as he wound his way across the room, his hands in his pockets. "Forever's an awfully long time."

"It was from the moment you moved in, or near enough," Coxley said, watching his every move. "The instant you proved willing to put up with me, I was done for."

"You never said anything. Not even a hint."

"You don't get hints. They're wasted on you. And god, of course I didn't say anything! It's not done and you know it."

"You could have," Arthur countered. "By the time I proved willing to put up with you painting naked sex scenes all over the walls and hiring boys from the brothels to hang around your studio night and day— By that point, you should have known I'd be safe to ask."

As Arthur drew ever nearer, Coxley watched him with an impossibly soft expression. "But I didn't want you to say no."

Arthur came to a halt in front of him. "Well, ask me now, then."

"Arthur."

"Jules?"

"I'm going to kiss you."

Arthur broke into a smile. "That's not a question."

"No," Coxley agreed, and grabbed Arthur's tie to haul him down.

Their mouths met more fiercely than Elizabeth and Coxley had done. Years of familiarly lent them a desperation Elizabeth didn't have to offer—or at least, not yet. Instead, she watched how Coxley wrapped both arms around Arthur's neck to hold him in place, pressing their bodies close like their clothes were already shed and they were nothing but skin. When they drew apart, it was only far enough to breathe, reluctant to part further.

"I'm glad I came tonight," Coxley said presently while Arthur straightened his clothes. "I thought you were calling me back just to set me straight and send me packing, but this is an entirely more agreeable turn of events. Unexpected as it may be."

"It certainly wasn't how I imagined ending my week," Elizabeth agreed. "Why don't we have a bite to eat, and see where the evening takes us? Whether that's dessert and a plate of leftovers for you to take home or something more companionable, we can just…" She spread her hands. "Play it by ear, as it were."

"We discussed multiple outcomes prior to your return," Arthur added, coming up beside Elizabeth to slip his hand around her waist as he addressed Coxley. "Elizabeth had several suggestions, both imaginative and enthusiastic."

"I'm sure she did," Coxley said, eyeing her speculatively. "I'm amenable, in any case. A bite to eat sounds wonderful. Is the painting—did you leave that in the dining room? We never got the chance to—"

"It's beautiful," Elizabeth said. "Coxley, it's the most beautiful thing I've seen in my life."

"You outdid yourself," Arthur added quietly. "I'm sorry I rather ruined the moment for you."

"In your defence, you did have good cause," Coxley allowed. "But you liked it?"

"It's magnificent," Elizabeth said. "I have no idea where to put it. My mother is going to despise it, of course, but I can't bear hiding it away."

"I can just keep giving you paintings, so eventually you'll have one in every room and the choice will become a matter of sheer logistics rather than taste."

"Well, that's an idea," Elizabeth agreed brightly.

"And a commitment," Arthur noted.

"First, shall we have supper, or save that for tomorrow and move straight onto dessert?" Elizabeth asked.

The vote for dessert was unanimous. They congregated in the sitting room with their plates balanced on their knees, working their way through a pan of dark-cherry chocolate-cheesecake brownies Elizabeth had stress-baked earlier that morning. The painting stood propped against the far wall and Elizabeth wanted to stare at it and nothing else, losing herself in its details, but her companions were fierce competitors for her attention.

Despite their kiss, nothing seemed particularly changed between Arthur and Coxley. They fell into the same pattern of familiar arguments, finishing each other's sentences and communicating the rest through shared looks and aborted gestures. The only difference was that when Coxley looked at Arthur there was something more wondrous in his expression, and he didn't try to hide it anymore. For his part, Arthur sat a little closer and stared a little longer than before, his thigh pressed firmly to Coxley's as Elizabeth boxed the man in from the other side.

When Elizabeth couldn't possibly eat another bite, she knocked her knee against Coxley's to playfully nudge him towards Arthur. Coxley needed little coaxing to set his plate aside and catch Arthur in another kiss, framing his face with both hands as he leaned in, eyes closed. Arthur kissed him back with only the slightest hesitation—not out of unwillingness, but because he seemed so unused to kissing anyone but Elizabeth.

She watched them, toying with the beads in her dress, as the spectacle fanned the flame of her desire. It started low, a mere spark in the kindling, but as their kiss deepened and Coxley crawled into Arthur's lap, with Arthur dropping his arms around his friend's waist to pull him close, it burned hotter. She had never seen Arthur kiss anyone else before, and it inspired the opposite of jealousy. They complemented each other beautifully, Coxley's darkness to Arthur's gold, and though she would have been happy to watch them forever, her body kept inching closer without conscious input from her mind.

She fit herself to Coxley's back like a second skin and he arched cat-like against her, reaching over his shoulder with one hand to find her without breaking his kiss. Slipping her hands around his middle, she gave his shoulder a light kiss like testing the waters before diving in to mouth at his neck, tasting him. When she looked up, Arthur was watching her, dark-eyed and panting for breath. Coxley rolled his hips against Arthur's lap, just once, before they all went still.

Elizabeth's hands were very close to the top of Coxley's trousers.

They hadn't talked about how far they wanted to go that night.

"Just to check," she said: "Does anyone think we're moving too fast?"

Coxley glanced at her over his shoulder, then back to Arthur.

"Because if not," she continued huskily, "might I suggest we take us upstairs?"

"Jules?" Arthur said. "That's your call, chap. I think Beth and I are on the same page."

"I'm certainly not going to be the one to put a stop to things," Coxley said. "If you both say upstairs, then I'm with you. Let's go upstairs."

CHAPTER NINETEEN

A COMPLICATED MATTER OF LOGISTICS
(ALSO KNOWN AS A THREESOME)

They left their plates and the remains of dessert where they sat. Elizabeth took Coxley by one hand and Coxley took Arthur by the other, stepping on each other's heels in their hunger for closeness as they trailed from the room.

As Elizabeth led their procession upstairs, her anticipation mounted with every step, and so too did her nervousness. She had gone to bed with Arthur a hundred times, both literally and figuratively. They knew each other inside and out, his body as familiar to her as her own. The last time she had taken someone new to bed had been years ago, and the prospect of doing it again was both thrilling and terrifying.

Despite her nerves, she didn't hesitate as she led them to the bedroom, waiting for them to file in ahead of her. The bed was more than large enough to fit the three of them, though the pillows might get knocked aside.

As she clicked the door shut, they all froze in place for an instant.

We shouldn't have let up on the heavy petting, Elizabeth thought desperately. Kissing their way up the stairs might have slowed them down, but it would have kept their momentum intact and avoided this awkward hesitation.

Arthur gave a little cough. "Clearly, we didn't think this far ahead. One of us is going to have to make the first move."

"Though it may surprise you," said Coxley, "I have very little experience with arrangements of this nature. Threesomes, I mean."

"Have you ever, at all?" Elizabeth asked.

"Once again, rumours of my sexual appetites have been greatly exaggerated," he said wryly.

"You've painted enough of them, though."

"Enough to determine that the logistics seem more complicated than they're worth. Composing a painting is one thing; keeping track of that many body parts in action is quite another."

"So, you're not interested?" Arthur asked.

"I didn't say that." Coxley wet his lips. "I am emphatically interested."

It was going to be up to her to make the first move, Elizabeth realised. Otherwise, the whole night was going to get away from them without anything happening.

That was quite alright. Slipping the straps of her dress over her shoulders, she immediately drew both men's attention. The garment dropped to the floor in a heap and she stood covered only by the chemise they had both seen so many times before. Though they were familiar with her body in every state of undress, they looked at her as if for the first time, full of wanting and wonder. When she held out her hands, they walked to her like helpless moths to a flame, and the feeling of power was indescribable. She drew them to the bed and they followed her willingly, climbing onto the mattress in her wake until the three of them were sitting in a tight circle in the middle, close enough for their knees and shoulders to touch.

She kissed Arthur first. "This doesn't have to be complicated," she said, before turning to kiss Coxley next. "Can we just get each other off tonight and leave the more ambitious pursuits for next time?"

Arthur tipped forward with a laugh to lean against her shoulder. "Such a romantic."

"Are you complaining?"

"I'm not," Coxley said quickly, leaning in to run his hands up each of their thighs. "Tell me what you want me to do."

"You two first," Elizabeth said, bodily turning Coxley towards Arthur. "I was so determined to set the two of you up, and you've known each other for so much longer, it only seems fair that you should start us off."

"Are we only doing this in pairs?" Arthur asked. "It does seem easiest, but I thought if we were going to be sharing, we might share all together."

Coxley looked at Elizabeth in clear agreement.

Rolling her eyes with a smile, Elizabeth gave Coxley a little push towards her husband. "I'll join you shortly. Just let me watch you kiss first, if you don't mind."

"As you wish."

Coxley climbed into Arthur's lap as he had done on the couch downstairs, straddling his thighs and bringing his hands to Arthur's shoulders, every movement cautious.

Arthur settled his hands on Coxley's hips, his expression open and wondrous. "Hello," he said softly.

Smiling, Coxley rocked against him. "Hello," he echoed. "Can I...?"

"I'm hardly going to turn you down now, am I?"

They kissed open-mouthed like they were both starving for it, fumbling each other's trousers open in their hurry to touch. Elizabeth sat as close to them as she could, her self-consciousness entirely fled. They fit together perfectly, like they were still locked in step on the dance floor, though this was a dance that would only ever be performed behind locked doors. They crashed together, laughing as their noses bumped in a clumsy kiss they couldn't bear to break.

Elizabeth slipped one hand under her chemise.

"Wait," Arthur panted. She knew how he looked when he was close and she could tell he was hanging on by a thread, and assumed Coxley was in a similar state. "Should we wait?"

They both looked to Elizabeth for instruction, or maybe permission.

She shook her head. "I want to watch you finish."

With a groan, Arthur hooked his arms under Coxley's to lift him off his thighs and bowl him over backwards, pinning him against the mattress, with Coxley's head in Elizabeth's lap.

Arthur held him there for a second as if admiring the view before glancing over to Elizabeth. Tentatively, he asked, "Can I see?"

Coxley tipped his head back to look at her too, curious and clearly not knowing what the request meant.

Short of breath and burning with desire, Elizabeth had to pull herself together before she could summon her magic. With a shudder, she let it dance out from her fingertips, drawing patterns of silver and blue against her own skin. It felt good, like tiny sparks of electricity, and she shut her eyes and let her magic flow over the bed, lapping at Arthur's hands and knees where he knelt over his friend.

Coxley drew a sharp breath when her magic grazed him, and, with a quick look at Arthur like he was seeking permission, let his out to join hers. His forest greens and summer golds joined her hydrangea blues and purples until the bed was a shimmering pool of the stuff, like a blanket of mist with the colours swirling in and out of each other. For a second, Arthur was perfectly still, his eyes closed, before his lungs heaved and his arms trembled where they supported him. When he opened his eyes, Elizabeth and Coxley's magic was reflected in his pupils, and his irises held all their shifting colours of greens and golds and blues.

If Elizabeth could have given him her magic, she would have. If she could have fed it to him, her fingers pressed to his lips so he could swallow it down, absorb it and take it as his own, she would have offered it to him in a heartbeat. Coxley felt the same; she could see it in his face, his yearning to give Arthur every impossible thing in the world.

Arthur exhaled a soft sound that might have been their names, or a prayer, or wordless gratitude.

"Whatever you want," Coxley breathed, his hands cupping Arthur's shoulders. "Whatever, whenever, you only have to ask—"

"Just this," Arthur said, like having the two of them in his bed was all he could ever wish for.

Elizabeth stretched out alongside them, drinking in the show they put on, one hand between her own legs and the other resting on Arthur's back between his shoulders. She trailed little lines of magic between his freckles, leaving goosebumps in her wake. She liked the way his muscles bunched and how his skin got slippery as he worked up a sweat almost as much as she enjoyed the sight of them together. There was no finesse to their coupling, no elegance or sense that they were making love like something out of one of her romance novels. They were still half-clothed, their shirts unbuttoned and shoved halfway down their arms, and their trousers open but more or less on. Somehow, that only made them more attractive, like they were so desperate for each other that they couldn't even take the time to undress and set the scene. There would be time for that later, if all went well, but in the moment, Elizabeth wouldn't change a thing.

They finished with Arthur's face buried in Coxley's throat, Coxley with his eyes shut and his hands in Arthur's hair. Elizabeth squirmed in place, flushed hot from top to bottom, her thighs pressed together so tightly they were trembling as she tried to resist bringing herself off without waiting for them to touch her. She tangled her fingers in Coxley's curls to distract herself from how badly she wanted them both on top of her, or under her—anything and everything.

"Good?" Coxley managed eventually, raising his head just enough to catch Elizabeth's eye as he continued petting Arthur's hair.

There was another minute before Arthur moved, propping himself up on his elbows to look at them both, though he made no effort to remove himself from between Coxley's thighs.

"More than good," Arthur confirmed. "Although one of us should probably take care of Elizabeth."

"Yes, please," she said breathlessly, spreading her legs just a little where she knelt. "Either one of you, or both, whatever you like. I really don't care as long as someone comes here right now."

Coxley's gaze flickered to Arthur, who gave him a slight nod. Coxley didn't waste another second before twisting onto his stomach, still underneath his partner.

"Tell me if there's anything you don't like," Coxley said, gazing up at Elizabeth, his hands grazing her bare knees.

"I can't imagine," she breathed.

"Then lay back and let me know how I do."

She reclined against her elbows, watching as he situated himself between her legs, sliding her chemise up over her stomach with an expression of utmost reverence. His hands were warm and his hair was a disaster, and when he went down on her, he did it with such single-minded intent that her whole world imploded. While Arthur liked to take his time, Coxley went in like he wanted to see how quickly he could tip her over the edge.

"Oh, god," she gasped, wrapping her fingers in his hair as her back arched off the mattress and her thighs clenched on either side of his head.

When she came, Elizabeth let her magic out unrestrained and it burst over them like a sunshower, sparking against their skin like kisses before dissolving against the sheets as she pulled in a deep breath and took it back into herself. He guided her through it, not slowing down until she finally collapsed back against the bed. For his part, Coxley's magic expanded with a flash like the sun slanting through a canopy of leaves, only lasting a second before he regained control and shaped it into a handful of gently glowing orbs that bobbed around the bed like large, lazy fireflies.

"You look like you enjoyed yourselves," Arthur commented.

At some point during Elizabeth's orgasm he had to come to lay beside her. He looked satisfied, both from his own time with Coxley and from watching her, and when she dropped one clumsy hand in his direction, he caught it and pressed a warm kiss to her knuckles.

"You're very good at that," she told Coxley, dazedly.

He sat up, looking as satisfied as a cat that had got the cream. His lips and chin glistened wet with her, and he dragged his wrist carelessly across his face to clean it. "I'm happy to do it again whenever you like."

"I'll take you up on that, but not right now. I've only just noticed how exhausted I am."

With his mouth still against her knuckles, Arthur asked, "Can you stay awake long enough for me to get you off, too?"

"I couldn't possibly say no, but please don't be offended if I doze off before you're done."

Laughing, he settled in against her hip, trailing one hand along her innermost thigh. "I'll do my best."

Arthur had years of practice, and he knew exactly how to touch her. With her first orgasm still sending shuddering aftershocks through her body, he kept his touch firm enough that she wasn't tempted to flinch away. Her second orgasm came even faster than the first, barrelling into her like a freight train.

"Elizabeth…" Coxley sounded awestruck.

"Come to bed now," Elizabeth said, somewhat nonsensically, reaching for them both.

"I haven't got anything to sleep in," Coxley said.

"You can borrow one of Arthur's nightshirts."

"He used to borrow clothes all the time," Arthur said. "He would absolutely destroy them in his studio, and I could never borrow any of his in return because he's so short."

"I'm of perfectly average height," Coxley retorted, though he was smiling. "You're both just unreasonably tall."

"Then don't wear anything at all; I'm sure I don't mind."

Arthur shrugged. "Nor I."

"In that case…"

Coxley only hesitated a second before pulling his shirt over his head, though he was less quick to shed his trousers. For all the time he spent looking at other people's naked bodies, he seemed shy when it came to his own. Elizabeth coaxed him to her side as she folded back the covers to get between the sheets. Arthur mirrored her on Coxley's other side, husband and wife shuffling the pillows into place as they had done countless times. The only change was an added body between them.

"Good night," Elizabeth murmured, reaching for the bedside lamp. "We'll talk in the morning."

"Technically it's morning now," Coxley said, just for the sake of being contrary, and she smiled as she ignored him and turned the switch to bring them to darkness.

"The magic," Coxley said after a moment, still lying in Arthur's arms. "Do you do that often?"

"Not all the time," Arthur replied, absently running one hand through Coxley's hair.

"We haven't been keeping a tally," Elizabeth said.

"But it's something you like?" Coxley asked, searching Arthur's face.

Arthur didn't answer, just dipped his head in a fraction of a nod.

"Do you still have those dreams?" Coxley's voice was so soft it was all but inaudible.

"Not all the time," Arthur repeated with equal softness.

"Does it help?"

He was quiet for a long minute and Elizabeth held her breath waiting for his answer.

"It doesn't hurt as much as it used to," he finally said.

Slowly, Coxley shifted in Arthur's arms so they were nose to nose, raising one hand to the side of Arthur's face. The tiniest glimmer of magic unspooled from his fingertip and they both leaned in at the same time to meet in a kiss as Coxley's magic caressed Arthur's cheek.

Elizabeth watched their mouths move against each other for a moment before draping herself over Coxley to reach Arthur.

"I'll tell you about the dreams one day," he murmured against her hair. "I promise."

"You don't have to. Just let me know whatever I can do to make them better."

"Everything you've already been doing. And sleeping beside someone seems to keep them at bay. Most of the time, at least."

"A pity you and I never tried that earlier," Coxley said, biting at Arthur's ear. "I imagine being too worn-out from sex to dream helps keep them at bay as well."

"Unsurprisingly, yes, though I'm happy to test the theory more rigorously."

"An excellent plan."

Coxley was warm and naked, his body bare to hers beneath the covers. Elizabeth lay facing him, her knees tucked in to brush against his. It was too dark to see him, but she could feel the slow and steady rhythm of his breaths, and on his other side, Arthur was the same. The day caught up to her in a rush and she let her eyes drift closed, one hand resting on the pillow, just near enough to touch the tips of Coxley's hair.

"Is it really alright?" Coxley said softly, after some time.

Elizabeth was nearly asleep, drifting in that heavy, blue-tinged sea of semi-consciousness.

"Yes, really." Arthur's voice was no more than a murmur. "I just wish you had said something sooner. Were you really pining for years?"

"Pining. You make me sound like a schoolgirl."

"Jules."

A beat of silence.

"Yes. It was years."

Arthur exhaled in a rush.

"Don't feel bad for me. I was happy enough. And it wouldn't have done for me to say something all that time ago—what if you'd fallen madly in love with me then, old thing? You'd never have met Elizabeth."

"I suppose not."

Another breath. Elizabeth wandered through her wedding day, everything champagne and gold in her memory, dancers flitting by like butterflies.

"She's remarkable," Coxley said. "I can't be sorry for falling for her like that."

"No, nor I."

The silence stretched and Elizabeth trailed further into her dreams. There was a rustle of sheets, the sound of something warm, like a kiss or an embrace, and then she was asleep.

CHAPTER TWENTY

A HOUSEHOLD OF THREE

When Elizabeth woke, the dawn light was slipping gently through the curtains, and Coxley was watching her. She stretched and yawned, pushing her hair back from her face, and offered him a sleepy smile.

"Good morning," she murmured. "Have you been awake long?"

"I like watching how you change in the light."

"I would have thought you'd grown bored of watching me by now." But then, he'd never grown bored of watching Arthur, so perhaps she shouldn't be surprised.

"Never," he vowed with a soft smile. He made no move to touch her, laying back just enough to give her space. On his other side, Arthur slumbered on.

"I thought you might leave in the night," she confessed, bridging the gap between them to clasp his hand.

"I considered it," he admitted. "But it was nigh impossible to sneak out from the middle of the bed. I assume you positioned me here purposefully."

"As insurance," she agreed, and squeezed his hand. "I want you to stay. You do understand that, don't you? I want you both to stay with each other, and with me."

He hummed thoughtfully and dropped his gaze to their joined hands, turning hers over and tracing the lines of her tendons through the back of her hand and along her fingers. His touch was so delicate, as if she herself were a work of art.

"How did you know?" he finally asked. "That I loved him, I mean. Or was I simply so excruciatingly obvious?"

"It was in your sketchbooks. All those portraits. I mean, yes, you were quite obvious once I thought to look for it, but it was the drawings that gave you away."

"You knew that before you sat for your portrait?"

She nodded.

"And you never begrudged me for it?"

"For a love you'd never once mentioned nor acted on, outside the confines of your own private work? No. All I wanted was to understand you better, and in the process, Arthur too. And then…" She shrugged, her smile tugging at the corners of her mouth. "Here we are."

"Indeed. What a mess we've made for ourselves."

"I don't see a mess. I see potential. Like the sketch before a painting: we're rough yet, and unfinished, but once we put the work in we have the chance to become something beautiful. Don't you think?"

He laughed too loudly. "First an artist and now a poet. What other depths are you hiding?"

"She contains multitudes," Arthur said, rolling over to blink at them with sleepily unfocused eyes. "It's early. What on earth are you talking about with sketches and poetry?"

"Us," Elizabeth replied simply. She reached over Coxley to run her fingers through Arthur's hair in a silent good-morning.

"We were waiting for you to wake."

"How kind." He yawned hugely, his jaw cracking. "And what will you do now that I'm awake?"

"I thought I would kiss you," she said, "and then I thought we might pick things up from where we left off last night. If that's agreeable?"

They both looked at Coxley.

"Yes." He broke into a smile, his eyes glittering. "Let's do that."

♦ ♦ ♦

"Well," said Coxley, collapsing onto his back some time later, "that was informative. Arthur, I had no idea the secrets you were keeping!"

"I was in the army," Arthur said lightly, coming up to drop one arm over Coxley's side and tangling his fingers with Elizabeth's. "I would have been hard-pressed not to learn a thing or two."

"If your main takeaway was that this was 'informative' then we're going to have to try harder next time," Elizabeth said, though she wasn't really cross. She was too wrung out, her body hot and lax, muscles well worked and satisfied from their tumble to do much more than sigh against the pillows and fix Coxley with a mildly reproving glare.

"I apologise, my dear," he said immediately, pressing a kiss to her temple where her hair clung to her forehead, sweaty and mussed and in desperate need of a bath and a comb. "I was at a loss for words. I should have said—pleasurable. Passionate. Earth-shattering. Life-changing." He punctuated each word with a kiss. "Are those better suited to your tastes? Your pride assuaged?"

"Those are better," she allowed, catching his mouth with hers on the next pass. "And I feel much the same."

"You don't need a recitation from me as well, do you?" Arthur asked, drawing lazy patterns on Coxley's skin as he gazed over at her.

"I don't know; it might be nice to hear."

He rolled his eyes fondly. "I love you very much."

"I know you do."

Dawn rolled into midmorning before they made any attempt to rise. Arthur called into work—they could manage without him for a single morning, he said—and they fell to kissing again, and then stroking and grasping and more besides, before rolling over to doze in the shared warmth beneath the covers. Finally, Elizabeth's stomach protested, demanding breakfast, and she propped herself up on both elbows to make a move towards beginning her day.

"Surely you could call for Mrs. Patel to bring up some food?" Coxley suggested, still sprawled on his back, one arm looped around Arthur's shoulders.

"I hardly think this is a sight she needs to see," Elizabeth said. "Besides which, I specifically told her not to come in today."

Coxley waved one hand. "She'll know about us as soon as she does the laundry. Impossible to avoid. We didn't even pretend the guest room was in use." He paused. "Are you concerned she might talk?"

Elizabeth considered it. Between servant rumours, her solitary visits to Coxley's studio, and the painting itself, was there any avoiding the gossip to come? "I don't think she will," she said slowly. "She's not given to fits of moral outrage."

"She's on good terms with her daughter, for whatever that's worth, and Deepa has done far more scandalous things than this," Coxley offered. "Though I suppose her mother doesn't have to clean up after her."

"Mrs. Patel is well-paid and well-appreciated here, and she knows it," Arthur said. "Other than that, well, what's one more scandal to weather?"

Downstairs, they found the last few cherry-cheesecake brownies from the previous night in the sitting room, and though Elizabeth was tempted to have dessert for breakfast, she set them aside in order to rustle up the leftover dinner she had made earlier on

Sunday. Tender roast beef, baby potatoes, carrots and parsnips in a brown sugar glaze, and soft white rolls all got reheated in the oven as Elizabeth, Arthur, and Coxley traded tiny kisses and little smiles in the morning sunbeams. Coxley was in one of Arthur's nightshirts after all, each of them dressed the bare minimum to make themselves decent. When the food was warm enough to eat, they sat clustered around one end of the dining table, tucking in with well-earned appetites. Elizabeth's cooking could hardly compare to Mrs. Patel's, but she could turn out a respectable meal, and she managed to feed herself and Arthur on the weekends when their housekeeper was off.

When they were halfway through their breakfast, Coxley finally asked, "So, how is this going to play out? Am I to be a regular guest here, dropping by for dinners and the occasional night, or?"

"It could be, if that's what you want," Elizabeth said. "Arthur and I hadn't talked about a long-term arrangement." But she wanted one, desperately, and Coxley's suggestion sounded so terribly casual, as if he expected to be used as was convenient, and nothing more. She caught Arthur's eye over the table. "Darling?"

"The French call it a ménage a trois," Arthur said, cutting his roast into squares, apparently unaffected by the weight of the conversation. "A 'household of three.'"

Her heart leapt.

"That sounds terribly domestic, considering the deviancy of the act," Coxley commented lightly.

"It could be, though," she said. "If you wanted. A domestic arrangement, that is. Something permanent."

"You said yourself you haven't found a new flatmate yet," Arthur said, still more concerned with his breakfast than anything else. "So, sell the old place, keep your studio, and move in here. The guest room is perfectly serviceable." He glanced up. "Assuming that's agreeable to you, darling."

"It is," she said quickly. "Yes, Coxley, do join us. I've been saying all this time that the house is too big for just the two of us."

"And when your parents come to visit? Or any other guest?"

She rolled her eyes and waved her hand. "A problem easily solved when it arises."

"Your mother dislikes me. She hid it very well when I met her at your engagement party, but I have a sense for these things."

"Then you shall just have to win her over, as you did me," Elizabeth said. "Now that you and I are friends, I'm sure she'll thaw to you after a few lunch dates together."

In her head, she was already planning how to approach her mother. They would start with brunch over the coming weekend; perhaps she could be wooed with a painting. She was fond of flowers, so long as they were more benign than Coxley's orchid offering. Elizabeth was confident Coxley could charm her mother, and as long as she was less astute than Mrs. Patel as to the true nature of their living arrangement, she didn't foresee any problems.

"And if you want children? What then?"

She and Arthur exchanged looks. They had discussed it, but only in passing, and certainly nothing was in the immediate works.

"If we want children, which is not to say that we've decided any such thing, it won't be for some years yet, and there's no reason they shouldn't grow up with an uncle in the house."

There was silence all around for a moment.

"I never wanted children of my own," Coxley said eventually. "They're sticky little devils, and I wouldn't trust them around my paints." He took a long drink from his tea. "But I can appreciate that other people's sometimes have a certain charm. The kind I can entertain for a short time and then return to the parents, you understand."

Elizabeth hid her smile behind her own cup. "It's a conversation we might have at a later date," she suggested. "Once things have settled. If you want to settle, that is."

"I do."

As they went back for seconds, it became increasingly obvious that Arthur's nightshirt was far oversized for Coxley's frame, as it kept slipping off his shoulders.

"This is only slightly ridiculous," Coxley observed, taking his seat again with a freshly-heaped plate. "You know, I generally sleep in the nude, so as to avoid these problems."

"I remember," Arthur said, long-suffering. "I walked in on you more than once."

"And I walked in on you once or twice in the bath, to even things out," Coxley said cheerfully. "Entirely by accident, of course."

"It was like living with a cat. No sense of boundaries whatsoever, and of course there was no point in trying to enforce them."

"And despite this, Arthur never modelled nude for you?" Elizabeth asked.

"A lost opportunity," Coxley mourned.

"You did use his likeness, though, didn't you? The golden youth, the one you said was your favourite. He has Arthur's eyes."

"You mean the one with the big, black—"

"Yes, that one."

"I told you I hired a boy to model for that painting, and that was the truth. But yes, I may have gone looking for someone who matched my very specific physical criteria."

"What painting is this?" Arthur asked, looking between the two of them.

"You don't know it," Coxley said. "Not that I hid it from you, but I haven't shown it anywhere yet, and you were out of the flat often enough. Busy on your dates and whatnot, which I certainly didn't resent at the time."

"Now that things have shifted between us," Elizabeth said to Arthur, "would you model for him?"

"Do you want me to?" Arthur asked Coxley.

"Always," Coxley said immediately.

"As if you haven't drawn me enough already." Arthur rolled his eyes, though he clearly didn't mean it.

"Yes, maybe. Not nude, though. I'll leave that to someone more daring."

"I found it quite freeing, personally," Elizabeth said with an easy shrug. "Maybe you'll like it."

"Maybe later on."

Coxley and Elizabeth exchanged a knowing glance. That was far from an outright refusal. If Arthur really didn't want to, he would have been stern about it. As it was, he'd likely be posing nude on Coxley's chaise within six months, and Elizabeth couldn't wait to see it.

◆ ◆ ◆

That afternoon, Arthur reluctantly slunk back to the office, but Elizabeth let her shop stay closed in order to lounge around the house with Coxley, poking at her typewriter.

"I promised my publisher one last M. Hayes book by the fall, before all this nonsense with Johnson came to a head. I expect they would let me out of it, all things considered, but I hate to renege on a promise."

"Have you definitely decided to let the pen name go?" Coxley asked from where he was sprawled across the couch to the side of her desk. "Because I don't mind pretending to be M. Hayes if you want to keep writing the books. I think it could be rather fun."

"I don't know. It might be time for a change." Elizabeth ran both hands through her hair before turning the movement into a full-body stretch, enjoying the way Coxley's gaze raked her frame, making no effort to hide his appreciation. "Last night in bed, I was hoping to find inspiration in our situation, but the truth is, I might be happier doing something else entirely. I've written over a dozen romances and I don't particularly feel as if I need to write another dozen. Especially not when I'm actively living two at the same time."

"Would you want to give up writing altogether?" Coxley asked curiously.

"Oh, no, though I wouldn't mind a bit of a holiday from it. I think all I really need is a change of pace, and I'll find my passion for it again."

"What about mysteries? You could immortalise that idiot Johnson in your work and repeatedly defeat him in as many different guises as you like. I imagine it would be remarkably cathartic."

She huffed out a laugh. "Yes, especially as I doubt I'll ever see justice done to him in the real world. Fiction is always more satisfying in that respect."

"Well, he certainly won't be working in London again. Bringing those letters to the party ensured that much, even if he won't be facing charges."

"I do rather like the idea of bashing him in a book series," Elizabeth admitted. "Though I don't know if I would want to spend so much time dwelling on him. To say nothing of the fact that I'm not convinced he would make a very good villain in a mystery. I'm afraid readers would write in to complain about how clumsy and ill-planned they found his actions. He's really quite farcical."

"Something to consider, in any case," Coxley suggested.

Elizabeth had to admit, there was a certain appeal in authoring a string of pulpy mysteries. She felt sufficiently energised to begin poking at a new idea, and a mystery novel was a significant change from her romances. It might be just the breath of fresh air that she needed to rejuvenate her interest in writing.

But she wasn't about to start writing it then and there. She would mull it over, sleep on it, and pick up the latest Agatha Christie book that was all the rage. Alphonse adored the Poirot stories; she would pick his brain about the genre over lunch later that week, perhaps.

And it wasn't as if she desperately needed the money.

As if reading her mind, Coxley said, "You know, if Deepa wears one of your dresses to just the right event, that may prove to be the only exposure you need to launch them into the stratosphere. That would afford you some time away from writing, if you need to refill the creative well."

"I would like it if my dresses could stand on their own legs instead of needing to be propped up by my royalties," Elizabeth mused.

"And you couldn't ask for a more flattering model."

Elizabeth felt a flutter of excitement regarding her dressmaking business for the first time in ages. "I have to meet with her, first," she said, more to caution herself against wild hope than to subdue Coxley's. "It could yet fall apart."

Coxley snorted. "That's the spirit."

"In the meantime." She picked up her latest project, which she had been using as a distraction from both her writing and her dressmaking. It sat innocuously in a little sewing tin beside her typewriter, shining in the sun.

"What are you working on?" Coxley asked, peering curiously up at her desk.

"A variation on those good-luck charms I use in my dresses. I thought I might dabble in jewellery or accessories. More as a hobby than a serious business venture, I think."

She held out the charm for his inspection. It was a simple thing, a solid magic sphere about the size of her thumbnail, with all the properties of a glass bead, similar to the flowers Jasmine sculpted from her magic. It was a deep, rich blue with varying shades throughout it, and the tiny sigil marked on it that served to attract good luck was silver, almost white.

"Very pretty," Coxley said admiringly.

"It's not especially strong. It can't protect from bad luck or accidents or anything of that nature, but it attracts a certain amount of common good luck. The kind that leads to finding a coin on the ground, or good weather when you need to step outside, or catching the first cab you hail when you're in a hurry. That sort of thing."

"Do you feel like you particularly need an extra spot of good luck right now? I remember your wedding dress with its charms served you well that day, and again at the garden party."

"It never hurts to ask the universe for a little extra help. I thought I would run a cord through it and wear it as a pendant." She held the bead up against the centre of her chest, testing the length of the imaginary cord. "Something like this."

"I would wear it," Coxley said. "I think it would add to the bohemian look I'm cultivating."

"At least wear it under your clothes," Elizabeth chided. "You still need to pretend to look respectable, for the sake of your clients, if not your personal taste."

"Would you make me one if I promised to keep it hidden so as not to detract from my respectable, gentlemanly aesthetic? Or, sell me one, rather," he corrected. "Seeing as you insisted on paying for your portrait, I must insist on paying you for your craftsmanship as well. It's only fair."

"Yes, of course," Elizabeth replied, neatly sidestepping the fact that she would never allow him to pay for something she considered a mere trinket. It was hardly comparable to a portrait that had been so many weeks in the making. Rolling the bead between her fingers, she asked hesitantly, "Do you think Arthur would wear one?"

"If you made it for him and asked him to? Of course, unquestionably."

"You don't think it would make him uncomfortable? The magic, I mean. Having such a constant reminder against his skin."

"I think he's the only one who can answer that," Coxley said gently, "but from what I've seen? No, I think he would cherish it. Especially if it's yours."

Elizabeth hummed thoughtfully, playing with the charm and letting the sun glint off its surface as an idea took shape.

◆ ◆ ◆

Over breakfast on Tuesday morning, Elizabeth couldn't take her eyes from the two of them. Mrs. Patel, who had returned from her impromptu vacation, served them poached eggs on toast with sides of baked beans, sausages, and rashers of bacon, and though she eyed them critically, her gaze lingering in particular on Coxley, who was nonchalantly wearing one of Arthur's robes, she acted as if nothing were unusual.

As Coxley got dressed to head to his studio and Elizabeth and Arthur were preparing, however reluctantly, for their respective workdays, Mrs. Patel drew Elizabeth aside for a quiet word.

"Should I expect Mr. Coxley at suppertime for the foreseeable future?" she asked.

"Yes, please," Elizabeth said as casually as she could as she pulled on her hat and cardigan.

"Shall I make up the guest room?"

"Ah." Elizabeth faltered. "Yes?"

Mrs. Patel hummed, looking Elizabeth up and down with a knowing expression. "Of course, ma'am. Very good."

"That won't be a problem?" Elizabeth asked carefully. "I know you only signed on to cook and clean for two."

"It's no problem, ma'am. I owe Mr. Coxley my position here, after all, to say nothing of my daughter's success. A household of three is not significantly more difficult to manage than that of a married couple."

"Oh, good," Elizabeth said faintly, caught off-guard by how easily Mrs. Patel could read the situation. A household of three, indeed. "I'm glad you think so."

"If I may say, it will be good for him. That man needs looking after."

"Yes, I know your insistence on seeing him fed," Elizabeth said with an airy laugh, trying to deflect from just how willing she was to look after him.

Mrs. Patel levelled her with a look suggesting that Coxley's eating habits weren't what she had meant at all.

Elizabeth's laugh turned into a little cough. "Anyway. I hope you had a good weekend?"

"It was unremarkable, which is how I like it, thank you, ma'am. I heard your garden party proved entertaining. I hope you enjoyed yourselves."

Whether Mrs. Patel had heard the precise nature of that entertainment, Elizabeth couldn't tell. She needed to phish out how much, exactly, Mrs. Patel knew and what else she might have inferred. The blackmail was one thing; she assumed all of London knew about that by now. Johnson's accusation that Elizabeth and Coxley were having an affair, however, might need to be handled more delicately, especially as Mrs. Patel was already making certain deductions about Coxley's place in the house.

So, Elizabeth plastered on a smile and deflected. "Yes, I finally met your daughter! You must be terribly proud of her. Did she tell you about it?"

"She mentioned a few things, but she is hardly the sole source of gossip when it comes to such an event. But I thought you might be pleased to know that the former private investigator Mr. Johnson has left London."

Elizabeth perked up, and when Arthur passed by at the end of the hall, she waved him over, with Coxley following in his wake, both of them looking brightly interested.

"I never did like that man," Mrs. Patel confided in them.

"Did you know him?" Elizabeth asked.

"Certainly not. He has a monthly column in the paper, and he always came across as the most pompous, insufferable fool." Mrs. Patel gave a delicate sniff. "Pardon my language, ma'am."

"Don't apologise," said Coxley, sounding delighted. "We agree entirely. Did you happen to hear the manner of his departure?"

"I believe his house was the victim of some minor vandalism on Saturday night after the party, and he left town sometime late on Sunday, under cover of darkness."

"Like a rat from a sinking ship," said Arthur.

"What sort of vandalism?" Elizabeth asked.

"I heard his front step was pelted with spoiled eggs and rotten fruit."

"That's very satisfying," Elizabeth admitted.

"And also a considerable amount of black paint," said Mrs. Patel. "A creative response to his alleged blackmailing, I should think. There were pictures in the gossip section of the Monday paper."

Arthur and Elizabeth both stole a glance at Coxley, who immediately raised his hands in innocence.

"I had nothing to do with either the rotten food or the paint, though I wish I'd been in on both. Unfortunately, I spent Saturday night drinking myself to sleep in my studio. I would have been thrilled to run the man out of town, but I'm afraid I can only take credit for what you saw during the party itself."

"Indeed," said Mrs. Patel. "The word is that Mr. Johnson's own wife was responsible for the paint. Furthermore, Deepa tells me that Mrs. Johnson has years of dirty laundry from their marriage, and that she is determined to air it in as public a manner as she can manage. She has spent the weekend talking to reporters and tabloid journalists, Deepa says."

"Good for her," said Elizabeth.

"Johnson will have to change his name if he wants to stay in the country, and even then, he won't be safe," Coxley said.

"Is it true that he asked Grace to lighten her hair to look more like me?" Elizabeth asked Coxley.

"Oh, I have no idea. I made that up on the spot, but it could be true. Her natural colour is mousier, though her temper certainly wasn't, by the end of things."

"Well, good riddance to bad rubbish, however it came about," said Arthur. "It's only a shame that we'll never see the case of that jewel thief resolved without him. Repulsive as he was, Johnson seemed to be Scotland Yard's only chance of closing that one."

"Oh, let the thief go free," Elizabeth said carelessly. "It's not like they're hurting anyone, and all those jewellery shops are insured anyway."

Mrs. Patel bade them good day and retreated, presumably to suss out what mess they had made in her absence. Elizabeth tried not to feel too self-conscious about the state in which they'd left the bed.

"You could write your own ending to the case," Coxley said, nudging her with his elbow. "Fiction is always more satisfying than fact, didn't you say?"

"Are you writing mysteries now?" Arthur asked, donning his cap as they headed to the door.

"I might be. What do you think? Should I aspire to be the next Agatha Christie?"

"That sounds marvellous, darling. Count me ·in to proofread them and be sure to mention me in the acknowledgements when they inevitably take off."

"He's much more enthused about this line of writing than when I suggested I might write homoerotic filth," Elizabeth told Coxley in an aside.

"I should be delighted if you penned some homoerotic filth," Coxley said, linking their elbows as they stepped outside. "Do you need an illustrator for those volumes? And have you considered distributing them underground in the French market?"

Arthur threw his head back with an exaggerated groan as he took Elizabeth's other arm. "I see how this is going to be," he declared to the sky as he pulled the door shut behind them. "I'm outnumbered. Together you're going to drag me into hedonism. Devils, the both of you."

"Yes, darling," Elizabeth said, pressing a kiss to his cheek, "but you like that about us."

After a quick glance up and down the street to ensure their privacy, Coxley gave him a matching kiss, leaning around Elizabeth to do it. "Second thoughts, old boy?"

Arthur tucked Elizabeth in closer against his side, drawing Coxley in by extension. "None."

"Wait," Elizabeth said before they descended the steps to the street. "I have something for you both." From her clutch, she drew three pendants, and, untangling the cords, handed one to Arthur and one to Coxley, keeping the third for herself. "You don't need to consider this a serious commitment," she said, feeling suddenly awkward as they each took their necklace from her. "I just thought it would be nice to have a little something just between the three of us."

"Charms?" Arthur asked softly, holding his up to the sun. When the light glanced through it at just the right angle, it looked less like blue glass and more gold, like it had a little flash of amber caught in its heart.

"Did you make them both yesterday afternoon?" Coxley asked. "After you showed me that first one?"

"You said you'd like one, and they don't take long."

She had kept that first one, the one that looked bluest, before carefully sculpting the other two from her magic, injecting the tiniest bit of colour to personalise each one. Like crystals, their colours varied when held to the light. Hers was more silvery, Arthur's amber, and Coxley's had a touch of green, turning it almost turquoise in the right conditions.

"Arthur," she said quietly, rocking her shoulder against his. "I wanted it to be a surprise, but I should have asked you first. You don't have to wear it if you don't want to."

"Don't be silly, Beth," he replied, his tone reverent. He held the charm between both hands like a bird that might fly away from him at any second. "I love it." He kissed her, quick and sure. "Let me put yours on you."

The cords were long enough for the necklaces to go on overhead without having to fiddle with any clasps. As Elizabeth draped Arthur's around his neck, fussing with his shirt collar so the charm lay against his chest under his clothes, Arthur settled Elizabeth's against her breast on top of her dress, a subtle little statement piece. When that was done, they both turned to Coxley, sharing his necklace between them to draw it over his head.

"You're quite sure you want to keep it hidden?" Elizabeth teased as she straightened his tie.

Smoothing one hand down the front of his shirt, Coxley caught her fingers in a quick kiss. "I rather like keeping this secret just between the three of us," he said in a low voice. "It's no one's business but our own."

"They're less formal than wedding rings," Arthur said casually as the three of them got back in a row to step onto the street. "What?" he added, at Coxley's startlement. "Is that too much, too soon? I know you were never keen on marriage as an institution, but really—"

"You can always give it back if you decide you want out," Elizabeth added.

"No," Coxley said cheerfully, insinuating himself between them and taking both their arms. "You gave it to me, and you can take it back over my dead body, thank you very much. I'm afraid you're stuck with me, now."

The sky was bright and the sun was hot, and Elizabeth soaked it up as surely as she soaked up her partners' attention and the solid feel of their arms joined through hers. The little charm around her neck glinted in the light like a spark, and the knowledge that Arthur and Coxley each wore one to match warmed her more than any amount of summer sun. Warm, too, was the fact that all three of them would be climbing into the same bed that night, sleeping under the same sheets, and breathing the same air. Sharing the same hopes and dreams and familiarity with each other's bodies.

Elizabeth pulled them both into a quick embrace, her step so light she felt weightless, and when they parted to go about their separate workdays, they parted with the confidence that they would shortly reconvene in the place that all three of them could call home.

ABOUT THE AUTHOR

Arden Powell is an author and illustrator from the Canadian East Coast. A nebulous entity, they live with a small terrier and an exorbitant number of houseplants, and have conversations with both. They write across multiple speculative-fiction genres, and everything they write is queer.

Printed in Great Britain
by Amazon